AUTUMN & ALIBIS

THE HEARTH & QUILL MYSTERIES
BOOK 1

JULES MOTSCHALL

CROWN JULES, INC.

AUTUMN & ALIBIS

Book 1 of The Hearth & Quill Mysteries

Jules Motschall

Crown Jules Press

For additional books by Jules Motschall, visit her website at
julesmotschallauthor.com.

For exclusive news on upcoming releases, updates on your favorite
characters, and free bonus content, sign up for her newsletter at
julesmotschallauthor.com/newsletter.

ISBN: 979-8-9918665-1-4

The Library of Congress has established a record for the title.

Library of Congress Control Number: 2025917450

Editor - Courtney Aussem

Formatted with Vellum.

For everyone who knows that the best months of the year end in 'ber. Because jeans and sweatshirts are far better than shorts and tank tops, I've created a world where it's always autumn. Grab a PSL, light a candle, and get cozy.

PROLOGUE

ct 18, 2024

Prudence Sherman pulled her jacket tighter, her fingers brushing over the envelope tucked safely in her inside pocket. Inside it was the quill. The sun shone, and a cool October breeze rustled through the apple trees, gold and red leaves dancing in the wind. She made her way through Sullivan's Apple Orchard. Soon, she would be free of the quill and could focus on truly important matters.

Ahead, leaning against an old apple tree, a figure waited, barely distinguishable from this distance. As she approached, the person pushed off the tree, but their stance was tense. Prudence felt a flicker of satisfaction. *Good. Let them be uneasy.* She was a woman of principle, and she had done the right thing.

The person greeted her with a terse nod. "Prudence."

"Let's not waste time with pleasantries," she replied coolly, stopping just a few feet away. "Where is she? I told you I would give it to *her*."

They stepped closer, the weight of their gaze cutting through the sunshine.

"I'll give it to her and we'll return it. You have my word"

Prudence's hand tightened around her jacket. She had no intention of letting it go.

"I'll be the one returning it," she said, her voice steely. "And I'm going to let Harper know *exactly* where I found it."

Silence stretched between them, thick and charged. The person's stance grew rigid, their tone sharpening.

"I can't let you do that," the person said, voice low and taut with anger. "We'll return it, but no one can know what happened."

Prudence let out a soft, mocking laugh.

"You don't have a choice here. I agreed to meet you, but this was clearly a waste of time. "

Turning on her heel, Prudence started to walk away, but before she could take more than a few steps, a hand clamped painfully around her upper arm, yanking her back. She gasped, heart hammering, as she twisted to face the person, but their grip held surprisingly firm.

"Take your hands off of me!" she snapped, her voice wavering for the first time.

"Give me the quill," the person said, their voice laced with an edge she hadn't expected.

They said nothing for a tense moment. Prudence struggled to get away, but the grip tightened.

"You're hurting me," she said, her voice shrill in the crisp afternoon air. "Let go!"

Squeezing hard, the person reached into Prudence's purse, rooting around and finding nothing. Roughly, they shoved their hands into each of Prudence's pockets until they discovered the envelope containing the quill. A slight smile appeared as they pulled the envelope from her pocket, released her arm and withdrew the quill. It was cream - colored with delicate gold stripes throughout the feather and a gold tip. It glinted in the warm sunshine as the person held it up to inspect it.

Prudence's heart raced, her voice nothing more than a broken whisper.

"Give that back...!"

She tried to snatch the quill back, but the person held it away from her. They fought for several moments, Prudence scratching and hitting. Then in a swift, brutal movement, the person thrust the quill down, driving it into Prudence's neck. The pain was sharp and immediate, and Prudence stumbled back, a strangled gasp escaping her lips as she clutched the wound.

Her legs buckled, and she sank against the rough bark of the apple tree, pressing her hand to the warmth spreading down her neck. She looked up at her assailant in stunned disbelief.

"You...stabbed me. You'll never... get away... with this," she choked, her voice strangled and barely audible.

The attacker remained silent, watching as she struggled, face in shadow against the glowing sunshine, their expression unreadable. As her consciousness faded, Prudence's last thought was one of bitter regret: she should have never gotten involved.

CHAPTER 1
AUGUST TO AUTUMN

Harper squinted and leaned forward as the windshield wipers struggled to keep up with the downpour. She popped a few gummy bears into her mouth and sang along to the radio. A few minutes later, the small, weathered, green and white sign on the side of the road came into view: "**Welcome to Fall, Michigan. Pop. 4,682.**" An enormous sigh escaped her involuntarily. Yesterday, she'd left Atlanta—one of the biggest cities in the United States. She had crammed everything she owned into a U-Haul trailer currently bouncing along behind her SUV. Here she was, moving to a town so small it barely existed on the map.

She pressed a little harder on the gas pedal and tried to ignore the knot of doubt twisting in her belly. She'd traded skyscrapers and a bustling, vibrant city for this microscopic dot on the map. What if this was the worst mistake she'd ever made?

After a few minutes, the sprawling fields of grass gave way to rows of corn lining both sides of the road like a natural corridor. The corn, standing five or six feet tall, stretched for over a mile before it transitioned to row upon row of apple trees. She was admiring the sprawling orchard when a large, burnt orange billboard came into view. "Welcome to Fall, Michigan... where it's always autumn!" was written in soft, white lettering on the billboard. Painted pumpkins and gourds and apples bordered the playful, bouncy letters, and autumn leaves artfully scattered along the edges of the sign.

Cute, Harper thought. As she drove through the outskirts of town, old farmhouses sat proudly on wide lots, set back from the road and surrounded by weathered fences and sprawling front yards. These gradually gave way to quaint cottages, charming bungalows, and grand Victorian and Colonial homes closer to the town center. Each Victorian had a generous front porch, some of which were adorned with wicker chairs, wooden rockers, or porch swings. Through the rain, Harper could see pumpkins, gourds, and fall-colored flowers decorated all the porches, hinting at the ever-present spirit of autumn, regardless of the actual season.

It was a warm August evening, yet Harper felt as if she'd driven straight through a portal into the heart of autumn. *Those decorations must be artificial,* Harper thought to herself.

Harper slowed as she approached an area that looked like the center of town, where surprisingly stately, crimson brick municipal buildings lined the road on both sides. There was a sign for the Fall Police Department, the Grand Traverse County Sheriff, and the Fall Fire Department. The buildings stood prominently in front of large, well-kept lawns and a modest sign in front of the Town Hall that read: *"Mayor Tom Gillespie welcomes you to Fall."*

"Well, thanks, Mayor Tom," Harper said into the silence of the car.

Downtown Fall appeared to be the epitome of quaint, small-town charm. The rain drummed steadily as Harper navigated the downtown streets. Historic brick and wood-sided buildings lined the streets. The buildings were painted in rich autumnal tones, creating a warm tapestry that practically screamed October. The storefronts were an eclectic mix of old and new, but each oozed seasonal character. Hand-carved wooden signs hung over doorways, proudly displaying the names of long-established local businesses. As Harper slowly drove by, she read the names aloud, *"Autumn's End Antiques, Cedar and Spice Tavern, Sweater Weather Wares, The Candle Cottage, Sullivan's Apple Market, Spin Me A Yarn, Woodland Whimsy, The Cozy Blanket Shoppe, Maple and Crumb, Harvest Thyme Spice Shop, Autumn Moon Gallery..."*

Harper smiled as she drove, completely charmed by what she was seeing. The town had wholeheartedly committed to its 'perpetual autumn' theme. There was a warmth and coziness here that Harper could feel even in the rain. Fall, Michigan, wasn't just a place; it was a whole vibe, an atmosphere that was enveloping Harper like a cozy blanket.

Up ahead, Harper spotted a picturesque town square that looked like it belonged on a postcard. It was empty now, due to the hour and the rain, but Harper could imagine it full of people. Encircling the square were a dozen shops and restaurants, each housed in two- and three-story buildings with large, inviting picture windows. Hanging signs and awnings marked each business; the awnings displayed varying shades of rich rust, copper, warm yellow, and off-white. It was as if every detail of this place immersed visitors in the warmth of autumn at every turn.

Harper's overall doubt gave way to a little swell of delight. The entire town seemed plucked from her favorite October daydream. *Maybe this wouldn't be such a bad move after all.*

Harper's phone buzzed. She glanced at her screen and saw a group chat titled *ATL Girls*, her never-ending conversation with her two closest friends back in Atlanta.

ATL GIRLS 🍂🍷🥧

Amanda: Have you made it to Fall yet?

Erin: Are you there?? How is it??

Harper quickly typed back.

Harper: Just got here! It's raining, but it's definitely charming. They're committed to the whole fall vibe, for sure! 🍁
    Amanda: Ugh, jealous! 😩 Send pics ASAP!
    Erin: Can't wait to hear all about it! XOXO Love you! 🖤

It was almost 8 p.m. when Harper pulled up in front of her destination. She knew the exploration should wait until the next day, but her curiosity was killing her. She couldn't wait another minute to see the shop. The rain had intensified, drumming steadily on the windshield in a thundering rhythm. Across the square was a cozy-looking coffee shop called Harvest Roast, though it sat dark and shuttered for the night. The thought of a hot cup of coffee tugged at her so strongly she could almost taste it, and a pang of disappointment settled in her chest.

Harper refocused and spotted the corner storefront she'd been searching for—a warm, reddish clay-colored building with a sign that read *"Hearth & Quill Bookstore"* in soft, gold lettering.

"There it is," she murmured to herself, her words barely audible over the steady rain.

The bookstore was huge, impressive, and though dark, somehow inviting, even on a rainy evening. It took up an entire town block, with one side of the building facing the town square and the other stretching down the side street. The shop was three stories tall, the entire facade was made up of massive picture windows, and an oversized door on the corner. The top two floors featured beautiful arched windows, and a small balcony on the third floor overlooked the street and the square. A crooked *CLOSED* sign hung from a hook above the mail slot. Its untouched facade suggested that it had been left alone for a while; however, its imperfections charmed.

The window displays, meant to draw in curious passersby, were covered in brown craft paper. *It looks as though it's being renovated,* she thought, though she knew better. The book store had been shuttered for months, since her Aunt Eleanor had died.

She squinted through the rain and she leaned forward. Her eyes traveled upward. Intricate molding crowned the building in colored stone that contrasted beautifully against the rich red brick. As Harper's gaze reached the top of the building, she noticed an ivory stone set into the brickwork, its surface carved with the date: *1884.*

"141 years old and still looks great," she whispered, feeling a touch of fondness for the place. It might be a little rough around the edges, but it was beautiful.

Stifling a yawn, Harper reached into the center console of her SUV and pulled out a ring of keys she'd received from her aunt's estate attorney. The rain had intensified, drumming relentlessly against the roof of the car. *Of all the times not to have an umbrella,* she thought. Bracing herself, she took a deep breath and swung the door open, leaping out into the downpour. She slammed the door behind her and sprinted toward the front of the shop. The rain soaked her in seconds, and she yelled out as it continued to pelt down.

Harper shoved the first key into the lock, but it didn't fit. She tried the second with the same result. By the time she reached the third key, frustration was creeping in. The fourth and final key slid into the lock, but refused to turn. The rain beat down harder, soaking her curly hair and running down the back of her shirt.

"Oh, come on!" Harper groaned, rain running down her face as she jiggled the key, pulling and pushing on the door with mounting frustration. She closed her eyes for a moment and took a deep breath, and started over, convinced she missed the proper key. She wiped the rain from her face with the back of her hand and tried again, pulling the door toward her as she twisted the key. The lock shifted just the tiniest bit, a subtle give that gave Harper hope. She gritted her teeth and leaned against the door with her shoulder, twisting the key harder. A faint jingle echoed from the other side, the bell on the door teasing her with each shove.

It was after 8 p.m. and because of the raging storm, the night was growing dark quickly. Exhaustion was creeping in. Hunger gnawed at her, reminding her just how long it had been since she'd eaten anything other than gas station junk food. With a sigh, Harper decided it was best to leave the exploration for the morning. *Not a very good start to my new adventure*, Harper thought to herself.

———

The street lay empty. It was a little creepy without a single car or person in sight. It was as if the entire town had vanished. The silence was eerie and thick enough to feel, but she reminded herself it was late and stormy. Hardly the hour or weather for anyone to be out walking.

The Waze app on her phone told her The Copper Fox Inn was just a few blocks away. She navigated her SUV and trailer down the deserted street until she arrived at the inn. Her huge vehicle took up almost three parking spots and she cringed at the sight. She turned off the engine and her stomach rumbled loudly.

The inn stood before her, an impressive Victorian mansion with a steeply pitched roof, towers and turrets, rounded cupolas and a wrap around porch with space for dozens of people. The copper-colored exterior was accented by shutters and rich, chocolate brown trim. A large oval sign hung from a polished newel post in the front yard, its bold letters reading, The Copper Fox, est. 1881. The inn exuded grandeur and warmth and the inviting glow of lights in the windows beckoned Harper inside.

Although drenched, Harper grabbed her purse and her weekender tote from the backseat, shirt clinging to her skin, and dashed for the front porch to escape the downpour. The rain was relentless, and the shelter of the porch was a welcome reprieve.

She pushed open the front door, stumbling slightly as she

stepped into the foyer. A bell chimed softly overhead, announcing her arrival. Harper stood for a moment, dripping wet, taking in the warmth and coziness of the inn's entryway. She was finally out of the storm.

"Well, good evening! I wasn't sure if I'd be seeing you tonight," came a warm voice from across the room. Harper spun around and saw an attractive man in his mid - thirties seated at a small front desk, a paperback book in hand. He wore a button-down shirt with sleeves rolled up to his elbows and had a friendly smile that reached his blue eyes, which crinkled at the corners beneath wire-rimmed glasses.

"Hi," Harper managed, suddenly self-conscious. She must have looked like a drowned rat, rain-soaked and bedraggled. Dropping her bag, she instinctively crossed her arms in front of her chest, trying to appear a little less disheveled.

Paul, according to the small brass nameplate on the desk—turned over his book, leaving it splayed open on the counter. At his feet was a small round dog bed with an impossibly cute Cavalier King Charles Spaniel curled up inside. The dog lifted her head with interest and watched Harper.

"Please come in," he said with a welcoming smile. "Welcome to The Copper Fox Inn! I'm Paul, the owner."

"Hi! I'm so sorry," Harper said with a sheepish grin, glancing down at the puddle forming on the mat around her feet. "I'm getting your floor all wet."

"Don't be silly," Paul replied, waving a hand dismissively. "That's what the welcome mats are for! You're not the first, and you certainly won't be the last. Come in, come in. Let me grab you a towel."

He slipped out from behind the desk and disappeared through a doorway, returning a moment later with a plush, copper-colored towel. The dog barely lifted her head. As he approached, Harper noticed he was wearing well-worn jeans and a pair of plaid slippers. When he caught her glance, he chuckled.

"Here, dry yourself off," he said, extending the towel toward her with a smile. "And forgive the slippers—my feet were soaked earlier, so I swapped out my shoes and completely forgot about it!" He laughed, wiggling his toes in the cozy slippers as if to prove his point.

Harper looked down at her own drenched Converse, her smile widening. "Hey, you've got the right idea. Those look perfect for a night like this." She took the towel gratefully and wrapped it around her shoulders. It was unbelievably fluffy, and Harper swore it felt warm, almost as if it had just come out of the dryer. The faint scent of vanilla clung to the fabric, and she felt a rush of gratitude for the warmth as she used the towel to squeeze water out of her long, curly hair.

"Adorable dog!" Harper said, nodding towards the dog.

"Oh, thank you. That's Lady, the resident expert when it comes to treats," he said with a laugh. He added, "Her full name is Lady von Trapp. We're big fans of The Sound of Music around here."

Harper laughed and watched as Lady yawned, stretched, and then walked in circles around her dog bed, finding just the right position before curling up in a ball again and closing her eyes.

"I got into town a lot later than I expected," she admitted, wiping at her face. "I've got an SUV pulling a trailer parked out front. Is there somewhere secure I can park it overnight? A parking lot or somewhere off-site?"

Paul shook his head with an apologetic smile.

"I'm afraid we don't have a parking lot, but you're fine where you are. You won't bother anyone there, and no one will bother your vehicle. Fall's one of the safest towns in the entire state," he added, his voice brimming with pride. "Most folks don't even bother locking their doors around here."

Harper's eyes widened slightly. That differed from her house in downtown Atlanta's Old Fourth Ward neighborhood.

"Really?" she asked, unable to hide her surprise.

Paul grinned.

"Really. You're in excellent hands here. Now, how about we get you checked in?" He moved back behind the desk, shuffled through some papers, and glanced up at her. "I'm guessing you're Harper?"

"Whitmore, yes," Harper confirmed, smiling.

"Yes, here we are," he said, pulling a paper from a folder with a little flourish. "You're in The Fox Suite. You're going to love it—it has a private bathroom with a clawfoot tub, a plush queen bed, and an original fireplace that we converted to electric. Just flip a switch, and voilà, instant fire!"

"That sounds perfect," Harper replied, signing the paper and passing it back to him. "Also, I'm starving. I've eaten nothing but candy since Ohio. Can you direct me to the nearest restaurant?"

Paul winced apologetically.

"Ah, I'm afraid everything closes early on Sundays. Nothing's open until breakfast. But," he added quickly, "I've got extras from tonight's guest dinner—my famous roast chicken with mashed potatoes and green beans, plus pumpkin pie for dessert. How about I bring a plate up to your room once you're settled?"

Harper's eyes widened in disbelief. "That would be amazing, thank you!"

"Don't mention it," Paul said, his calm tone exuding warmth. He handed her a keychain. There was a small brass key on it, and a delicate metal disk with a fox's head, intricately etched with tiny whiskers and fur. The craftsmanship was beautiful, and she smiled at the charming detail.

"We just know that you're going to fall in love with Fall," Paul delivered the line like it was a well-rehearsed mantra, but with a wink that made Harper chuckle.

"The Fox Suite is just up the main stairs, second door on the left. There's a plaque on the door—you can't miss it. Can I help with your luggage?"

"Oh, no thank you," Harper said with a smile, adjusting her weekender bag on her shoulder.

13

She found the room easily enough. The name was carved into a plaque on the door, and underneath it was an oval-shaped copper strike plate with a brass fox head door knocker. She lifted the fox head gently and let it fall, hearing a soft 'ting' as the fox head struck the plate. The wood above the knocker displayed the words "The Fox Suite," etched and filled with gold leaf, causing it to shimmer. It was beautiful.

Once inside, Harper let out a sigh. She dropped her bag and collapsed into an overstuffed chair just inside the doorway, feeling her exhaustion hit her all at once. She knew she would eat dinner, wash her face, and be out like a light when her head hit the pillow.

CHAPTER 2
HEARTH & QUILL

Harper stirred early the next morning, blinking groggily at the soft light filtering through the curtains. Her body seemed to have a built-in alarm clock, no matter how exhausted she might be. She glanced around the room, taking in the quiet stillness, but there was no clock in sight. With a resigned sigh, she reached for her phone on the bedside table, tapping the screen. *5:47 a.m.* Of course.

She groaned inwardly, closing her eyes and trying to will herself back to sleep. But it was no use—once she was awake, she couldn't get back to sleep. She lay there for a few more minutes, eyes shut, knowing the effort was futile. Her mind had already started ticking through the day's to-do list.

She sat up and looked around the room, taking it all in. Last night, in her exhaustion, Harper had barely noticed her surroundings, but this morning, she saw everything. She lay on an impressive oversized four-poster bed. The dark and richly grained wood framed a mattress that was the perfect balance of firm and indulgently soft. A cozy throw draped neatly across the footboard, layered the thick quilt wrapped around her.

Warmth radiated throughout the entire room. The wall color was a soft, earthy brown and the fabrics included rich oranges, warm yellows, creamy whites, and deep cranberry reds. Every detail was thoughtful and inviting. Across from the bed, against the wall, stood a stunning antique armoire, its polished wood gleaming faintly in the morning light. There were a few copper sconces on the walls, and two cozy side chairs nestled near the door to the bathroom, perfect for reading or unwinding. Harper swung her legs over the side of the bed and stretched, then she padded across the plush rug and into the bathroom.

A pleasantly hot shower melted away the last remnants of travel fatigue. Harper slipped into her favorite jeans, a well-worn Emory University T-shirt, and her trusty gray Converse. She was happy to find that after being under the radiator overnight, her shoes were perfectly dry. She left her curls damp and swiped on a few coats of mascara. A quick glance out the window reassured her that her SUV and trailer were still right where she had parked them, safe and sound.

Harper grabbed her bag and the charming, fox-shaped room key and quietly opened the door. The moment she cracked it open, the comforting sounds of breakfast drifted toward her—the soft clink of silverware on plates, the indistinct murmur of conversation, and, most importantly, the intoxicating scents of coffee, cinnamon, and sizzling bacon. Her stomach growled in anticipation.

Harper made her way into the cozy breakfast room, which was beautifully decorated. Copper-colored tablecloths draped half a dozen cafe tables, and small bookshelves filled with well-worn novels and cookbooks lined the walls. A handful of guests sat quietly, chatting over breakfast or reading their books and newspapers, the peaceful morning hum filling the air.

Against the wall stood a large antique sideboard. Pitchers of water and freshly squeezed juice, bowls of vibrant fruit, trays of flaky pastries, and a small handwritten sign reading, "For those in need of a 'grab and go' breakfast," were arranged on it. The scent of cinnamon and freshly baked bread lingered in the air.

A small plaid dog bed lay against the wall, and inside was Lady, sitting primly, watching the breakfast scene before her.

Paul appeared and cheerfully said, "Good morning, Harper. Can I get you some coffee?"

"Oh yes, please," she replied. "And good morning." She found an empty table near the bookshelves and sat down.

Paul reappeared moments later, carrying a large rust-colored coffee mug. With a practiced hand, he poured the steaming brew, and the rich, heady aroma immediately enveloped Harper, its warmth cutting through the lingering brain fogginess of the morning.

After adding a splash of cream and a spoonful of sugar, she inhaled deeply, then took a tentative sip. Her eyebrows shot up in surprise; the coffee was smooth, bold, and utterly perfect. Far better than she'd expected, and a welcome comfort after the previous two days of travel.

"Wow," she said, her lips curving into a smile over the rim of the mug. "This might be the best cup of coffee I've ever had."

"The secret is nutmeg and cinnamon in the grounds before brewing." Paul said conspiratorially, grinning.

"It's delicious!" Harper said.

"Thank you. I hope you slept well."

Harper nodded. "I did. I was out the moment my head hit the pillow. The bed was so comfortable. And your roast chicken was to die for!"

Paul beamed.

"I'm so glad to hear that! Why don't you review the breakfast menu, and I'll be right back."

Paul circled the room efficiently, filling coffee mugs and clearing a few plates with a practiced hand. He chatted with guests, answered questions, and directed one couple by pointing out local sights on a town map.

Maple Pecan Pancakes
Fluffy pancakes infused with maple syrup and topped with toasted pecans, served with a side of warm maple syrup and a dollop of spiced butter.

Sweet Potato & Sage Breakfast Hash
A hearty hash made with roasted sweet potatoes, crispy bacon, fresh sage, and a sprinkle of goat cheese. Served with sunny-side-up eggs on top.

Maple-Glazed Bacon
Crispy strips of bacon brushed with a maple glaze and cracked black pepper, offering a sweet-savory flavor.

Cinnamon-Spiced Granola with Greek Yogurt
Homemade granola with oats, almonds, dried cranberries, and a hint of cinnamon, served with creamy Greek yogurt and fresh fruit.

Fresh Baked Apple Scones
Light, buttery scones filled with chunks of spiced apples and served with cinnamon-honey butter.

Everything sounded incredible. When Paul came back around, Harper ordered the Sweet Potato and Sage Breakfast Hash, and he refilled her coffee mug.

She perused the shelves next to her, absentmindedly picked up a copy of a book and started reading. Within a few minutes, she became completely engrossed in the mystery novel. Her food arrived, smelling incredible, and she continued reading as she ate. Far too quickly, the plate was empty. The food was exceptional. When Paul returned to check on her, she told him so.

"Thank you. The hash was my mother's recipe." He wiped his hands on a yellow, gingham-checked towel and threw it over his shoulder. "This was her inn until she passed six years ago. I inherited her recipes - and have created a few of my own. But the hash has always been a guest favorite."

She smiled. "I can see why. That goat cheese was incredible."

"All the cheese comes from a local dairy farm," Paul said. "You can't get any fresher than Maple Grove Dairy, just outside of Fall."

"Well, that explains it," she smiled. "I am a bit of a foodie, so that was heaven."

"You know what? Hold on a second," Paul said, heading back to the kitchen. Harper waited, shelving the book and making a mental note of the title, *Murder on Mackinac Island* by John Thorston.

Paul returned with a white bag and dropped it on the table.

"This is an apple muffin with a brown sugar streusel topping. I've been playing with the recipe, trying to get it perfect. I feel like something is missing. Try it and let me know what you think?"

Harper peered into the bag at the enormous muffin. Her mouth watered, despite being so stuffed she wished she could unbutton her jeans. "Sure, I'd love to. But can I try it later? I'm stuffed!"

Paul's smile was as big as the muffin. "Of course! I'll see you later!"

Harper spent a few minutes checking out the inn, mesmerized by the details. In the parlor—the plush velvet armchairs were a gorgeous cranberry color, the cozy sofa and chair were upholstered with a fox motif, and the deep green wainscoting that ran along the lower half of the walls contrasted perfectly with the soft cream above. Copper accents glinted throughout the room, complementing garlands of autumn leaves, miniature pumpkins, and clusters of branches artfully arranged throughout the space.

Over the mantle hung an oversized, framed oil painting of a fox curled up in a forest of golden leaves. The mantle was full of a collection of brass and copper candlesticks in varying heights, their polished surfaces catching the light. In each room, she saw a small dog bed for Lady. Harper was utterly charmed by the bed and breakfast. The place was more than just beautiful—it felt like a home, steeped in history, care, and a love for autumn.

It was a beautiful, warm morning, so Harper walked to Hearth & Quill from the inn. The warmth of the day was a pleasant surprise, though it shouldn't have been. It was August, and summer was in full swing. But after just 12 hours in Fall, she was so enchanted by the autumnal *everything;* she was convinced that it was October.

As Harper walked, passersby greeted her with a smile, a nod, or a friendly "good morning." She passed a handful of restaurants just opening for breakfast, a few charming shops with fall displays in the windows, and an outdoor outfitter with a bright red kayak dangling from the roof like a beacon. Soon, she reached the corner of Willow and Main, where the towering double oak doors of Hearth & Quill stood waiting. The bookstore stretched nearly a full block in both directions, its massive windows catching the morning light as if they were holding their breath. She pulled out the jangling keyring, trying each one like she had the night before. The third slid into place, and with a twist and a satisfying click, the deadbolt gave way. The door creaked open—but stopped short. A heap of untouched mail had built up behind it, blocking the threshold. With a sigh, Harper leaned her shoulder into the heavy wood and gave it a firm shove. The door inched open, then gave way with a ring of the bell, sending the pile of mail cascading across the carpet in a soft avalanche. Despite the warmth of the morning sun behind her, the inside of the bookstore was cool, dim, and hushed—like stepping into another world that hadn't stirred in quite some time.

"Wow," Harper breathed, taking in the enormous space before her.

From the front door, she could see nearly the entire two-story shop. The entrance opened into a cavernous room centered on a massive stone fireplace that looked like it belonged in a mountain lodge. Above the hearth, an intricately carved wooden mantel held antique lanterns, small potted plants, and a collection of framed literary quotes leaning casually against the chimney.

An oversized leather sofa sat in front of the fireplace, flanked by four high-backed chairs and two side tables fashioned from stacked antique suitcases. Books covered nearly every surface—neatly, mostly. Some were stacked on the floor in waist-high towers; others tumbled from toppled piles under the coffee table. Wood-and-wrought-iron tables dotted the space, also laden with books, while a patchwork of overlapping, timeworn rugs softened the floor beneath it all.

Harper tried to step forward but was stopped by the heap of mail at her feet. She crouched, scooped up some of the mail from the worn rug, and carried it to the long, leather-topped counter beside the door. The surface was smooth with age, the leather buttery beneath her fingertips. An antique brass cash register gleamed faintly in the dim light, a quiet relic of another era. Beside it, a neat stack of bookmarks and magnets read *Hearth & Quill Bookstore, Fall, Michigan*, each printed with a burnt-orange maple tree in full autumn glory. She made several more trips before all the mail was piled on the countertop.

The walls of the shop featured floor to ceiling bookshelves, complete with massive wooden ladders that slide back and forth on a metal rail. Harper could picture herself sliding back and forth like in a scene from *Beauty and the Beast*. One ladder dangled precariously off the rail on one wheel, ready to topple at any moment. Harper could see a wrought-iron spiral staircase, just barely visible from her vantage point. In the back right corner was an oversized grandfather clock, easily 6 feet tall and 4 feet wide.

"Incredible," Harper whispered, her voice sounding almost too loud in the hush that filled the space.

Harper let out a breath she hadn't realized she was holding. The bookshop might be a lot more work than she'd expected. She hadn't really considered that it would need much attention—but now, looking around, she saw signs of neglect everywhere. A broken ladder. Books scattered across the floor. Little repairs needed in every corner. And all of it was now her responsibility.

She swallowed hard.

She looked around and saw the massive wrought - iron and wood chandelier suspended high above her. The fixture was enormous, maybe six feet across, and shaped like a tiered wedding cake, with 3 levels of candle-shaped light bulbs. It looked like something out of a grand old estate—a relic from another time.

Harper found the switch panel and flipped each of the six toggles but nothing happened. The chandelier stayed dark, and the shadows clinging to the corners of the shop remained heavy and still. *Of course,* she thought. *The power's probably been shut off.*

Flanking the front door were two large display windows—one facing Willow Street, the other overlooking Main Street and the town square. But they were more than just windows. Aunt Ellie had turned each into a cozy seating nook, complete with three overstuffed chairs and an old steamer trunk used as a coffee table. Harper could almost see herself there, curled up with a book, sunlight pouring in, and the quiet rhythm of the town just outside.

She couldn't see out now—the windows were covered in brown craft paper—but golden light streamed through the glass panes of the door, casting long slants across the floor. Behind the counter sat a cushioned chair with a cardigan draped over the back, as if her aunt had just stepped away for a moment and might return any second.

Harper walked slowly between the rows of shelves, the hardwood floors creaking pleasantly beneath her feet. Across the shop's width, she saw some shelves tilted slightly from age, and every shelf was crammed with books. The shelves that lined the walls loomed over her, stacked haphazardly with books—some brand new and pristine, and others worn and weathered, their spines cracked from years of love or neglect. Dust motes floated lazily in the air, catching the rays of sunshine like tiny sparks suspended in time.

She wandered deeper into the shop, trailing her fingers along the worn edges of the shelves as she moved toward the fireplace. Handwritten signs marked each section—*Classic Mysteries, Historical Fiction, Local Legends*—their faded ink and curling corners adding to the store's charm. The air was thick with the scent of aged paper, old wood, and the lingering trace of spiced candles, wrapping the space in a sense of warmth and quiet, timeless comfort.

Harper stood still for a moment, torn between pride and panic. The shop was incredible—far more beautiful and substantial than she'd expected—and the fact that it now belonged to her filled her with a quiet, startling sense of wonder. But beneath that wonder was a rising current of stress. She did not know where to begin. Ten years in advertising hadn't prepared her for bookstore inventory, building repairs, or the sheer volume of dust on every surface.

And yet... she felt strangely at ease here. Comfortable, like the space had always been waiting for her. *How is that possible?* she wondered. How could something feel like home so quickly?

It hit her then just how much had changed. A few days ago, she'd still been an Atlantan. A week ago, she had a job in advertising. A month ago, she was engaged to be married.

Now, she was none of those things.

Now, she was *here*.

CHAPTER 3
MAGGIE

Deciding she needed coffee before diving any deeper into the bookstore, Harper grabbed her bag, pulled the door shut behind her, and headed a few shops down to a place called Harvest Roast.

As she walked, a handful of people passed by—each offering a smile or a polite nod. She smiled back, wondering if they somehow knew who she was, or if everyone in Fall was just this friendly to strangers.

The moment she stepped inside the coffee shop, the scent hit her —rich, warm, and impossibly inviting. She nearly said *mmmmm* out loud.

There weren't many things Harper loved more than a good cup of coffee.

"Hey there! What can I get started for you?" asked the woman behind the counter, smiling as Harper approached. She looked to be in her thirties, her name tag reading *Melanie*.

"Hi! Do you have hazelnut coffee?" Harper asked, hopefully.

"For sure," Melanie said, already reaching for a large to-go cup and a marker. "Cream and sugar?"

"Extra of both, please," Harper said with a grin.

"You got it." Melanie smiled as she scribbled the order on the cup. "What's your name?"

Harper gave her name, then took a seat at the small table nearest the door, smiling politely at the people coming and going. A minute later, the door swung open and a tall blonde woman bounded in, radiating energy. She wore yoga pants and an old The Avett Brothers t-shirt; her hair was piled on top of her head in a carefree, messy bun. Her grin was wide and unbothered, like someone who knew everyone and had been up for hours already.

"Hey, Mel! How are you?" she called out, not even fully through the door. "Can I get my usual, please?" Her words came fast, her smile never faltering. She turned—and spotted Harper.

"Well, hi there! I'm Maggie," she said brightly, striding over with theatrical flair. She offered her hand and gave a playful little bow, like she was greeting royalty.

Harper laughed, standing and shaking her hand.

"Hi. I'm Harper Whitmore."

"Whitmore. As in Ellie?" Maggie said, tilting her head.

"Yes! She was my great aunt. Love your shirt," Harper said, gesturing towards Maggie's t-shirt.

"Thanks," Maggie said, glancing down at her shirt with a grin. "I've seen The Avett Brothers live—like, seven times. Totally obsessed."

"Wow, you've got me beat. I've seen them 5 times. They're just phenomenal live, aren't they?" Harper asked.

"Oh, for sure! They're amazing. So what brings you to town? Wait—*ohmygod*, are you here to take over the bookstore?" Maggie's words tumbled out in a rush, her excitement bubbling over until they nearly ran together. Harper couldn't help but smile. It was like Maggie was in a hurry to become friends—and Harper found that oddly endearing.

"Well," Harper said with a laugh. "Yeah, I guess I am."

"Ohthankgoodness," Maggie said. "Headquarters has been

closed since April, when your Aunt Ellie passed. Gosh, I miss her - and the bookstore- terribly."

"Headquarters?" Harper asked.

"Hearth & Quill, H&Q, HQ, Headquarters," she explained with a cheesy grin.

"Hazelnut coffee, extra cream, extra sugar," Melanie called out.

Harper laughed at Maggie and went to the counter to retrieve her coffee. She took a sip. It was incredible and Harper told her so.

"That's how I take my coffee, too. Light and sweet. But I like French vanilla," said Maggie.

They chatted easily while Maggie waited for her coffee, quickly discovering a shared love of music, books, and strong coffee. Both were in their early thirties, both single, and both seemed equally surprised by how natural the conversation felt.

Their differences, at least on the surface, were mostly physical— Maggie was tall and blonde, with the lean grace of a former dancer, while Harper was brunette, average height, with a strong runner's frame and the muscle tone that came from early morning miles and years of discipline.

Harper learned that Maggie had been close to Aunt Ellie. She'd worked at the bookstore in high school, studied there throughout college, and stayed in touch long after. Maggie spoke of her with fondness and ease, the kind that only came from a genuine connection.

"Okay, gimme your phone," Maggie said, holding out her hand.

"Uhhh. Okay," Harper said hesitantly, a small smile tugging at her lips as she handed it over.

"We're clearly going to be besties," Maggie said. She took Harper's phone and added her name and phone number to Harper's contact list. Then she went to fluff her hair, but remembering it was in a messy topknot, she struck a pose with an exaggerated kiss face and added her photo to the contact card as well. Harper had a huge grin on her face. Before she handed it back, Maggie called herself from Harper's phone, sharing Harper's contact info with herself as well.

"There. Now, how's the shop look inside?" Maggie asked.

"Well..." Harper hesitated. "Uhh. I haven't seen it since I was a kid, so I have nothing to compare it to. But it's a little rough. I've never seen so much dust. It needs a good cleaning. I'm overwhelmed, so I was stalling by getting coffee."

"Well, I can help. In fact, I could bring a few people over this afternoon and we could have a little cleaning party," Maggie said.

"Oh, no," said Harper, shaking her head. "Absolutely not. I can't ask you to do that."

"You didn't ask - I offered," Maggie said matter-of-factly. "You don't know how much we all miss Ellie and HQ. It's almost selfish of me to offer to help because I really just want the doors open again!"

"I mean - I could definitely use the help. But I don't even have power inside yet. I need to call the power company, but —" Harper said.

"Did you try the fuse box in the back room?" Maggie asked, blowing on and then sipping her coffee.

"Uh - no. I didn't even *find* the backroom yet," Harper said.

"Well, come on. Let's go see what we can do," Maggie said, opening the door and holding it for Harper.

———

Within two minutes, they were in the bookshop, and Maggie confidently led Harper to the back of the store. There was a small hallway with 3 doors. Straight ahead, the door had an 'Exit' sign, on the left, the sign read 'Restroom' and on the right was a sign that read 'Private.'

Harper opened that door and was surprised to find a short hallway and two more doors, one on the left and one on the right. To the left was a storage room with commercial metal racks stuffed from floor to ceiling with cardboard boxes. There were boxes of toilet tissue, coffee mugs, Keurig K-cups and other inventory. The second door led to a medium-sized office.

"Here it is," Maggie said, reaching into the storeroom and opening a metal breaker box cover. "And voila," she flipped a switch, and the lights came on, bathing the office and storeroom in light. "That's terrific, thank you so much!!" Harper said appreciatively.

Harper peeked into the office, a dark space with dust-covered laminate shelves sagging under the weight of forgotten books and files. It was a disorganized mess, with papers spilling from drawers, boxes stacked haphazardly, and a thick layer of dust coating every surface.

In the main bookshop, Harper looked around, admiring the lighting. The shop was washed in a warm, golden glow that felt cozy and welcoming. The chandeliers were stunning now that Harper could see them fully illuminated.

"Isn't it magical?" Maggie said, turning around slowly. "It's the bookstore of my dreams."

"You can say that again," Harper said. "I think it's the bookstore of everyone's dreams. I've never seen anything like it."

As they walked toward the front of the store, Maggie shared how she used to come in everyday after school to study.

"Aunt Ellie basically tutored me through geometry," she laughed. "Eventually she just gave me a job shelving books because I was here so much."

Her voice softened as she looked around. "This place always felt like a second home. Even after college, I'd come by a couple of times a week—just to read, answer emails, or work in the quiet. It was the only place I could actually breathe."

They stopped in front of a section of crime novels, and Harper absentmindedly picked up a book and flipped it over to read the back page.

"I convinced your Aunt Ellie to have this true crime section a few years ago," Maggie said. "Mostly because I'm true crime obsessed, but it's been surprisingly popular."

"What? I'm a true-crime girlie, too. Do you listen to pods?" Harper said excitedly.

"Absolutely! Crime Junkie is my favorite," Maggie put a hand to her heart earnestly.

"'*And I'm Brit*'," Harper said, grinning and duplicating the way the podcast's costar introduced herself each episode.

Maggie roared with laughter. "You nailed it!"

"I've never missed an episode," Harper laughed. She put the book back on the shelf and started walking again. "It seems like you were close with my aunt, and you obviously love this place. Maybe she should have left the bookstore to you."

"Oh, no. No, no, no," Maggie closed her eyes solemnly. "I adore reading and true crime, but the true love of MY life is sweets. I own the bakery a few blocks over, Maple and Crumb."

"Ohhhh... my first genuine friend in town AND she owns the local bakery? This is going to be bad for my waistline," Harper laughed, stopping by the spiral staircase.

"Hey, I have daily gluten-free, sugar-free, and keto options!"

"That's good to know," Harper said. "But I'd rather eat the real deal. I'm a total foodie!"

"Same, girl, same," Maggie said. "Speaking of love... my love for Hearth & Quill started right up those stairs in the loft."

"Oh?" Harper said. "I didn't check it out yet, since I couldn't find the lights."

"Now *that* might be the most special place in the entire shop. It's the kid's loft." Maggie said, taking a sip of her coffee. "C'mon, let me show you."

Harper and Maggie started up the sturdy spiral staircase tucked in the back of the store. Harper's gaze was drawn to the railing. What looked like plain black twirling wrought-iron balusters was, in fact, a series of balusters twisted into the shapes of characters from famous children's books. One baluster started at the floor, twirled and twisted, and about halfway between the stair and the handrail, it stretched into a small rabbit checking his watch, the famous character from Lewis Carroll's children's book *Alice in Wonderland*. A few more steps up, Harper saw the famous Sorting Hat from the *Harry Potter* books and tiny shields for each house in the novels, all in wrought-iron form. *The Very Hungry Caterpillar* twirled its way up another baluster, eating its way through fruits and *Winnie the Pooh* with all his friends. The attention to detail on this staircase was beautiful. A skilled blacksmith must have created it.

"This is incredible," Harper said, touching the balusters.

"It started with just one, the white rabbit. She added a new one every few years. The last one was the sorting hat from *Harry Potter*." Maggie got to the top of the stairs and plopped down on a cushion nearby, allowing Harper to explore the space.

The loft was open to the main floor, allowing light from the large picture windows to stream in. A low wall around the space meant the kids were safe while enjoying the loft. All around were hanging lights with cream-colored drum shades, each featuring little hand-drawn vignettes from children's books. The effect was magical. Soft rugs and floor cushions in muted fall colors filled the space. The effect was calming, peaceful and autumnal in its coziness. Low bookshelves were filled with brightly colored covers and whimsical tales. Board books were lined up with covers facing out so that little ones could see the titles.

"So what do you think?" Maggie asked after a minute.

"It's..."Harper began, putting her coffee cup down on a nearby table. "Well, it's absolutely perfect."

Harper let her fingers trail slowly over the spines of the books, reading the titles. She noticed some from her childhood, and others she'd never heard of before. As she passed over *Corduroy*, a wave of nostalgia washed over her. The bright red book featured a little brown teddy bear wearing overalls, bending down to pull what he believed to be his missing button off of a mattress. Harper remembered her mom reading her *Corduroy* when she was a child. It was one of her absolute favorites. Her heart swelled.

A cozy nook with a window seat and a round window looked out over Main Street and the town square - perfect for parents to sit with their children as they read together. Wooden beams crisscrossed the ceiling above, and paper lanterns shaped like woodland creatures hung down, adding a playful, magical touch to the space. Tucked away in corners were little surprises—secret alcoves with more bookshelves, reading nooks hidden behind velvet curtains, small tables where visitors could sit and color or read.

Harper took a sip of her coffee, and her gaze drifted across the shelves.

"This bookstore isn't at all what I expected. There's something about it... I feel connected to it in a way I can't quite explain."

"That's a good sign," Maggie said with a knowing smile, sipping her coffee. "Your aunt felt the same way. This place meant everything to her."

Harper nodded, the feeling deepening. It was clear that this bookstore was more than just a business—it was something almost magical.

CHAPTER 4
ELBOW GREASE

A little while later, Maggie dashed off, promising to return around 3pm with reinforcements. Harper gave up protesting and thanked her. When she left, the bookstore seemed empty and cold, as if Maggie had given it life.

Harper found a small janitorial closet in the bathroom. She grabbed a caddy with cleaning supplies, rags, dusters and trash bags, carried it to the front of the store and set it atop the mail mountain, causing more pieces to slide down the counter.

First things first, Harper thought.

She looked behind the counter, found a paper bag and stuffed it full of mail. She would deal with it later, but for now, she needed to make some tidying progress. Harper filled up a second bag as well, then took the bags to the office and laid them on the desk.

Back out front, Harper pulled out her phone, turned on her favorite true crime podcast and popped in her earbuds. The podcasters' soothing voices filled her ears, and Harper let out a contented sigh. It was time to tackle the dirt and grime. She tied the apron around her waist, smoothed it down with her hands, and loaded it up with rags, products and other supplies. She started at the front of the store, cleaning the large picture window alcoves. With the crime story unfolding, she lost herself in the cleaning. She pounded the cushions on the furniture, used a broom to reach high cobwebs, and swept the dust and dirt into big piles in the middle of the walkways. She wiped tables and shelves, picked up books and piled them onto a few rolling carts with signs that said, "Changed My Mind," and wiped the wood trim and baseboards.

Once she finished with one of the picture window alcoves, she wiped down the front doors and moved to the other side of the shop, repeating her chores there. Finally, she tore down the brown craft paper from the windows, and let the light flood into the space. Instantly, Harper felt the late summer sun warming her through the glass. She wanted to sink into a nearby chair and take a nap like a cat. The podcast episode was over, so she took out her earbuds and took a moment to gaze through the panes across the street to the town square. She saw a few older men sitting drinking coffee, a group of young women doing yoga in front of the gazebo, and a few people walking through the square on their way to their destinations.

Harper hauled a ladder out of the storeroom to wash the picture windows. She cleaned each window three times, inside and out, before it was truly clean. Harper was happy with the difference she was already making.

Once the window alcoves were clean, Harper moved onto the cavernous open room. *'You clean from the top down,'* she could almost hear her mother saying, and Harper eyed the tall ladders nestled into the stacks. One more quick glance in the janitor's closet revealed a duster on a long, telescoping handle. As she inspected it, the bell above the door chimed and in walked Maggie with two women and three men, all around their age.

"Hey there," Maggie said. "You started without us!" She gestured towards the window alcoves.

Harper laughed and held up her hands in a "wait, wait' motion. "Now hold on, there is plenty of cleaning for everyone."

They laughed and introductions were made all around. Harper met Courtney, Hannah, Noah, Connor and Tyler. They were all friendly and warm, and Harper thanked them and promised pizza and beer for their trouble.

After a few minutes of chatting, they made a plan of attack. Connor, Noah and Tyler would move the heaviest things around as needed, while Hannah, Courtney, Maggie and Harper would clean and direct them what needed moving. They'd start from the front of the store and move towards the back door, working from the top of the store *down (ha! Harper felt vindicated!)*.

Maggie had brought two buckets full of cleaning supplies, a bottle of vinegar and a little basket filled with tiny bottles that Harper guessed were essential oils. Maggie saw Harper eyeing the bottles and said, "I stopped at Frost and Fire. They were happy to donate some supplies to help get HQ clean and tidy."

"Frost and Fire?" Harper repeated questioningly.

"The apothecary in town. They have a ton of cleaning products, plus essential oils. They also custom blend a scent for most of the shopkeepers in town. Your aunt had her own scent, and Agnes sent me a few bottles to give to you."

"Wow. This town keeps getting more charming. My very own custom scent?" Harper shook her head incredulously. Maybe that's why she kept smelling the incredible scent of vanilla and sandalwood throughout the store.

"Well technically it's the shop's scent," said Noah, smirking. "But I can guarantee Agnes will make a scent for you too once she meets you. It's sort of her thing."

Before long, they were climbing the ladders, dangling from the rungs, and wiping the shelves from top to bottom. Someone turned on music, and they cleaned and chatted, while rag after rag was tossed in an enormous pile, filthy with dust and grime. The smell of the cleaner filled the space, a pleasant mix of lemon and pine. Harper couldn't believe her good fortune in running into Maggie today, and to have six people helping her clean. She started the day completely overwhelmed, and with each swipe, she felt more and more relaxed. While Harper didn't enjoy cleaning, there was something satisfying about making things right. Each brass sconce was polished to a high shine. Each swipe revealed beautiful wood shelves, gorgeous leather-bound book spines in rich shades of brown and burgundy, and unique decor throughout the shop.

"Do you want me to shelve these books?" Courtney gestured to the stack of books on the side table near the hearth.

Harper considered it. "No, thank you. I'll do that. I think it'll help me learn the layout of the store if I put them away."

Her aunt had amassed a collection of antique quills that were on display in nearly every corner of the bookshop. There were quills encased in wood and glass display boxes mounted vertically and horizontally on the walls. There was a collection of quills standing in their original metal inkwells, which were made of pewter, silver and brass. The collection of ceramic inkwells with Asian markings on the side was stunning. And there was one extra-large glass display case resting on the mantle above the hearth with the most stunning quills Harper had ever seen. Eight quills lined up horizontally from smallest to largest. The most stunning one was the largest feather quill. The feather was cream colored and had the most delicate golden stripes throughout it. There was a gold tip on the end of the feather. It glimmered in the sunlight, almost glowing softly. At the other end was a very sharp gold nib for writing. Harper wondered what kind of bird had golden feathers? It was absolutely gorgeous.

She carefully cleaned each quill display case, polishing the glass and removing all the dust. Harper loved the quills and thought it was a quirky collection to see in a bookshop. Harper also noticed that at the front and back of the shop, where the walls weren't covered with bookshelves, they were covered in a light cream-colored wallpaper with a delicate golden quill pattern. It was absolutely stunning attention to detail.

After a few hours, they collectively paused to catch their breath. Harper threw her rag onto the enormous pile with the others and rubbed her lower back, stretching gently from left to right.

"Wow. This place looks incredible!" Courtney said, wiping her brow with the back of her hand. They all looked around, taking in the space.

"It really does," Noah agreed. "This would have taken Harper days on her own."

"Or weeks," Harper corrected, and they all laughed. "Seriously, I can't thank y'all enough."

"Many hands make light work," said Hannah, flopping down into an armchair.

"That's what we say at the orchard when we're harvesting," said Connor. To Harper, he explained, "I work there, too, during the peak season."

Just then, the bell overhead jingled and a large stack of 6 pizza boxes walked in, completely obscuring the person behind.

"Delivery for Harper?" came a muffled voice from behind the boxes.

"Perfect timing. Here, let me help," Harper said, rushing over to take the boxes and set them on the counter. There stood a young man in his early 20s, wearing a red windbreaker that said The Rustic Pie on the chest.

"Hi," Harper said.

"Hey, Ronnie," Connor called out from the couch. "What are you doing delivering pizzas?'

"Hey everybody!" Ronnie said, looking around. "Marco called out sick, so I had to fill in."

"Oh, you should have called me into work," Connor said. He laughed and said to Harper "I work there too, as a part-time delivery driver."

"Then you'd have missed the cleaning party, Connor," Hannah said, wiping her brow on her forearm. "Wanna join us, Ronnie?"

"Wish I could, but duty calls," Ronnie said, gesturing to the door. "But wow, it's looking great in here."

Then, looking at Harper, he smiled and gave her the total. Harper paid in cash and thanked him.

"You're welcome," he said with a grin. "There are plates, napkins and parmesan cheese in the bag. Have a great night."

Connor and Tyler went to the general store to pick up some beer and soda, and the group sat around the hearth, eating, drinking and laughing together.

By the time Harper returned to The Copper Fox Inn, it was well past 9 p.m. Her shoulders and hands ached from scrubbing, and her back and legs throbbed from hours spent balancing on ladders, lifting books, and hauling boxes. She could only imagine how Connor and Tyler felt after a full afternoon of hefting the heaviest items in the shop. The memory of them hoisting the massive Chesterfield sofa into the air while she and Maggie swept and mopped furiously underneath made her smile—she couldn't have done it without them.

Needing to unwind, Harper drew herself a hot bath in the antique clawfoot tub. As the water filled the basin, she discovered a small sachet of dried herbs on the counter, labeled "Compliments of The Copper Fox Inn." Curious, she poured the contents into the bath. Almost instantly, the room filled with the calming scents of orange, vanilla, and cloves. *Paul has impeccable taste*, Harper thought as she inhaled deeply, letting the comforting aroma settle over her like a blanket.

She stripped off her grimy clothes and slid into the bath, exhaling audibly as the hot water began easing her sore muscles. The tension melted from her body, and for a moment, she thought she might never leave the tub.

As she soaked, her thoughts drifted back over the day, marveling at how connected she had felt to so many people. From Paul's warm welcome to Maggie's infectious energy and the incredible group that helped her clean the shop, she couldn't believe the kindness of everyone in Fall.

During her long drive from Georgia to Michigan, she'd had plenty of time to second-guess her decision to move. Trading the hustle and vibrancy of a big southern city for the quiet, small-town life of northern Michigan had seemed daunting, and she had missed her friends back home before she'd even left Atlanta. She loved the big city. Leaving was heartbreaking, and starting over in a new place had felt like a serious gamble, especially in her 30s. But as she lay there in the soothing water, the scent of herbs lingering in the air, Harper thought something she hadn't dared to imagine on the journey north—this move might just be the best decision she'd ever made.

CHAPTER 5
TIME TO GO

Harper woke the next morning early. She turned over in bed and felt every muscle in her body ache. *Owww,* she thought. *Even breathing hurts.* Harper checked her phone... 5:57 a.m. She lay in bed for a while, scrolling through social media, watching a few reels, and catching up on texts. As she did, she rolled her ankles under the duvet, stretching her calves. Harper was used to running about 5 miles each morning, but the cleaning and lifting had been a welcome challenge to her muscles. It was 6:30 before she swung her legs over the side of the bed and stood up. She dressed in yoga pants, an oversized t-shirt and tennis shoes. Her long brown hair had dried weirdly after going to bed with wet hair, so she pulled it back into a ponytail. She grabbed her sunglasses, her bag and her fox room key and headed downstairs.

Harper walked into the dining room and sank in the first chair at an open table she came to. Lady padded over, sniffed her leg, and returned to her dog bed to lie down.

Paul appeared out of nowhere with an oversized coffee mug and said, "Good morning, Harper. Would you like some coffee?"

"Yes, please," she said with a groan.

"I have mimosas if you need a little hair-of-the-dog," he said with raised eyebrows as he filled her cup.

"No, just coffee is great," she said with a little laugh, adding cream and sugar. "I wish I were hungover... I'm just sore. I cleaned the entire bookstore last night. I had some outstanding folks helping me, which was amazing and unexpected. But it also meant I couldn't quit before they did. I'm beat."

"Ahh, so you *are* related to Ellie. I thought two Whitmores in one small town was probably not a coincidence, but I didn't want to pry," Paul said.

"Yes, she was my great-aunt. She left me the bookstore when she passed," Harper said.

"Well, that must have been a ton of work you did yesterday. Who came by to help you?"Paul asked.

She took a sip of her coffee and shook her head slowly.

"So dang good, Paul," she said, nodding towards her coffee mug. "I met Maggie at Harvest Roast, and she brought some friends to help me. Courtney, Hannah, Noah, Connor and Tyler."

" Oh, that's a great group of folks there. I'm so glad you're getting a warm welcome to Fall," he said." I just know you'll love it here. But first, breakfast. What'll you have?"

Harper looked down at the menu.

Pumpkin Spice Pancakes
Fluffy pancakes made with pumpkin puree,
cinnamon, nutmeg, and cloves, served with
maple syrup and pecans.

Sausage and Apple Breakfast Skillet
Breakfast sausage, diced apples and potatoes
with sage and rosemary, served with over-
easy eggs and a buttermilk biscuit

Cider-Glazed Ham Steak
Pan-fried ham glazed with a reduction of
apple cider, brown sugar, and Dijon mustard.

Cinnamon Pecan Granola Parfait
Layers of Greek yogurt, cinnamon, pecan
granola, and fresh seasonal pears.

Cranberry Orange Muffins
Orange-flavored cake with fresh cranberries
and orange zest, perfect for a grab-and-go
breakfast.

"Everything sounds amazing. I think I'll try the Sausage & Apple Breakfast Skillet, please. But could I have the eggs scrambled instead?" Harper asked.

"Sure, no problem," Paul said.

"Thanks," Harper said, taking a long sip of her coffee.

Paul refilled it before heading back to the kitchen, and Harper sat back with a satisfied sigh.

They chatted a bit when Paul delivered her meal and again when he cleared her dishes. Harper barely refrained from licking the plate clean; it was so good. As he cleared the empty plate, Paul said she could leave the SUV and trailer there again.

"Oh, I meant to tell you," Harper began, leaning in slightly. "That muffin from yesterday? It was *incredible*. I absolutely loved the little bits of apple in the cake, but the star was the crunchy brown sugar topping." She smiled a little sheepishly. "I actually ate the whole top of the muffin first—it was that good."

Her eyes sparkled as she remembered it, the perfect balance of sweet, tart, and buttery crunch. "Honestly, I could've eaten a whole batch of just the tops."

"I'm so glad you liked it. But doesn't it seem like it's missing something?" Paul sat down opposite Harper.

"I think it's perfect as is, but if you think it's missing something, maybe try some salt flakes. It sounds weird, but I have a few recipes that have exotic salts in them and it really makes the other flavors pop without being overly salty. Try black lava salt, Himalayan salt, or arctic salt flakes."

"What in the world has happened to salt lately?" Paul shook his head. "There used to be just... salt. And now, there are more varieties than I ever knew existed. But that's a good idea, thanks!"

"I am here anytime you need a food taster," Harper said with a smile.

"Tomorrow, I'll have a new scone for you to try," Paul said, standing up. "You have a great day, Harper!"

"Back 'atcha, Paul, thanks."

Harper knew what she needed most of all was a yoga class, but she'd settle for a long walk where she could work out the kinks in her body.

After a long walk that loosened the knots in her back, Harper stood outside Maple and Crumb, Maggie's cozy little bakery, with a basket tucked under her arm. It was late morning, but the shop's windows were framed with twinkling fairy lights, and the sugary sweet scent of cake and frosting wafted through the door as she stepped inside. Bells chimed overhead as Harper swung the door open.

The shop was warm, filled with the comforting hum of chatter and the soft clinking of coffee cups. A few locals sat at tables, enjoying their afternoon treats, while Maggie worked behind the counter, laughing with a customer as she handed over a bag of fresh pastries.

When Maggie spotted Harper, her face lit up. "Hey Harper!

How are ya? Whatcha got there?" she called out, wiping her hands on her apron.

Harper made her way to the counter, feeling a little shy despite Maggie's easy warmth.

"I wanted to bring you a little something," she said, holding up the basket. "Just to say thank you for everything you've done for me."

Maggie raised an eyebrow, a teasing smile spreading across her face. "You're bringing *me* a treat? Yay! No one ever brings food to the baker!"

Harper laughed, relaxing a bit. "I'm rethinking it a bit right now, actually. It smells heavenly in here...what was I thinking? I can't take credit since I don't have a kitchen yet - these are some pumpkin muffins from Paul's inn. "

Maggie's eyes widened with delight as she took the basket from Harper.

"Oh, yum. Paul's a terrific baker and those sound amazing!" She peeked inside and inhaled deeply, her grin growing wider. "You're officially my favorite customer."

"Well, I had to do a little something to say thank you. I really appreciate your help. You were so generous with your time helping me clean the bookstore, and in introducing me to some new friends as well..." Harper trailed off with a smile.

Maggie set the basket down and leaned against the counter, crossing her arms. "That's what friends are for, right?"

Harper felt a warmth spread through her, the kind that had been missing for a while. "Right. Honestly, this has all been really overwhelming, and you made it feel less so. I'm just really glad I met you."

Maggie waved it off but was clearly pleased. "Okay, now that we've got these amazing muffins, you're staying for coffee, right? I'm making a fresh pot, and I've got the best cinnamon rolls in town waiting. I'll trade you one for a muffin."

Harper laughed. "Deal."

Maggie hustled around the shop getting cinnamon rolls, mugs and coffee.

Harper looked around and said, "Speaking of besties... it seems like you know everyone in town."

"I do," she picked up a muffin and considered it. "But they're not all The Avett Brothers-loving, true crime-obsessed, coffee-drinking maniacs like you and me." She took an enormous bite and laughed.

"True," Harper grinned, picking up her cinnamon roll. "Have you listened to *Up and Vanished,* by the way? It's so good!"

"No, I haven't. I've been listening to *Criminal* and *My Favorite Murder* lately." She widened her eyes and looked at the muffin. "This is really good! Yum."

"Right?" Harper agreed. "Those pods are good. I'm all caught up on *Criminal*. Nothing is quite like *Serial* season 1...I've listened to that entire season 3 times, from start to finish. I really think Jay did it." Harper said conspiratorially.

"Ohmygosh," Maggie said, pounding the table with excitement. "Me too! It was totally Jay!"

They continued chatting about their shared love of true crime, and Harper couldn't help but smile. She already felt like she had a great friend in Maggie.

Harper was back at the bookstore before noon, ready to get to work. But she found herself daydreaming. She was curious about the house her aunt left her besides the bookstore. Aunt Ellie had kept it very secretive, only telling her she'd left her a home, but nothing more than that. She wondered if it was close to town so she could walk to the bookstore, or further out of town where she'd need to drive each day. She took out her phone and impulsively sent a quick text to Maggie.

"Hey, I forgot to ask you... do you know where my aunt's house is? The attorney didn't tell me."

A reply arrived almost immediately. "Yup. Above the bookstore."

Harper walked outside and looked up. Sure enough, the bookstore was three floors high, but the bookshop was only two stories. *I can definitely walk to work,* she thought. She couldn't figure out how to get up to the apartment. She walked around the front of the building, but there wasn't a door for access to the apartment there. Harper turned down the side street, walked the depth of the building, and then walked back up front again. There were no entrances to the apartment there, either. Around back, there was a small parking lot with six parking spots and a dumpster. Attached to the building, she saw a metal fire escape leading to a window, but it wasn't reachable from the ground. And a fire escape couldn't be the only way to get into a house. She spent another 5 minutes looking around the bookstore. The only doors lead to the office, storage room, bathroom, and exit out to the alley.

"Feeling dumb, but how do I get in?" She texted Maggie.

"LOL. Check the time.😊" Maggie replied.

It was 9:03 a.m. What did that mean? She wandered around the shop again, looking for a clock. The only one was a massive grandfather clock against the back wall of the shop. *No, it couldn't be,* Harper thought. *Could it?*

Harper inspected the grandfather clock closely. It was wider than most, and pressed against the wall tightly. She pushed and pulled on the face of the clock, then opened the glass front door of the clock. Harper closed the front door, considered it for a minute, then ran her fingers around the seam where the clock met the wall and felt a faint breeze. She slid her fingers up and around. As her fingers slide down the left side of the clock, she felt a small groove, just big enough for the tips of her fingers to settle into the wood. She gave a tug, and the entire clock swung towards her, away from the wall.

Harper was almost giddy with excitement. Behind the grandfather clock was a set of wooden stairs leading up over the office below, and disappearing to the left. The grandfather clock was a secret door! She felt like she was in a Nancy Drew novel. She reached inside for a light switch, found one and flipped it, flooding the wide staircase with light.

CHAPTER 6
THE APARTMENT

Harper climbed the wooden staircase with a grin on her face, her hand trailing along the old wooden banister that creaked under her touch. The steps groaned with each move she made. A faint smell of vanilla and aged wood hung in the air, mixed with the unmistakable scent of old books that seemed to follow her wherever she went in this place.

She reached the landing at the top of the stairs. A tarnished brass keyhole stared back at her. She fished out the keyring her aunt had left for her, trying each key until one slid into the lock with a satisfying click. Harper turned the knob and pushed the door open.

Sunlight streamed through the tall, arched windows, casting warm golden patches of light across the hardwood floors. Dust motes danced lazily in the beams of light. Just off the foyer was a cozy living area with a brown leather couch, a cream-colored overstuffed armchair with an ottoman, just begging for someone to curl up and read a good book in it. A blanket in tones of sage green and cream draped the arm of the chair. There was an industrial-looking coffee table with several old magazines on top, and a small fireplace with a mantel on one wall. A few old photos, a tiny brass clock, and an owl figurine lined the mantel. Harper saw a few potted plants, one of which was definitely dead, but several succulents and a fern were clinging to life by a thread.

A beautiful, surprisingly stylish kitchen was tucked against the far wall of the space. It was small but well appointed, with navy blue painted cabinets, gold hardware and butcher block countertops. A round dining table was in the corner by the window, with a navy blue checked cloth draped over it. Harper walked over to the table and saw that she had a perfect view of the street below and the entire town square. The trees outside were still green, but drying in the late August heat. She could almost feel the change coming, and couldn't wait to see the leaves change into shades of gold and crimson. The thought brought a smile to her face.

"Wow," Harper breathed, turning around slowly.

She hadn't been expecting much, but this apartment was absolutely perfect. It reminded her of a loft apartment that she'd had in Atlanta years ago. It was as if it had been picked up and placed in the middle of a charming small town. Harper wandered farther into the space, her footsteps echoing softly. There were two bedrooms, though one was functioning as a craft room and office space. The other was set up as the primary bedroom. Both were perfectly cozy and welcoming. The iron-framed queen-sized bed had a fluffy ivory duvet and, at the foot of the bed, a chunky sage green blanket was draped, just waiting to be pulled up on a chilly evening. Next to the bed, an old-fashioned wooden wardrobe stood tall, its door slightly ajar, revealing a few hangers and a scarf that had belonged to Aunt Ellie. In the living room, a double set of doors led out to a small balcony. She stepped out and realized that the entire balcony space was hidden from the street below. There was a railing, and it hid the balcony behind the facade of the bookstore. If she leaned out over the wall, she could be seen from the street, but just sitting on the balcony, it was totally private. Two chairs and a small round bistro table filled out the space, as well as a few dead plants. Harper loved the balcony and could picture spending lots of time out there, enjoying the hidden space and fresh air.

But it was the bathroom that made her giddy. There was an enormous clawfoot tub, beautiful white subway tiled walls and the floor was timeless marble hexagonal tiles. A white shower curtain and fluffy rug gave the bathroom a clean feeling that Harper liked.

Harper stood in the living room. The apartment needed a little paint and a deep clean, but just like the shop below, it had an undeniable charm that was drawing Harper in. She felt a knot of doubt unravel deep in her belly. This was more than she had expected. It wasn't just a place to stay. It was a home.

She pulled open the windows a little wider and breathed in some of the final scents of summer, mingling with the cozy promise of her new home above the bookstore. The apartment seemed to breathe with her, like it was settling into this new chapter, and as Harper took her first real look around, she couldn't help but feel that this place—dust, quirks, and all—was exactly where she was meant to be. It felt like the fresh start she needed.

Harper pulled out her phone and opened the *ATL Girls* group chat.

ATL GIRLS 📓🍷📚

Harper: Okay, so you know how I've been staying at the B&B until I can move into my aunt's house?

Erin: Yes.

Harper: Well y'all, I found the house. It's an apartment above the bookstore and...

Harper: THERE'S

Harper: A

Harper: HIDDEN

Harper: DOOR

Erin: What?!

Amanda: I'm sorry, did you just casually say that??

Harper: I know, right? The only way to get into the apartment is a door behind the grandfather clock. It's like something out of *Nancy Drew and the Charmingly Dusty Attic Apartment.*

Amanda: STOP

Erin: Do you have a flashlight and a bat??

Harper: LOL...once you go through the clock, it's pretty normal. It's a staircase up to a door. But man, it's cool to walk through that clock!

Amanda: I swear, if this becomes a full mystery novel, we are flying in!

Erin: Same. I'll bring wine and a Ouija board.

Harper: Pls, no ghosts, just dusty secrets and the occasional scone 😂

Amanda: Is the apartment cute??

Harper: SO cute. Exposed brick, sloped ceilings, stained-glass window in the bathroom for no reason.

Harper: It's like living inside a vintage storybook.

Erin: Ugh! Rude

Amanda: I hate you in the most supportive way

Harper: I miss you girls ...but I think this place might be something special

Amanda: Aww

Erin: OMG Harper's catching feelings for her apartment

Harper: Honestly? I'm not even denying it . 😂

Harper set her phone down and smiled. And even though her life had changed so much, her connection to her friends from Atlanta felt as strong as ever.

Early the next morning, Harper laced up her sneakers and pulled her long, unruly curls into a ponytail. She stepped out onto the front porch of the bed-and-breakfast and took a deep breath. The air was cool and still. This was great running weather. The town was cloaked in a soft pre-dawn hush, the sky just beginning to pale at the edges. She stretched slowly, shaking out her legs and rolling her shoulders.

Harper popped in her earbuds, tapped the start button on her running watch, and set off at a gentle pace, letting her body warm up as she trotted past storefronts. She weaved through downtown, over streets named Elm and Sycamore, Fig and Acorn. She ran past the municipal complex, where the firehouse and police station stood quiet. Then, as she headed out of town, the buildings slowly fell away, replaced by stretches of open fields and apple orchards and rows of corn.

Her stride lengthened, and she picked up speed, letting the rhythm of her breath settle into something steady. Out here, with only the sound of her footfalls and the muffled beat of music in her ears, Harper felt light and free. The rural roads curved gently, lined with split-rail fences and the occasional sleepy farmhouse. Morning fog clung low to the ground, hovering just above the rows of corn.

She passed over an old stone bridge where a creek cut through the woods and under the road. Harper checked her watch - she'd gone about 4 miles out of town. She pulled out one earbud and listened— to nothing. No cars, no voices, just the rustle of trees and the distant caw of a bird. It was so different from running through Piedmont Park with the tall city buildings surrounding the space in every direction. Or her morning jogs on The Beltline in the Old Fourth Ward neighborhood of Atlanta. There, the old railroad track had been turned into a running and walking path, bordered with incredible art installations and murals. Those had been her favorite places to run before she moved to Fall. Running in the silence and seclusion of a truly rural area with nothing to see and no one else around for miles was a big shift. Harper was surprised just how much she loved it.

Turning back, she pushed to a faster cadence, her body loose now, her thoughts surprisingly clear. She let them wander—thinking about her friends back in Atlanta, her new friends here in Fall, the bookstore, her Aunt Ellie, and more.

As the little town came back into view, beautiful in the early light, Harper pushed her pace one last time. Then she slowed to a jog as she passed rows of now-awake storefronts. The scent of fresh coffee hit her from across the square. She slowed even more and breathed deeply, enjoying the endorphin rush that always came after a great run. As she walked the last few blocks back to The Copper Fox Inn, her sweat cooled against her skin. Harper stopped her watch - just over eight miles - and smiled to herself. Morning runs were her favorite way to start the day, but coffee was a very close second.

CHAPTER 7
MEET GABE

After a quick breakfast, Harper retrieved her SUV and trailer and drove over to the bookstore. She attempted to maneuver into the tiny parking lot behind the building. It took three or four tries—each attempt more frustrating than the last—to get the trailer fully inside without it sticking out into the street. Finally satisfied, she shut off the engine and climbed out, heading to unlock the trailer.

Harper pulled out the first box, hefting its weight awkwardly into her arms. *What is this, books?* She thought. As she turned around, she collided hard with someone. The impact jolted her, and the box slipped from her grasp. It slammed into her shin before sliding down her leg and hitting the pavement with a heavy thud. The sharp pain made her wince, and she groaned. "Oww." She glanced down at the box—yep, definitely books.

Before she could gather herself, a set of powerful hands gripped her forearms, steadying her.

"Whoa there," came a warm, deep voice. "Are you okay?"

Harper looked up and found herself face-to-face with a man who seemed like he'd stepped straight out of a rugged, outdoorsy catalog. His dark hair peeked out from under a worn baseball cap, and his sun-kissed skin contrasted against the rolled-up sleeves of his flannel shirt, revealing muscular forearms that looked like they belonged to someone who worked with his hands for a living. The edge of a black tattoo showed from beneath the cuff of his shirt, but it was his stunning hazel eyes—sharp, warm, and flecked with gold—that caught her off guard. They seemed to shimmer with amusement as he looked at her, a smile tugging at the corners of his mouth.

"I'm... uh, yeah. I'm fine," Harper stammered, feeling heat rush to her cheeks. *Oh, nice, Harper. Real smooth,* she scolded herself inwardly.

The man's smile grew into a grin, one that crinkled the corners of his eyes in an effortlessly charming way. "Good to know," he said, his voice deep and slow, carrying a hint of humor. He released her arms gently, but not before giving them a reassuring squeeze.

"I'm sorry. Let me help you with that," he said with an easy smile, effortlessly scooping up the box as if it weighed nothing. "Where can I take it for you?"

Harper swallowed hard. *My God, he's good-looking.* Naturally, she was sweaty and still in her workout clothes, her hair pulled back into a ponytail and not a stitch of makeup on. Of course.

"Oh, that's okay," she blurted, her voice a little too high. "I can take it from here."

"I insist," he replied, flashing a lopsided grin that made her heart do a ridiculous little flip. "I ran into you. The least I can do is make up for smashing your foot."

"Shin," she corrected weakly, inwardly cringing. *Seriously? Could I be more awkward?* She could feel her face heating, and she mentally begged herself to act normal.

Clearing her throat, she tried again. "I mean, it's fine, really. I'm moving in, and the apartment's tricky to get to. You can't reach it directly—it's kind of like a secret door situation—so I can just—"

He chuckled, cutting her off. "Moving in?"

"Yes, I own this bookstore—Hearth & Quill," Harper said, her words coming out faster than she intended. "It was my great-aunt Ellie's shop before she... well, she left it to me when she passed. So now it's mine. Uh. Like I said."

She mentally cringed at herself for over-explaining, but the way he was watching her—attentive, with that faint smile—only heightened her nerves.

"Ahhh, so you are taking over Ellie's shop," he said, recognition lighting up his eyes. "She was such a sweet lady. I used to bring her the best Honey Crisps—they were her favorite."

Harper must have looked puzzled because he shifted the box in his arms and extended his hand with an amiable smile. "I'm Gabe Sullivan, owner of Sullivan's Apple Orchard, just outside of town."

The moment clicked, and Harper's expression softened. *That explains his hands,* she thought. *He was an apple farmer. An apple grower? Applist? Whatever - he worked with apples.*

"Nice to meet you, Gabe," she said, returning his smile. "I'm Harper. Harper Whitmore."

Her hand practically disappeared in his, his grip strong but gentle. His warmth was palpable as he shook it.

"That's a noble name... Harper Whitmore. Sounds like an author," Gabe said with an amiable smile, the kind that lit up his entire face. In one smooth motion, he turned his baseball cap backward—a gesture so practiced, it made Harper's heart skip. He somehow looked even more attractive with the hat on backward, the casual move making her knees feel a little weak.

Gabe reached into the trailer and hoisted another box, barely breaking a sweat. "Why don't you grab a box, and we can get these upstairs to your apartment?" he said, already heading toward the back door of Hearth & Quill.

The next 20 minutes passed in a blur of trips up and down the stairs. Gabe, effortlessly carrying two boxes for every one of Harper's, held the back door open for her with his foot each time, his movements smooth and natural. He navigated the shop as if he knew it like the back of his hand, which left Harper curious.

"How do you know the place so well?" She asked, panting slightly from the effort.

"I renovated Ellie's bathroom a few years back," he said with a chuckle. "It was very... pink before I got my hands on it."

Harper laughed. "Oh, the bathroom is beautiful! I love the hexagonal tiles."

Gabe's grin widened. "Thanks. I used to work in construction, still do some handyman projects for friends and family," he added, leaning casually against the doorframe as Harper set down her last box.

"How did you get into apple growing?" she asked, balancing the box on top of the growing stack.

"I guess I've always been in the apple business," Gabe said with a smile, his eyes crinkling at the edges in a way that made him even more charming. "It was my dad's farm, so I grew up in the orchard. Some of my earliest memories are of walking the rows with him, checking the apples. I went into construction for a while, but he got sick about four years ago, so I stepped up and took on more of the business."

"I'm sorry to hear that," Harper said softly.

"Thanks. Luckily, he recovered, but he retired—to Florida of all places. Can you imagine? Where it's always summer? Sounds miserable to me," he said with a mock scowl, before breaking into a laugh. Harper couldn't help but laugh with him. He had infectious energy. "Anyway, now Sullivan's is all mine. I want to make sure he's proud of the legacy he built, and maybe one day I'll pass it on to my kids."

Harper's heart dropped.

"Oh, how old are your kids?" she asked brightly, trying to mask her sudden disappointment.

Gabe chuckled and shook his head. "Oh, no, no kids yet. I'm not married. I just mean my future kids," he said, flashing that affable grin again.

Harper's heart soared unexpectedly, and she mentally scolded herself. *Get a grip, Harper. He's just making conversation—this is not a rom-com.*

"How about you?" Gabe asked, casually taking off his hat and wiping his brow with the back of his wrist before replacing it.

"Me? Nope, no kids. And I'm not married. I just went through a breakup, actually," she said, her voice a little more relaxed now.

"I'm sorry to hear that. Is that why you moved to Fall?" he asked, watching her intently.

"Sort of," Harper replied. "When my aunt passed, I was planning to sell the shop and go back to Atlanta. But I felt conflicted about it. The breakup made it a lot easier to consider moving here and taking over, like Ellie wanted me to. And then my agency lost a major client - I was in advertising - and it seemed like a sign to come to Fall."

"Well, we're certainly happy to have you," he said with unwavering eye contact that made her heart race.

"Water," she blurted out suddenly, then cringed at her awkwardness. "Sorry, I mean, can I offer you a bottle of water? I haven't been to the grocery store yet, but I have a case of water..."

Gabe grinned, then glanced down at his watch. "Actually, I really need to get going," he said, a hint of apology in his voice.

"Oh, of course," Harper replied, masking her disappointment with a forced brightness.

"But I'll take a rain check," Gabe added, his tone hopeful as he met her eyes again.

"Anytime," Harper said, smiling. "And thanks again for the help. I really appreciate it."

"No problem. And sorry again for crashing into you," he said with a playful grin. "But welcome to Fall. You're going to love it here."

She walked him downstairs to the front of the bookstore, watching as he stepped out into the late afternoon sunlight. Harper lingered for a moment, then pulled out her phone, Googling the nearest U-Haul return location. She would return the trailer and swing by the hardware store for some essentials. Anything to get her mind off the gorgeous Gabe Sullivan.

CHAPTER 8
WINE AND CHEESE

The late afternoon sun bathed Fall in a warm, golden light as Harper made her way back to The Copper Fox Inn. She was eager to have a break after another long day. Tonight, Paul was hosting a wine and cheese happy hour for guests, and after moving boxes and shelving books all day, Harper couldn't think of a better way to unwind before bed.

The inn was welcoming, with its front porch wrapped in twinkling lights and the faint sound of soft jazz music drifting out through the open windows. Inside, the smell of freshly baked bread mingled with the earthy scent of wine, drawing Harper into the cozy living room. Paul was setting up the last of the wine glasses on the rustic wooden table when she walked in.

"Hey, you made it!" Paul greeted her with a warm smile, standing behind a tray filled with fresh cheeses and a selection of bottles. Lady stood next to him. "I was thinking you'd gotten buried under all those boxes."

Harper laughed as she approached, shaking her head. "Not quite, but it was close. I swear I've discovered whole layers of dust that I didn't even know could exist."

"Well, that sounds like a good reason to have a glass of wine," Paul said, pouring a generous amount of red wine into one glass and handing it to her. "You deserve it after all that hard work."

Harper took the glass, grateful for the break, and swirled the deep crimson liquid before taking a sip. The rich flavor was smooth and calming, just what she needed. "You're right. This is exactly what I needed."

Paul chuckled, grabbing a glass for himself before motioning toward a pair of comfortable armchairs near the large bay windows. "Come on, let's sit and chat. How's the shop coming along?"

They made their way to the chairs, Harper sinking into the plush cushions with a sigh of relief. She patted her lap, and Lady jumped up and laid across her lap. She nuzzled Harper's hand to get petted. Harper smiled and began petting the tiny dog. Her coat was silky soft.

"It's getting there," she said, reaching for a slice of cheese from the platter on the small table between them. "I didn't think it would take this long just to clean. I still have weeks of sorting ahead of me. I didn't realize how much stuff Ellie had collected over the years. There are books I haven't even heard of tucked on the back shelves—old classics, first editions, even some rare titles. It's overwhelming but also kind of exciting."

Paul leaned back in his chair, nodding as he sipped his wine. "Ellie was always one to hold on to things. She had an eye for treasures, that's for sure. Sounds like you're discovering a few of your own in there."

"I am," Harper agreed, smiling as she thought about the books she'd uncovered. "I found this beautiful edition of Jane Eyre today, the kind with gilded edges and a leather cover. It was like finding a hidden gem."

Paul gave her an approving nod. "That's the right attitude. It's a treasure hunt! I know it's a lot of work right now, but you've got the whole town behind you."

Harper felt a wave of gratitude for his encouragement and sipped her wine again. She scratched Lady behind the ears. "Thanks, Paul. It helps to hear that. It's been a busy few days, and I've wondered a few times if I would ever get there. But I have to remind myself, I just got here, and I'm making significant progress so far."

"I'm sure that you are. Taking over a shop that someone else ran for so long has got to be hard. Have you figured out her inventory system?"

"What inventory system?" Harper said wryly. "Aunt Ellie doesn't even have a computer, let alone a POS inventory system. From what I can see, she accepts only cash. No Venmo, Apple Cash or even credit cards. She's got an old-fashioned cash register. So, there's definitely some modernizing that needs to be done. I don't know how many books are in the shop, what titles, or the pricing. I have to physically be holding a book in my hand to get any information."

Harper let out a loud sigh, and said, "Enough about me. How's your day been? Anything exciting at the inn?"

Paul grinned, shaking his head. "Oh, you know how it is—nothing too wild. We had a couple check in from Chicago earlier, celebrating their anniversary, and I had to fix the Wi-Fi for one guest who needed to do some work. But mostly, it's been quiet. Just the way I like it."

Harper raised an eyebrow playfully. "The glamorous life of an innkeeper."

Paul laughed, lifting his glass in a mock toast. "Exactly. Though, truth be told, I wouldn't trade it for anything. There's something I love about making this place feel like home for people, even if it's just for a few days."

Harper nodded, understanding. "It absolutely feels like a home. It makes me want to stay forever."

"You're welcome to!" Paul laughed.

They continued chatting as the evening went on, with the wine flowing and the conversation light and easy. Harper relaxed more and more, the weight of the day slipping away as they talked about the town, the people who lived there, and each of their visions for the future of their businesses.

"Well," Harper said, and Lady stood up, jumped to the floor and trotted over to her dog bed. The dog had an uncanny way of knowing just where to be. Harper stood up and placed her empty wineglass on the table. "I better head back and get some rest before tomorrow's round of cleaning. Can I help you clean up?"

Paul stood as well, smiling warmly. "Absolutely not. You're still a guest, and I love taking care of my guests. Sleep well!"

"Thank you, Paul," she said, laughing. "I think all the Cabernet will ensure that."

With a wave, Harper headed up the stairs to her room. Harper lay on the bed, fully dressed, and stared at the ceiling, trying not to think about Gabe Sullivan.

5:41am. Harper really wished she could sleep in. She loved watching movies where people slept in, then luxuriated in their beds for a while before rising to start the day.

Harper skipped the shower, threw her hair in a ponytail, and headed downstairs to the dining room, excited about what Paul would have in store for her today.

He was sitting at one of the small bistro tables with Lady at his feet, coffee cup in hand, when Harper entered the room. He started to stand up and she stopped him.

"Sit, sit," she gestured to him. "I can get my coffee."

He smiled and settled back into his chair, yawning.

"Thanks. Breakfast service starts at 6, I was just enjoying a quick cup myself with my last few minutes."

Harper strode over to the sideboard and served herself a steaming mug of coffee. She saw the menu, printed and displayed on a little easel.

Apple Cinnamon French Toast Bake
Thick slices of brioche soaked in cinnamon custard, layered with spiced apples, and baked to golden perfection, served with powdered sugar and warm apple compote.

Autumn Harvest Eggs Benedict
Apple-sage sausage patties, perfectly poached eggs, crispy fried sage leaves, and a light and velvety butternut squash puree in place of traditional hollandaise sauce. Served on toasted English muffins or roasted sweet potato rounds.

Apple Sage Sausage Patty
A savory blend of seasoned pork and fresh sage, perfectly balanced with the natural sweetness of grated apples. Pan-seared to golden perfection, with a crisp exterior and tender, juicy center.

Pumpkin Spice Granola Parfait
Layers of spiced granola, creamy Greek yogurt, and pumpkin purée, topped with a drizzle of honey and roasted pumpkin seeds.

Pumpkin Cream Cheese Muffins
Moist pumpkin muffins with a rich cream cheese center, topped with a cinnamon streusel.

"Oh my gosh, today's menu sounds incredible. How is each day better than the last?"

Harper added cream and sugar and turned to face him.

"I'm an insomniac," he said. "I plan menus when I can't sleep."

"Oh, that's the worst," she said, taking a sip of the hearty brew. "I can always fall asleep, but I'm a chronically early riser. If I wake up at 4 a.m. to use the bathroom, I'm up for the day."

"Same here," he agreed. "I usually can't fall asleep until 1 or 2, even though I'm exhausted, and then something will wake me up around 4 or 5 and that's it. I'm awake."

"People who can sleep well will never understand our struggle," Harper said.

He stood, finishing his cup of coffee in a long gulp. "No, they won't!" He said with a shake of his head. He scooped up Lady and planted a kiss on the top of her head before setting her back down.

"Oh, I know I promised you a new scone," Paul said with a playful grin, "but this morning, my heart is all about pumpkin cream cheese muffins."

Harper's eyes lit up as she sipped her coffee. "Those sound incredible."

Paul wiped a few imaginary crumbs from the counter, his expression softening. "Thanks! I love experimenting with new recipes." He paused, then asked, "So, what's the plan for today?"

"More exploring the shop," Harper said, a hint of excitement creeping into her voice. "Oh, and I found my aunt's apartment above the store yesterday, and it's even more charming than I imagined. But I was actually hoping to stay here for a while so I can clean it out and do some painting, and repairs?"

Paul leaned against the counter, a warm sideways smile spreading across his face. "The suite's yours for as long as you need it. I kept it open just in case. Figured you'd want to spruce up your aunt's place a bit before officially moving in."

The day passed in a blur of unpacking and cleaning. Just before bed, Harper picked up her phone and scrolled through her messages until she found the group chat with her girlfriends: *ATL Girls*.

Her fingers hovered over the keyboard before she finally started typing:

ATL GIRLS

Harper: So, Fall, Michigan... where do I even start?

A response came almost immediately.

Amanda: OMG, spill the tea! Is it *actually* like a Hallmark movie??

Erin: Yes! Give us all the cozy details. Flannel? Hot cider? Cute small-town guys??

Harper: It's like stepping into another world. Seriously, this town *lives* for autumn. Everything is golden leaves, pumpkin patches, and cider mills. It's like perpetual fall here!

Amanda: Ugh, jealous. I want that life. All I have here are traffic jams and pumpkin spice lattes from Starbucks in September and October. 😩

Erin: Sounds dreamy. So, what's the catch? There's always a catch. 👀

Harper: None yet. There's something about this place that feels like... maybe I belong here. Or at least, I need to see what happens next. 🍂✨

Amanda: Sounds like a romance novel waiting to happen! 😏

Erin: Girl, keep us posted on all the cute small-town guys. I expect full updates.

Harper: LOL. I will. You'll be the first to know! Miss you guys.

Amanda : Miss you more! 🖤. Keep the updates coming. And seriously, find some flannel.

Harper put her phone down. This town was unique, but maybe that was exactly what she needed.

CHAPTER 9
FRIENDLY TOWN

And so it continued that way the first two weeks that Harper lived in Fall. She would go for a run in the morning, indulge in an incredible breakfast at the B&B, then head over to her shop and apartment to get to work. Harper knew she would miss Paul and his delicious food, but she was eager to settle into her own place, too. So she tackled the apartment first, wanting to move out of the B&B and into her own home.

Harper scrubbed every inch of the apartment, from the dust-caked ceiling fans down to the scuffed baseboards. Along the way, she tackled minor maintenance tasks—replacing burnt-out bulbs, tightening loose door handles, and fixing the torn window screen in the bedroom. Then she had high-speed internet installed in both the apartment and the bookstore, bringing a modern touch to her new life in Fall.

Next, she painted a few rooms in the apartment and unpacked all of her boxes, stocked the pantry with essentials, and replaced the worn-out pots and pans. She treated herself to a new set of kitchen knives and added a few potted plants to bring a bit of life to the space.

Once Harper was satisfied with her cozy new apartment, she left the bed-and-breakfast and moved into her new home. Next, she set her sights on Labor Day weekend for the grand reopening of Hearth & Quill, a date Maggie assured her was the perfect kickoff to Fall's bustling autumn tourist season.

Thanks to Maggie and the group that had helped her, the shop was clean, but it was still cluttered with stacks of books everywhere. Her first major task was to sort and remove the dozens of books scattered across the floor, tables, and tucked into every corner. As she shelved the books, she was also discovering the shop, learning its layout and sections until she could almost navigate the aisles without a second thought. With each book she put away, the space felt lighter and more open. The shop was literally getting bigger, as each aisle was free of stacks of books and there was more space to move around in. It was a far cry from the dusty, cluttered store she had inherited just a few weeks before.

With the front of the bookstore coming together, she turned her attention to the storage room, where she discovered an abundance of branded items like stickers, paper bags, t-shirts and sweatshirts, all emblazoned with the store's name and logo. Eager to bring order to the chaos, Harper broke out her label maker and created neat signs for every shelf in the storage room. She organized the janitor's closet with new shelving and a hanging rack to keep the brooms and mops off the floor.

Little by little, the bookstore was growing into Harper's vision for the space. Every thoughtful update, every careful touch, brought it closer to feeling like an extension of herself. The once-cluttered space was tidier and more organized every day, and the space was filled with her personality. Hearth & Quill was beginning to feel like home.

One morning in late August, Harper was walking down Main Street, just after a glorious long run. She loved strolling through town, looking through the storefront windows. The shops were impossibly quaint, each window dressed in pumpkins, corn husks, and twinkly copper lights although it was summer. She found herself in front of a jam and jelly store and admired the display: tiny jars of spiced jam and handwritten labels that said things like "Autumn in a Jar" and "Sweater Weather Spread."

"Hey girl, mind lending a hand?" came a voice from behind Harper.

Harper saw Maggie and rushed to take two of the bags weighing her down. "Sure. What's all this?"

"Just flour, sugar and cinnamon. I was running low," Maggie said as she pushed open the door with her hip. "But come in and try a snickerdoodle."

Ten minutes and one warm cookie later, Harper was back on the sidewalk with Maggie, carrying 4 boxes of baked goods. Maggie had another 8 boxes in her hands, and she used her chin to hold them in place as she walked.

"I'm glad you stopped," Maggie said. "Now, want to come with me to make the rounds?"

"The rounds?" Harper asked.

As they walked, Maggie explained.

"Mrs. Lindstrom at the flower shop needs help to move her mums outside, and then I promised I'd take a box of candles over to Nora at The Candle Cottage. And Harold from the movie theater can't get on the ladder anymore to lift the marquee letters — he had back surgery last month. So I need to spell out *HOCUS POCUS MARATHON* on the marquee."

"I'm sweaty and a tad underdressed," Harper said. "But count me in. You do this every day?"

"Only during months that end in 'ber,'" Maggie said with a laugh. "Just like when we came to help you clean - in Fall, we really look out for one another. If you ever need anything, we'll all pitch in to help."

This was so different from the big-city vibe in Atlanta. The people there were very nice, but nothing could compare to the warmth of a small town like Fall. They reached Mums the Word, where an older woman with large glasses and a knit cardigan was struggling with a cart full of oversized, potted chrysanthemums.

"Maggie, sweetheart, thank you!" Mrs. Lindstrom called. "And you brought help!"

"I did," Maggie said, handing over a box of snickerdoodle. "These are fresh from this morning."

Harper grabbed one of the heavy pots and smiled. "I'm Harper. I just moved here a few weeks ago."

Mrs. Lindstrom gave her the once-over, then nodded approvingly. "Strong wrists. You'll do just fine."

After unloading the mums and chatting briefly with Mrs. Lindstrom about the squirrels eating her cornucopia wreath (again), Maggie tugged Harper along to the next errand. The next stop was The Candle Cottage, a narrow shop that smelled like toasted marshmallows and amber. Inside, Nora—dressed in a flowing scarf and surrounded by towering candle displays—handed over a box and insisted Harper take a free "Falling Leaves" votive for her troubles. Maggie gave her a box of snickerdoodle as well, and Nora beamed.

"You're officially one of us now," Nora said to Harper, laughing. "Your hands smell like autumn scents and wax."

By the time they stepped back out onto the sidewalk, Harper was grinning.

"This was not what I planned to do today," she said. "But it's making me feel great to help others. I know firsthand how it can feel when you have a monumental task ahead of you. When others show up to help, it suddenly feels doable."

Maggie grinned. "That's Fall for you. People come for the leaves, but stay for the friendship and community."

A quiet minute went by.

"So," Maggie said, nudging Harper with her elbow, "what do you think about our little autumn wonderland? Really."

Harper glanced down at her shoes and back up. "You know, when Aunt Ellie passed, I thought I would come and settle her affairs, maybe sell the bookstore and go back to Atlanta. Then my ex and I split up, and my ad agency lost its biggest client, which meant I was out of a job. So it just felt like everything was falling apart so that something *else* could fall together, you know?"

Maggie raised an eyebrow. "I totally do!"

Harper hesitated. "Now that I'm here, there's something about this place... it's different. It's slower. Warmer. I didn't expect that."

Maggie grinned. "Careful. You're sounding like a lifer."

Harper and Maggie crossed the street and waved hello to a man standing near a ladder in front of the cinema. As they approached, he called out, "You must be Harper. Ellie always said you'd come one day."

Harper blinked and widened her eyes. "She did...?"

"She said this town would find its way into your bones," Harold said, smiling and adjusting his cap. "Looks like it has."

Harper smiled and held the ladder steady for Maggie to climb up and adjust the marquee. As they stood on the sidewalk in front of the old movie theater, Harper wondered if maybe Fall was just where she was.

ATL GIRLS 🖊️🍎🍷🎞️

Harper: So I accidentally joined a work crew today.

Amanda: Is this code for something??

Erin: Did you finally go on a date?? 😉

Harper: LOL no. I was walking around, exploring the town, and ran into Maggie. She's got such good energy and an enormous heart. She kind of kidnapped me...but in the friendliest way possible?

Amanda: Omg I KNEW you'd get adopted by someone within a month.

Erin: Does she have cult leader energy or more PTA president with a wine rack?

Harper: Somewhere in between. Picture if Miss Frizzle owned a bakery and emotionally bullied you into carrying mums for old ladies.

Amanda: I love her already. 🩶

Erin: Same. Please keep her.

Harper: She made me laugh like five times in an hour. And everyone in town seems to know her.

Amanda: You needed a new ride-or-die.

Harper: I'm not replacing you!

Erin: You already have.

Amanda: We've been Fall-dumped 😭🍂

Harper: OMG STOP.

Harper: I'm starting a new life, not erasing my old one. You're still my girls.

Amanda: Ok but does Maggie drink wine and gossip?

Harper: She bakes incredible snickerdoodle, and we stopped at the local brewery for a hard cider after our chores. And she gave me at least three bits of unverified local drama.

Erin: She's in.

Amanda: Add her to the group chat. 😂

CHAPTER 10
NEW IDEA

The following afternoon, Harper was shelving books when Maggie breezed in with a bright smile on her face.

"Hey there, " Maggie said. "What are you up to?"

"Oh, hi! I'm glad you're here," Harper said brightly. "I had an idea on my run this morning that I wanted to chat with you about."

"Sure, hit me. But can we grab a coffee?" She said, jerking her thumb towards her shoulder in a 'let's go' motion.

"Yes, please!" Harper agreed.

As they walked to Harvest Roast, Harper told Maggie about her idea.

"So I found this long, sturdy table in the back of the storeroom," she started. "It's a wide, narrow display table. First, I thought I could set up a display of local Michigan authors. But we already have that great section in the middle of the store with the display shelf, you know the one?" she asked.

Maggie held the door to the coffee shop open to her, saying, "Yup, I know the one."

"So then I had this wild idea," Harper continued. "What if I set the table up in one of the picture windows and set out an assortment of products from local businesses? People visiting Hearth & Quill can discover new products from all over town while they shop for books."

"Ohhh, sort of cross-promotional type thing," Maggie said, her eyes widening appreciatively.

"Exactly!" Harper agreed. They paused their conversation while they ordered their drinks, a pumpkin spice latte for Harper and a chai for Maggie.

"Do you think the other shops in town would like the idea?" Harper asked once they'd ordered and paid.

"Are you kidding? I think they'd love it," Maggie said enthusiastically. "Especially some shops on the outskirts of town. You've got a prime spot with your shop facing the town square. A lot of the autumn tourists come to visit the town square and the shops right around it, without always exploring every side street."

"Oh, that's a good point. Seeing the products of those businesses might draw them out to the outskirts. Maybe I could have a sample of products from Sullivan's Apple Orchard, to encourage folks to take a trip out there during their visit," Harper said, her mind racing.

"Great idea! I can introduce you to the owner, Gabe Sullivan," Maggie said. "He's a great guy."

"I met him, actually. I ran into him - literally," Harper recounted the story to Maggie, who laughed good-naturedly with her friend.

"That sounds exactly like Gabe to stop whatever he was doing to help a neighbor," Maggie agreed. "And he's not bad to look at, either, am I right?"

She raised her eyebrows comically and wiggled them up and down at Harper, who burst out laughing.

"You are so ridiculous," Harper laughed.

"I'm not wrong, though," Maggie said. "He's got that rugged exterior and soft inside thing most women swoon over."

"Most women, but not you?" Harper asked, lifting her eyebrows questioningly. She took her coffee from Melanie and thanked her.

"Nope, not me," Maggie said, taking her chai from Melanie. "I like my men like I like my handbags. Small, fancy, and preferably, Italian."

Harper threw her head back and laughed while Melanie looked on, shaking her head with laughter at the two of them.

Harper spent the next week visiting local businesses. At each shop, she shared her vision for the local business display at Hearth & Quill and, as Maggie had predicted, the community embraced the idea. Each shop owner was eager to take part. Harper worked out an arrangement: for items under $50, she would purchase them upfront and recoup the cost when they sold in her bookstore. For more expensive items, she offered a consignment model—taking the items, issuing a receipt, and paying the shopkeeper once it sold. Harper enjoyed the opportunity to explore the businesses of Fall. Throughout the week, she spoke with nearly every shopkeeper and business owner in downtown Fall, making new friends and introducing herself to the town.

At Fall in Love, an autumn-themed souvenir shop, the owner agreed to provide an 'Adore Autumn' gift box, which was full of autumnal items and town-themed items. Melanie at Harvest Roast provided several bags of coffee beans and coffee mugs, some with the Harvest Roast logo, some autumn themed, some bearing the town name.

Maggie agreed to provide a weekly assortment of items from Maple and Crumb, primarily individually wrapped, iced sugar cookies decorated in autumnal themes. There were cookies in the shape of maple and oak leaves, acorns, pumpkins, and cornucopias, plus square cookies with the town name and autumnal decorations drawn on with icing. The designs were charming and reflected the town perfectly.

Harper met with Paul and the owner of the Amber Lantern Inn, Martha, about her idea. They provided a stack of business cards and brochures to be displayed, and Paul agreed to bring over baked goods once per week to show his baking. Martha offered to create postcards with printed schedules of upcoming Fall events as well.

At Harvest Thyme spice shop, Harper pushed open the door and was enveloped by a warm wave of fragrant cinnamon, cloves, and cardamom. She inhaled deeply and looked around at the shelves lined with colorful jars and burlap sacks filled with spices created a cozy atmosphere.

Indira looked up from behind the counter, a bright smile lighting her face. "Harper, right? Just the person I wanted to see!"

They exchanged introductions, and Harper said "I've been thinking of adding some local products to the bookstore – would you be interested?"

Indira's eyes sparkled with excitement. "Funny you should say that. I've been crafting some special spice blends that I think would be perfect to sell at your shop."

Harper leaned in, intrigued. "Tell me more."

"Well," Indira said, reaching for a small, elegantly labeled tin, "this is *Cinnamon Classics* – a cinnamon and vanilla sugar blend meant for tea or baking. And here's *Dark Roast Mystery*, a smoky chai with a hint of clove, inspired by classic whodunits."

Harper chuckled. "I love those names! I think these would be perfect to sell. It'll bring a whole additional layer of coziness to the shop."

Indira smiled warmly. "I'll prepare some samples and bring them by later. Let's see if your readers *fall* in love with them."

Up next, the The Cozy Blanket. Harper adored the shop as soon as she walked in. She bought two afghans for herself, plus owners Liz and Mary offered Harper five afghans and throw blankets to be displayed around Hearth & Quill.

Harper shopped for almost an hour at Autumn's End Antiques before she even chatted with the owner, Neil, about her idea. During that time, she bought a small entryway table for her apartment along with several decor items for both the apartment and the bookstore.

Neil provided baskets and some pottery and dishes in autumnal colors for the display table.

The Candle Cottage offered half a dozen candles in dreamy autumnal scents, including mixes of caramel, cinnamon, nutmeg, pumpkin spice and apple. Mums the Word florist offered to bring by a few mums for the coffee table in front of the hearth and to be placed on either side of the front door, with a small sign advertising that the flowers were from the shop.

Harper couldn't believe her success. She also couldn't believe her rapidly declining bank balance as she shopped throughout Fall's downtown area. The shopping was better than in any beach town she'd ever visited. There were incredible collections of items at each shop.

Harper spent a small fortune at the Steeped in Joy tea shop. She loved loose-leaf tea, so she picked up a variety of flavors, plus a small teapot and strainers. Anne, the owner, provided a small assortment of tea leaf blends in small gift boxes, plus accessories like a small teapot, an assortment of loose leaf tea strainers, and a honey jar with a small spoon.

Frost & Fire provided an assortment of items. The owner of the apothecary, Agnes, was passionate about her essential oil roller blends and her beef tallow hand cream. Harper had to admit it was terrific. She bought a few for herself and secured a few for the store.

Laden with bags, Harper walked into Sullivan's Apple Market, which was just a few streets over from the bookstore. Harper was expecting to see Gabe, but met Annie, the general manager, instead. Annie explained that the in-town Market was the storefront for Sullivan's Apple Orchard, which was about a 4-minute drive outside of town. Annie liked the idea of the Local Business table, and recommended Harper visit Gabe at the orchard to discuss what he wanted to display at the bookshop.

So, later that day, Harper found herself at Sullivan's Apple Orchard wandering through rows of apple trees, their branches heavy with fruit, casting dappled shadows on the ground. She hadn't realized the orchard was so big, sprawling in all directions and leaving Harper feeling as though she was in her own little world. After wandering for a while and getting pleasantly lost, Harper followed the little signs that would lead her back towards the main entrance. Just as she rounded the bend between two trees, her foot caught on a stray tree root hidden beneath the fallen leaves. She stumbled, her ankle twisting beneath her, and she fell forward.

The ground came up fast, but instead of landing in the dirt, she found herself tangled in a set of muscular arms.

"Whoa there," a warm, deep voice said, steadying her. "You okay?"

Harper looked up to see Gabe, a broad friendly smile on his face. *Not again,* Harper thought to herself. Gabe was wearing jeans and a white shirt with a plaid flannel shirt over it. The sleeves were rolled up and his arms and hands were covered in dust and bits of leaves from working in the orchard. Harper immediately noticed his eyes again. The hazel was striking, and they twinkled with amusement.

"We've got to stop meeting like this," Gabe said, a soft smile tugging at his lips. He let go of her arms and her skin felt cold after his warm touch.

"Sorry! That root came out of nowhere," Harper managed lamely.

"At least it wasn't my fault this time," Gabe answered with a laugh.

"Definitely not," Harper agreed with a tinkly giggle that didn't sound like hers.

"Actually, I was hoping to run into you," Harper said. "I mean, not literally run into you, but, um, I'm here to chat with you. Do you have a few minutes? I was hoping to talk about carrying your apples and products at the bookstore."

Gabe's smile grew wider, and he crossed his arms over his chest and looked at her appraisingly. "I've got all the time in the world to talk with you. I just assumed you were here to steal my apples."

Harper laughed, this time a genuine laugh that felt like it bubbled up from her toes. "You caught me. I have a plan to sneak out of here with as many as I can carry," she teased, playfully gesturing to her leather Michael Kors tote bag.

"Well, if you're going to steal apples, at least let me help you pick the good ones," Gabe said with a wink. He reached towards her, then up behind her and plucked a perfectly ripe apple from a nearby branch, rubbed it against his shirt to shine it, and handed it to her. "Here. Try this Honeycrisp - on the house."

Harper took the apple, feeling the smooth surface under her fingers. She took a bite, the crispness of the fruit and the sweet flavor making her eyes close in delight. "Wow, you weren't kidding. This is amazing."

"I know my apples," Gabe said, looking confident and proud. "Why don't you let me give you a proper tour? If you're going to carry my products, you should at least know where it comes from."

"Sure, that sounds... nice," Harper said, feeling a brief flutter in her chest. It had been a while since she'd felt this kind of excitement, and she welcomed it.

"Great. After you, Miss Whitmore," Gabe said, gesturing in an exaggerated 'after you' motion. Harper walked down the rows of trees, the smell of apples and warm soil filling the autumn air.

CHAPTER 11
COLLECTING A MOUNTAIN

As Gabe led her deeper into the orchard, Harper could feel the world around her transforming. The sounds of the town faded away, replaced by the rustling of leaves and the occasional distant chatter of visitors enjoying their apple-picking adventures. Now and then, a burst of laughter or the delighted squeal of a child drifted over to them, carried by the gentle autumn breeze.

"I love it out here," Harper said. "It's so peaceful."

Gabe shoved his hands in his pockets and walked next to her, looking down at his boots. He had a way of leaving long pauses between the ends of her sentences and the beginning of his, so she wondered if he was waiting for her to say more.

"It's my favorite place on earth," he said, looking around with a soft smile. "I know every tree. It feels so familiar, like home to me. I guess that might sound a little odd..." he trailed off.

"Actually, I think I'm starting to know how you feel. It's not even been a month and I'm having the same feeling about Aunt Ellie's store. I've spent so much time in there cleaning and shelving books, I know every section, every row, and almost every shelf. I certainly don't know every category or every book, but maybe one day," Harper said with a little laugh. "It feels really familiar and comforting to be there."

"Fall has that effect on people," Gabe twirled a leaf in his hands, then let it float to the ground. "It wraps you up in a big flannel hug, makes you want to stay awhile. Your great-aunt was like that - she always treated everyone around her like family. I wanted to be around her and HQ. She made this town better just by being here."

"Thank you," Harper said, feeling a pang of emotion. "It's nice to hear that people thought of her like that. I'm nervous about filling her shoes. It's like... how can I possibly keep that magic going?"

"Magic doesn't go away," Gabe said thoughtfully, pausing by a tree with bright yellow apples. He reached up to pluck one, admiring it and shining it on his shirt before handing it to her. "It just changes hands. And from what I see so far, you're going to do just fine. "

Harper smiled, a blush creeping up her cheeks, and she quickly tried to hide it by focusing on the apple he handed her. She took a small bite, savoring the sweet-tart flavor. "Mmmm. What's this one?"

"That's a Ginger Gold," he said.

"Never heard of it, but I like it," she said. She considered the fruit and then thought about what he said about magic. "I hope you're right about continuing the magic. I wasn't expecting much from Fall. As a city girl, I was sort of dreading the small town, if I'm honest. But I've been pleasantly surprised by how warm and welcoming the people are."

Gabe chuckled, the sound rich and comforting. "We're a friendly bunch. And speaking of which..." He gestured ahead to a cozy little shed tucked between the trees, its wooden structure painted a deep red to match the apples hanging overhead. "This is our cider press. Want a peek behind the scenes?"

Harper's eyes lit up. "Absolutely! I love apple cider. "

Gabe pushed open the door of the shed, and Harper followed him inside.

Inside, the air was warm and heavy with the scent of spices—

cinnamon, nutmeg, clove—and of course, fresh apples. A large wooden press stood in one corner, and baskets of apples were lined up beside it, ready to be transformed into Sullivan's famous cider.

"Wow," Harper breathed, taking it all in. "This is... amazing."

"Here you go," Gabe said, handing her a freshly poured cup of cider. "Freshly made this morning."

Harper needed no more encouragement. She took a sip and let out an involuntary hum of approval. "Oh my gosh," she said, her eyes widening. "This is delicious."

Gabe spent a few minutes explaining cider making and showed her how the machines worked. They continued chatting while Harper finished her cider.

"Why don't we go up to the market stand near where you parked?" Gabe started. "We can grab some fresh donuts and talk business in my office? Unless you're all "appled out"?"

She shook her head. "Not even close. I love autumn so much I'm in heaven."

He grabbed the jug of cider and led the way. Within a few minutes, they were at the market stand. He led her over to a donut display, where she chose one powdered and one cinnamon - sugar.

Harper took a bite. As the powdered sugar melted on her tongue, she said, "Mmmm...wow, those are perfect."

"Careful," Gabe teased. "They're addictive. You wouldn't be the first person to lose all self-control around these things."

The two of them stood there, sharing cider and donuts, letting the conversation flow naturally. Harper laughed more than she had in months. They talked about everything and nothing—the quirks of the town, the regular customers who came to the orchard, even the best recipes for apple pie.

Gabe also seemed genuinely interested in hearing about her plans for Hearth and Quill. He was enthusiastic about her plan for the local product table. He promised to deliver a bushel basket of fresh apples each week, as well as an assortment of packaged products like Sullivan's apple butter, jam, jelly and salsa. In the golden afternoon light, surrounded by apple trees and the comforting scent of autumn, Harper felt like everything was falling together perfectly.

After four days of visiting local shops and stores, Harper had an overflowing pile of merchandise and goods to display. She also had a ton of brochures and business cards from shops and restaurants that had nothing to display. Harper had also collected menus from all the restaurants in town: *Bennett's, Golden Crust Sandwich Co., Thyme & Table, Rustic Pie Pizza* and a few others.

She suddenly felt overwhelmed and was second-guessing her idea. She was just a few days out from its grand reopening; her shop was a mess, and she had turned her bookstore into an *everything* store. What was she thinking?!?

She panic-texted Maggie and asked if she could come by and help in exchange for free coffee. Maggie said she'd be there in 30 minutes. In the meantime, Harper grabbed two coffees from Harvest Roast and headed back to HQ.

Maggie breezed through the door a few minutes later and saw the pile of products.

"Holy smokes," she said, eyes wide. "You weren't kidding!"

"I told you! I think maybe this was a mistake. At this rate, I'll never be ready for the Grand Reopening," Harper said with a groan.

"No, no," Maggie said reassuringly. "We just need to make a plan. Let's start with the table itself. Where is it?"

"It's by the back door. It was too heavy for me to move myself."

Within a few minutes, they'd carried the table to the front of the store, found the perfect spot for it and set it up near the front picture window. They started by spreading a rustic linen table runner in soft cream across the length of the table, giving it a simple yet elegant look.

Like a shark, Maggie circled the pile of housewares and decor items Harper had to display. She pulled out a collection of ceramic plates and bowls in rich shades of burnt orange, deep cranberry, and soft sage green. She artfully stacked the plates and arranged the bowls, creating height and balance to the display. Harper added small, mismatched vintage glass jars and bottles in amber and clear hues, filling them with sprigs of eucalyptus and faux wildflowers.

Harper set a crate from the antique store up on its end, added products across the top, and nestled the bushel of apples inside the crate, some of the fruit tumbling out casually.

"Ooooh, yes, I love that," Maggie said encouragingly. They tried products on the table, moving them left to right, forward and back until they found the perfect space.

On the small shelf underneath the table, Maggie added a pair of brass candlesticks with long, tapered beeswax candles, plus the basket with the handmade afghans, layered perfectly and spilling out invitingly. She also added a section for the business cards, brochures, and paper menus. Maggie added tiny white pumpkins and pinecones in shades of copper and gold around the products as a final decorative touch.

When Harper stepped back, she was stunned by how professional the display looked.

"Ohmygosh, I absolutely love it," Maggie said, throwing her long hair behind her shoulder.

"Me too," Harper said, amazed at seeing her vision come to life. " It's exactly what I wanted, but couldn't put into words."

Maggie put her arm around Harper's shoulder.

"I told you that you'd be ready to reopen!" Maggie said, excitedly.

Harper was organizing books at Hearth and Quill when her phone buzzed in her pocket. She pulled it out and saw the group chat lighting up: *ATL Girls.*

ATL GIRLS

Amanda: Harper!! How's life north of the Mason-Dixon line? Miss you!! 🩶

Erin: Yes, miss you so much! Tell us what's new in Fall. Any more small-town drama? 👀

Harper smiled, leaning against a bookshelf as she typed back.

Harper: Hey, ladies! Miss you too. Things are good! Today is my shop's grand reopening!

Amanda: Yay for the grand reopening! You're going to do great! How's Maggie? You two still hanging out?

Harper: Yep, I see her everyday. We're becoming really good friends. 🩶

Erin: Love that for you! So, any cute small-town guys? Are they all lumberjacks with beards and flannel?

Harper: You know I can't resist a guy in flannel. :) There are some cuties, but nothing serious. Just getting my bearings for now.

Amanda : Girl, you better keep us updated when Mr. Flannel shows up!

Erin: Agreed! And make sure to save us some of Maggie's treats when we visit.

Harper: Done! Miss you both so much. Let's plan a call soon?

Amanda: YES! We need an ATL/Fall crossover ASAP. Miss you, Harp!

Erin: Miss you tons! Have an awesome grand opening! Talk soon!

Harper put her phone back in her pocket, feeling a warm sense of connection.

CHAPTER 12
GRAND REOPENING

The morning sun streamed through the freshly polished windows of Hearth & Quill. The bookstore absolutely gleamed. Autumn garlands twined around the doorframe, baskets of gourds flanked the entrance, and a chalkboard sign stood proudly out front:

"GRAND REOPENING CELEBRATION TONIGHT!"

Inside, Harper stood in the center of the shop, arms crossed, turning in a slow circle. Everything was *just right*. She took a deep breath, then exhaled slowly. Her stomach fluttered with nerves and excitement.

The bell over the door jingled.

Harper turned, expecting Maggie—or maybe Gabe, checking in before the crowd—but instead, a tall man in a forest green windbreaker stepped inside, carrying an enormous bouquet. Burnt orange dahlias, golden roses, burgundy mums, and sprays of eucalyptus spilled from a deep amber vase tied with a silk ribbon.

"Delivery for a Harper Whitmore," he said, glancing at the card.

"That's me," Harper replied, eyes widening. "Wow. That is stunning."

The delivery man set the bouquet on the counter with a grin. "Someone's got great taste. Good luck today, Miss Whitmore." He tipped his cap and was gone.

Harper reached for the small cream envelope tucked into the flowers and slid out the card.

Congratulations on your Grand Reopening, Harper! We're SO proud of you. Wish we could be there to toast your bookshop in person, but we'll settle for wine and a FaceTime date soon. Break a leg! Or a bookshelf! Love, Amanda & Erin

Harper laughed, her eyes misting. She brushed her fingers over the petals, then reread the note, this time smiling through the lump in her throat. She placed the bouquet on the checkout counter just inside the front door, where everyone would see it. Then she picked up her phone and snapped a photo, sending it with a caption:

"I can feel your love all the way from Georgia. And your bouquet is front and center for the celebration! Love you girls! 🩶"

As she put the phone down, the bell jingled again.

"Wow! Who sent those gorgeous flowers?" Maggie asked, sweeping in with a basket of mini apple cider donuts.

"My friends Erin and Amanda," Harper said, still grinning.

"Aww...that is so thoughtful. Looks like this day's already off to a beautiful start." Maggie plucked a donut from the basket and handed it to her. "Eat. Caffeine and carbs before chaos."

Harper took a bite, the warmth of cinnamon and sugar grounding her. Through the front windows, she could see townsfolk ambling by, starting their day. She looked around her bookstore—her home, her new beginning—and let the joy bloom in her chest.

Hours later, the finishing touches were in place. Hearth & Quill had been given a warm, welcoming makeover for its big night. There was a fire roaring in the hearth. The shelves were lined with bestsellers, indie picks, and a special section. Harper gathered all the books she found in the upstairs apartment into a small display titled Ellie's Picks. She figured her aunt had literally selected them, so it made sense.

Harper had added a little extra fall decor by putting some pumpkins on the mantle and near the hearth, added some rustic crates, and hung up some string lights to frame the room, with candles flickering softly on the tables. A local acoustic duo were setup just inside the picture window, softly playing covers from Fleetwood Mac to Florence and the Machine. The music floated on the breeze throughout the space, and spilled out onto the sidewalk, where people mingled and chatted. It was the perfect vibe.

It seemed like the entire town was there. The atmosphere was warm and relaxed, and Harper mingled and chatted with people all night. Her 'Local Business' table was an absolute hit, with several shop owners asking if they could copy the idea. She enthusiastically agreed, thinking it could only be good for everyone's business to support one another. Harper was grateful she had gone around to so many local businesses to collect items. Despite being new to town, everywhere she looked was a friendly face, someone she had chatted with, bought items from, or arranged consignment with.

Maggie had encouraged Harper to hire Becky, from Sullivan's Orchard to staff the cash register for the evening, and Harper was glad that she'd agreed. There was a steady line of customers at checkout all night, and if Harper had been at the cashier's desk, she wouldn't have had nearly any time to mingle and connect with people.

Maggie also recommended three recent graduates of Fall High School to work as servers for the night. Harper was grateful for them circling the bookstore and the sidewalk in front of the shop with trays of food that she had catered from local restaurant, Thyme and Table. The owners, Ross and Mike, had even decided on the menu with no need for any input from Harper, which she was grateful for. About an hour into the party, Maggie came rushing up.

"This party is fabulous, girl. And have you had the bite size grilled cheese? They're ah-ma-zing!"

"No, every tray is empty before they get to me!" Harper moaned. "I really want to try one!"

"I'll see if I can grab you one. I think it's gruyere," Maggie sing-songed, disappearing into the crowd.

Around 7pm, as the party was underway, someone tapped a wine glass and shouted "speech!" Harper felt her stomach flip-flop, having not prepared anything for the occasion. But one glance across the room and she saw the friendly faces of Paul, Gabe, Maggie, Melanie, Courtney, Connor, and all the business owners she had met over the last few weeks and she felt herself relax. Harper was touched so many people had come out to support her. She realized that every face in the shop was a friendly one.

Harper took a breath and smiled.

"Good evening, everyone. I'm so grateful for how you've all welcomed me to Fall. I've never experienced such a warm welcome anywhere, or made so many friends so quickly. I'm learning what you already know - that we have something very special here in this little town. With the bookstore's grand reopening, I hope to continue my Aunt Eleanor's legacy. Thanks for being a part of the next chapter...! Let's raise a glass to new beginnings, the stories that we'll share and to Hearth & Quill. "

Harper raised her glass, and the crowd raised theirs and said 'cheers.' There was some light applause and people resumed their mingling.

Maggie came back around, a fresh glass of champagne in her hand, but no food.

"Nice speech. No grilled cheese in sight, sorry. But the caterer said some are gruyere and some were brie. They're to die for."

Harper groaned. "Brie is my favorite. Come on, don't tease me! "

Throughout the evening, Harper met a few local authors. Grant Bishop was a middle - aged man wearing a tweed jacket with suede elbow patches who wrote nonfiction books about the state of Michigan and the Great Lakes. He had an upcoming book launch about the wilderness in the Upper Peninsula and Harper agreed to take a call from his publisher to set up a book reading.

Vivian Hawthorn had lived in Fall for decades. She was in her late

50s or early 60s and was absolutely stunning. She wore flawless makeup, smelled of expensive perfume, and wore just a touch too much jewelry. She effortlessly glided around the room, including over to Harper to introduce herself as a friend of her Aunt Eleanor.

"I was so sorry to hear of her passing," Vivian said softly. "Eleanor and I shared a love of old things. I'm delighted you're keeping the shop going."

"Thank you," Harper said. "Aunt Ellie was wonderful and Hearth & Quill is really special. I have grown quite fond of it already."

"It certainly is special. Congratulations on your reopening and best wishes. It was lovely to meet you, dear," Vivian purred, and drifted away to chat with other guests.

"Nice to meet you, as well," Harper called after her.

Betsy Hawkins was a local children's author and a family therapist. Her books were geared toward early childhood and taught kids how to deal with big emotions. Betsy was soft - spoken and kind and Harper liked her instantly. Betsy lived between Fall and Traverse City, and loved Fall's atmosphere. She had a new book coming out in January. They made plans to chat about a bookstore event to promote the book and social-emotional learning for kids. Agnes from Frost & Fire greeted Harper warmly and gave her a gift bag full of the scent she'd created for the bookstore. The combination of vanilla and sandalwood was one that Harper already loved and associated with the shop. She tucked the gift bag away in the office and rejoined the festivities. Harper turned the corner, finally free to go in search of mini grilled cheese sandwiches, when she nearly ran into Gabe.

"Hi, Harper," Gabe said, leaning towards her and giving her a quick hug. "Congratulations. The bookshop looks incredible."

Harper breathed in deeply. Gabe smelled phenomenal, like a warm mix of leather, whisky and sandalwood, combined with a faint note of pine. Harper wanted to wrap herself up in the smell and live there forever.

"Hi, Gabe. Thank you, and thanks for coming," she said with a smile. She noticed he held a book in his hand and she gestured to it. "What do you have there?"

He held up the book, "Oh, I found this up in the Local Author section. It's an older book from a local author I like, John Thorston. It's called '*Murder on Mackinac Island*'."

"What a small world. I actually started reading that book a few weeks back," she said, surprised."Paul has a copy over at the inn. I read some of it during breakfast, but didn't finish it."

"It *is* a small world. I could tell you how it ends... that is, if you play your cards right," he smiled and raised his eyebrows comically.

"Oh, really?" Harper laughed, the champagne making her feel more bold than usual. She took a sip of her champagne, maintaining eye contact with Gabe as she did, a smile playing on her lips. She tried to think of something witty to say. "I hope Becky told you that you get a raffle ticket with your purchase." *Jeez, Harp. Not exactly what I'd consider top-notch flirting.*

"She did," he said, his eyes locked on Harper's. "I'm dying to know, Miss Shop Owner. What can I win?"

Harper grinned and leaned in to be heard over the crowd.

"A collection of bestselling books, a gift card to a local business, or a basket of baked goodies from Maple and Crumb," she trailed off, struggling to remember all of the items.

"That's a shame," he said, leaning in even closer and speaking into her ear to be heard. She could feel his breath on her neck. "That's not what I was hoping for...."

She swallowed hard. *Oh dear god.* "Oh?," she whispered, her heart rate jumping. "What were you hoping for?"

He looked around quickly and leaned into her so close that she could feel the heat from his skin against hers.

"Some of those bite - sized grilled cheese sandwiches," he said, breaking the flirty tension with a laugh.

Harper threw her head back and laughed. Gabe laughed with

her, his eyes on hers. Across the room, Maggie could spot the chemistry between them and almost squealed with excitement.

It was after 11:30 p.m. when the last of the guests cleared out, and Harper and Maggie flopped onto the sofa in front of the hearth.

"What an incredible night," Harper sighed contentedly, a soft smile on her face. She kicked off her heels and groaned with relief.

"I feel like everyone in town came out," Maggie said. "I had so much fun."

"I did, too!" Harper took one last sip of her wine and set down the glass. "I did good business, too. I sold a ton of books and met local authors that I'm going to connect with going forward. It was really fun."

"That's great," Maggie said, pulling her feet up underneath her. "Speaking of connections..."

Harper laughed and tried to look innocent. "Yes?"

"Don't even try that with me. Spill it," Maggie said. "I saw you talking with Gabe."

"Spill what? We were talking," Harper leaned her head back onto the couch. "He's a nice guy. He's hilarious, actually."

"And...?" Maggie said animatedly. "When's the wedding?"

"Girl - he hasn't even asked me out. I'm not sure if he's flirting with me, or just really friendly," Harper said, closing her eyes.

"Um. I've known him for years, and he's never looked at me the way he looks at you. I can tell you that much." Maggie used her foot to nudge Harper in the thigh gently.

Harper smirked and pushed Maggie's foot away.

"Well, what's his story?" Harper asked. "Is he single?"

"Yeah, he's been single for years," Maggie wiggled her eyebrows up and down.

"How is a man like *that* single?" She said absentmindedly.

Maggie sat up a bit.

"He was dating a woman named Stephanie maybe 5 years ago? It was before his dad got sick. They broke up and she moved to Chicago. He hasn't dated anyone since."

"Hmmm. Maybe he's not over her. You never know," Harper said. She tried to change topics. "Want some water?"

"Sure." Maggie asked. "But you're not changing the topic that easily. Trust me, he's over her. And I see the way he looks at you."

Harper laughed as she crossed the room, poured two glasses of water from a pitcher, and returned to the hearth. "I'm not trying to change the topic. But there's nothing to say. He's a good looking guy and he seems nice. There, you happy?"

"Yes, I am," Maggie giggled. "Aaaaaand?"

"Aaaand, what?" Harper drew out the word questioningly. "What do you want from me? He smelled good tonight."

"Ohmygoshhereallydid, didn't he? Like whisky and an alpine wood," Maggie said, wistfully, taking a long sip of water.

Harper burst out laughing. "An alpine wood? You're so goofy."

Maggie nearly choked on her water, then wiped her mouth, smiling. "Harper! You could make little Alpine smelling babies with him!"

Harper cracked up.

They both calmed down, and after a minute, Maggie said, "You just moved here and already, I can't imagine Fall without you."

"Alright, alright, don't get all cheesy on me. " Harper laughed.

"OMG, those grilled cheese sandwiches!" Maggie exclaimed, wide eyed. "Girl. They were SO good."

"If you don't shush about those sandwiches... do you know I never got one?" Harper cracked up, moving to sit down again. She froze. Her gaze caught on one of the quill display cases above the mantle. One box was open, the door cracked an inch or two. She moved closer, examining the box. "Hey, look at this."

Maggie stood up and moved beside Harper. "What the...? Why is that open?"

Harper swung the door open further, revealing an empty case.

Maggie said, "You're missing a feather!"

"Those are antique quills. Like the ones that people wrote with back in the olden days. My aunt collected them," she glanced at the floor around her feet, somehow knowing it wouldn't be there. "The missing one is really beautiful...it's cream with this, like, gold veining throughout the feather. I noticed it when I was cleaning because it glowed in the sunlight. It's stunning."

"Someone stole an antique quill from your shop? Who would do that?" Maggie said, her brows furrowed.

"I have no idea, " Harper said, giving up and sinking down into the couch.

"Ohmygosh, it's our very own mystery!" Maggie said, then continued quietly. "We have a thief in Fall...for, like, the first time ever."

"We do," Harper said slowly, her brows knitted together. "But why would they steal my aunt's antique quill...?"

CHAPTER 13
BUSINESS BEGINS

A few days after the grand reopening, Harper stepped back to admire her new "Open" sign on the front door of The Hearth & Quill, feeling a thrill of accomplishment. The bookstore was alive again, infused with her aunt's warmth and charm, and Harper's touches, too. She loved the local business table and so did her customers. Her first official week in business was going very well.

The bell above the door jingled and Harper straightened, a warm smile ready as the first customer of the day walked in. It was a woman in her late 60s, tall and slender with sharp eyes that scanned the room like she was inspecting a fine wine. She had silver hair cut in a severe bob just below her chin and was wearing a knit top, cardigan and a sensible pair of loafers. She had a serious, stern look about her and clutched a small black purse under her arm.

"Good morning!" Harper called cheerfully. "Welcome to The Hearth & Quill. Let me know if I can help you find anything."

The woman's eyes landed on Harper, and a faintly disapproving smile flickered across her lips. "Harper Whitmore, I presume?" She adjusted her purse, clutching it more tightly.

"Yes, that's me." Harper extended her hand. "And you are?"

"Prudence Sherman." The woman's hand was cold and stiff in Harper's warm grasp. "I was a...friend of your aunt's."

"It's nice to meet you," Harper said, sitting down in the chair behind the counter.

Prudence's gaze swept over the bookstore again, her expression growing more critical.

"I couldn't make it to your grand opening celebration. I assume it went well?" Prudence pulled her cardigan down primly as she spoke.

"It went very well," Harper said warmly. "Thanks for asking."

"Did you know your Aunt Ellie took over this shop when she was just 25 years old. The dear spent her entire life here - 50 years."

Harper forced a polite smile, a bit offended at the underlying assumption that Prudence knew her aunt better than Harper.

"Yes, I knew that. I'm excited to carry on her legacy. She left some big shoes to fill!," Harper said with a warm smile. "I've added a few small updates like the Local Business table. Take a look and let me know your thoughts."

Prudence gave the corner a cursory glance and sniffed. "I see." She turned back, fixing Harper with a look that felt more like an appraisal than a greeting. "Your aunt was very particular. I do hope you're not planning to change *too* much."

"Oh, just small things here and there, a bit of organization, but keeping the heart the same," Harper smiled, keeping her tone light.

"Hmm," Prudence replied noncommittally, readjusting her purse strap on her shoulder. "Your aunt always knew exactly where everything was in here. You could ask her for a book, new or used, recent or old, and she could find it immediately. Your generation is so concerned with decluttering and organization." She walked toward the display of quills above the hearth and stopped short. "You're missing a quill here - this case is empty."

"Yes, I know. It went missing on the night of the reopening. I've been asking around, and I'm hopeful it will turn up soon."

"How could you misplace a feather quill?" She asked accusatorially.

"I'm not sure, " Harper said, growing tired of the conversation and Prudence's tone, so she tried a different tactic. "What can I help you find today, Mrs. Sherman?"

Prudence gave a stiff nod. "Yes, well. I'm looking for three books about pie making." She slid a small piece of paper over to Harper with the book titles.

Harper took the slip of paper, reading it as she walked to the cooking and baking section. *This would be easier if I could search my inventory in a computer database,* she thought to herself. It took her just a moment to find the section, and she was secretly impressed with herself. She was happy to find that there were quite a few books in the section, and they had two of the three books that Prudence was looking for in stock.

"I have two of those titles in stock." Harper walked back to the counter and placed the books on the counter. "Here you go. The third I don't have, but I can order it for you from a larger shop up in Traverse City. I should have it for you in just a few days."

"I suppose that will have to do," Prudence said with a sigh. She paid for her items and, at Harper's request, she wrote her phone number on the back of the paper.

"Great, thank you," Harper said. "I'll call you when I receive the last title."

"That would be fine." Prudence said haughtily.

The bell jingled as she disappeared into the brisk autumn air, leaving Harper standing in the quiet shop, feeling a lingering chill despite the crackling warmth of the fireplace.

"That sounds like Prudence, all right," laughed Maggie later that day. She had stopped by the shop with a coffee and a cookie for Harper, and Harper had filled her in on the exchange. "She's a tough ol' bird, but she's harmless."

"I don't know about harmless," Harper laughed. "She was one of my first customers of the day and she really bummed me out!"

"Don't let her get to you. She's just a sour ol' lady." Maggie said, popping the last bite of her cookie in her mouth.

"Okay, but you should have seen me, Maggie. I was so proud of myself. I knew just where to go in the shop, and I found the books right away. I felt like Aunt Ellie would have been so proud of me."

"She totally would have!" Maggie agreed animatedly. "And I'm proud of you, too. You're like, legit now. Harper Whitmore - bookseller."

Harper laughed and took a bite of the cookie and was pleasantly surprised. "Wow. What is this cookie? Lemon and...?"

Maggie opened her mouth theatrically in an excited look. "Rosemary!" She clapped her hands together excitedly. "What do you think?"

"It's good. Herby, but not too herby. The lemon is so tasty and bright, it's perfect."

"That's *exactly* what I was going for!" Maggie said happily. "Yay. Okay, I better get back. You have a good day. *And don't go changing anything around here.*" She imitated Prudence, standing rod-straight and holding her head rigidly.

Harper laughed. "No, of course I won't, *Prudence.*"

———

The bell over the door jingled as Mrs. Hastings bustled into The Hearth & Quill, her presence somehow bringing an air of both excitement and chaos into the quiet bookstore. Harper looked up from her spot behind the counter, a smile spreading across her face as the elderly woman made her way over, her gaze sweeping across the shelves with a look of intense concentration.

"Good morning, Mrs. Hastings," Harper greeted warmly. "What brings you in today? Looking for another mystery?"

Mrs. Hastings waved a dismissive hand, her many cocktail rings catching the light. "No, no, dear. I'm on a mission. I've had an idea to color code my entire house!"

Harper raised an eyebrow, intrigued. "Oh?"

Mrs. Hastings leaned closer, glancing around as if what she was about to say was a town secret. "Color-coding, dear. It's all the rage. Have you seen those girls who do the organizing show? It's amazing. And I'm going to do it!"

Harper let out a little laugh. "Yes, I believe it's called *The Home Edit*. They sure do color-code everything! How can I help?"

"I'm looking for a book on decluttering and organization," Mrs. Hastings said. "Do you have anything like that?"

Harper couldn't help but grin at the image. "I'm sure we do. Let's look in the home section."

Mrs. Hastings followed Harper to the section, and they spent a few minutes going over the titles that might be relevant for her. Mrs. Hastings picked up three books excitedly.

"These are perfect," Mrs. Hastings said, her eyes sparkling with excitement. As Harper rang up her purchases, she continued, "You know, you could do rainbow order books! A table with all reds, or all purples, something like that."

Harper glanced around, trying to picture her carefully organized sections reorganized into what would essentially be a giant rainbow. "I don't know, Mrs. Hastings. It would be hard to find a book based on color. I think I'll stick with the good old alphabetical order for now."

Mrs. Hastings let out an exaggerated sigh, placing a hand dramatically to her chest. "Fine, fine. But don't come crying to me when another bookstore color-codes and steals all your business!"

Harper laughed, patting Mrs. Hastings on the shoulder. "Tell you what—if I ever decide to reorganize, you'll be the first to know."

Mrs. Hastings gave a satisfied nod, her eyes gleaming. "Thank you, dear. And I'll also take that new mystery you've got up front. I like that it has a good, bold cover—I simply cannot abide pastels."

As Mrs. Hastings tottered toward the register, Harper couldn't help but smile. This town was full of characters.

Harper stepped out of the general store, balancing a paper bag filled with new dish towels, a jar of apple butter, coffee, a bag of apples and a cookie from Maggie's shop. The autumn air smelled of wood smoke and caramel apples, and the sidewalks were scattered with crisp red leaves that crunched satisfyingly underfoot.

"Looks like someone's up to something festive," came a familiar voice to her left.

She turned to find Paul leaning casually against a lamppost, a paper coffee cup in one hand and a leash in the other. Lady was sniffing around the grass looking for the perfect spot to do her business. Paul had a cheerful yellow knit scarf looped loosely around his neck.

"Paul," she said, smiling. "Don't tell anyone, but I think I've hit peak small-town cliché. I'm about five minutes away from starting a cinnamon stick collection."

Paul chuckled, pushing off the post and walking over. Lady followed, having taken care of her business. "You're basically a local. Next comes dressing in all fall colors and knowing everyone's dog by name."

"I already know at least seven," Harper said with mock pride. "Though one of them might be an enormous cat named Meatball."

Paul laughed and held out his coffee. "I'll trade you a sip of this for one of whatever's in that bag."

Harper peeked inside and pulled out a little wrapped cookie from Maple and Crumb. "Deal."

They made the exchange like pros. He took a bite and nodded in approval. "Maggie's baking is incredible, as usual."

"I know, " Harper sighed. "How's the inn today?"

"Busy," he said. "I've got a couple from Grand Rapids who came up just to 'smell the air' and one guest who's convinced our front porch is haunted because the wind keeps moving the rocking chair."

Harper grinned. "So basically, business as usual?"

"Pretty much. Busy, but it's a good busy." He looked at her a little more closely. "You holding up okay?"

She hesitated, then gave a small, tired smile. "Doing pretty great. The bookstore keeps me grounded. And I've got good people around. I'm feeling more settled here now."

Paul nodded, kind and steady. "Well, don't forget to take care of yourself, too. Hearth & Quill is lucky to have you—but so is the town."

Her smile widened. "Thanks, Paul. I'll stop by for some of your incredible coffee later this week."

"I'll save you the biggest mug," he said, tipping his coffee cup in farewell. "C'mon, Lady von Trapp. Let's get back to work."

As he walked off toward the inn, scarf trailing in the breeze, Harper felt a little lighter. Just one more reason she was starting to believe Fall, Michigan, might actually be home.

The bell over the bookstore door jingled just as Harper was trying—unsuccessfully—to tape a hand-drawn "Staff Picks" sign above a crooked bookshelf. She turned, tape sticking to her fingertips, and saw Connor standing just inside the doorway, hands in the pockets of his worn jeans.

"Morning," she said, brushing a stray curl from her face. "What's up?"

Connor cleared his throat and looked at her.

"I was wondering if you might be hiring. "

Harper blinked. "Me?"

"Yeah. I thought you might need help. You already know I can clean. But I can also do just about any repair you need done. Lug boxes of books around, organize the stock room, whatever you need."

She laughed. "You're a jack of all trades. You sound like a helpful guy to have around."

"I definitely am!" Connor said with a smile.

Harper glanced around and thought about her to-do list.

"You can ask Ronnie or Gabe for a reference," Connor continued. "I am a part-time delivery driver at Rustic Pie, and I work at the orchard seasonally as well."

Harper lifted her eyebrows appreciatively. "You're a busy guy! I'll tell you what... I can't hire you officially right now because I don't have a handle on the shop's books yet. But I can pay you cash for doing handyman work around here. Does that sound all right?

Connor grinned. "Sure, that would be great!"

Harper smiled, leaning on the counter. "What's your schedule like? Could you come in the morning? Say 9 a.m. to 1 p.m.?"

Conner said, "Sure!"

"Alright then. Is tomorrow too soon to start?" Harper asked.

"How about today? I'm free right now!" he said.

Harper laughed. "You're determined. I like that. Alright. I could use some help to hang this new light fixture in the bathroom, and then you could help me unload these boxes of new releases."

Connor grinned and rubbed his hands together. "Great."

Weeks slipped by in a gentle rhythm, each day blending into the next in a way that felt comforting, like a favorite old song. Harper sank into her new life with contentment. Every morning, she woke to the soft light filtering through her upstairs apartment. She'd go for a run or do yoga, and then grab coffee at Harvest Roast before heading back to open Hearth & Quill.

She'd flick on the warm string lights that lined the shelves and arrange a few new books on the front display. Connor would come in for a few hours and shelve books, repair items and build fires in the fireplace. Harper's shop had a steady stream of regulars: townsfolk who came in for the new releases or the cozy classics she kept stacked near the armchairs. Some people came in just to read. She'd chat with them, hear about their lives, and gradually, she felt herself becoming part of this quiet world. The bookstore was a gathering place as much as it was a store.

Maggie came by almost every day, sweeping in with her usual energy, her arms loaded with fresh pastries or treats from Maple and Crumb. Harper kept a spot on the counter clear just for Maggie's deliveries, a little corner that smelled constantly of cinnamon and frosting.

"Harper, you've got to try this one," Maggie would say, handing over a flaky apple turnover or a buttery croissant filled with homemade jam. "And this batch? It's my best yet!"

Harper always accepted the treats with a grateful smile. They'd sit together over coffee in the early afternoons, swapping stories about the customers who'd come through, sharing bits of town gossip that Maggie or Harper had heard. Over time, Harper's laughter became freer, her nerves less sharp. She thought less about her old job at the advertising agency, and less about her ex-fiance. Her heart felt lighter.

Afternoons were usually steady in terms of business, and Harper stayed busy. Some evenings, Harper would lock up and head upstairs, sometimes carrying a new book she'd saved for herself or an old favorite she'd been longing to reread. She'd curl up on the worn leather armchair by her window, watching as the golden autumn light softened, the quiet streets of Fall settling down for the night. The little sounds of the town—distant laughter from the Rustic Pie or Sullivans, music from The Fallen Leaves brewery—became familiar to her, part of her nightly soundtrack.

One evening in early October, Harper paused as she climbed the stairs to the apartment above. She looked around *her* bookstore. The smell of paper and ink, the low hum of the heater, the books resting peacefully on their shelves—she realized that all of it felt like home.

CHAPTER 14
FIREPIT AND FRIENDS

One afternoon, while the wind swept red and gold leaves across the sidewalks of Fall, Harper stood on a wooden step stool inside Hearth & Quill, hanging a garland of dried oranges and cinnamon sticks along the windows, the scent mixing with the faint aroma of book pages and the remnants of the morning's chai.

"You know you're officially one of us now, right?" Maggie's voice floated up from below. She was sitting cross-legged on the floor, organizing a basket of knitted bookmarks that someone from the Harvest Hall craft guild had dropped off.

"Because of the citrus garland?" Harper asked.

"Well, because you *care* about the citrus garland," Maggie replied, grinning. "Only real Fall residents get weirdly passionate about decorative produce."

Harper laughed, adjusting one final loop of twine. "I do kind of love it here."

"I'm so glad to hear it. Couldn't imagine this place without you," Maggie said.

"Awww, you're so sweet," Harper batted her eyelashes. "We better get going. I can't wait to try some cider."

Paul was already out back when Harper and Maggie arrived, stoking a small fire in a copper bowl behind the inn. String lights crisscrossed the patio above, flickering against the soft gray dusk. A few guests milled nearby with mugs of cider and small plates of warm brie and bread.

"Well, hello there!" Paul exclaimed when he saw them.

"Sorry we're late," Maggie teased. "We had to double back for an extra pie."

"And I brought a book of ghost stories, if the mood strikes us," Harper raised her eyebrows suggestively.

Paul handed Harper and Maggie mugs from a nearby tray.

"Try this one. Apple, cinnamon, a hint of rosemary and of course, whiskey. Might be my best batch yet."

Harper sipped and closed her eyes. "Okay, wow. That tastes like a hug."

"Told you," Paul said with a proud nod.

They settled into chairs around the fire pit, the glow warming their faces as the first stars winked through the canopy of trees. Paul passed around toasted pecans and little pumpkin hand pies, and the conversation meandered easily from Maggie's childhood Halloween costume disasters to Paul's cast of characters at the inn.

Paul chuckled. "It's never boring around here, that's for sure."

Just then, the gate creaked, and Gabe appeared. He looked incredible in jeans and a well-worn Carhartt jacket.

"Sorry I'm late. What'd I miss?" He said, settling into a chair next to Harper.

"You made it just in time for funny innkeeper stories," Harper said, enjoying the smell of his cologne.

"Oh, good," Gabe said. "I didn't miss any revealing Harper stories, then?"

She shook her head, smiling. "You're trouble."

As the evening wore on, the sky deepened into a blanket of navy and stars. Paul turned on a little portable speaker and soft jazz played low in the background. The fire crackled. Laughter came easily.

At one point, Maggie excused herself to the restroom, and Paul went inside to grab more napkins. That left Harper and Gabe alone, side by side, in the quiet.

"You like Fall so far?" he asked, his voice soft.

She nodded, eyes on the fire. "I really do. And I didn't expect to. I thought I'd come, sell the shop and leave. But something about this place... feels like home. It made me want to stay."

"Maybe it's the cider," he offered.

She shook her head and turned to look at him. "It's not the cider, though it is delicious."

Gabe looked back at Harper, smiling, and there was a pause. They were silent as a moment passed between them.

"Well, I for one, am glad you didn't leave," Gabe said, looking from her eyes to her lips.

"Me too," Harper said in a voice just above a whisper.

Just then, Paul returned with napkins and broke the moment. Harper felt a pang of disappointment and realized she couldn't wait to see where that moment was going to lead. Maggie came bouncing back a second later, waving a plate of cookies and declaring they needed to play some ridiculous game she'd just invented.

And Harper smiled, full and real. Because these people were so kind and had welcomed her in with open arms. She felt like she was part of something wonderful in Fall.

Back at her apartment, Harper kicked off her boots, grabbed a blanket, and sank onto the couch. The warmth of the evening still lingered, but so did something else – something she hadn't said out loud yet.

She pulled out her phone. It was time to update the group.

ATL GIRLS 🍂🍎🍷📚

Harper: Okay. So. I may have developed a tiny crush. Like, micro-crush. Barely noticeable. Probably seasonal.

Erin: OH!! DO TELL! Who's the Fall Farmer Bae??

Amanda:Wait. Is this the guy with the orchard? Gabe, right? 👀 The one with the flannel?

Harper: MAYBE. Okay yes. We ended up hanging out with Maggie and Paul tonight by the fire behind the inn. It was casual. Cozy.

Erin: And? You and Gabe locked eyes across the flames while someone strummed an acoustic guitar?? 😂

Harper:Lol no guitars, but... there was a moment. Just the two of us for a minute. The fire was crackling. He asked if I liked it here, and I told him I did. He said he was glad I stayed. And I think he meant it.

Amanda: Okay, but WAS THERE EYE CONTACT? WAS THERE A KISS?

Harper: No, but there was a serious lip glance. And I might have forgotten how to speak for like five whole seconds.

Erin: SAY LESS. I'M INVESTED.

Amanda: He sounds like the human version of a weighted blanket.

Harper: Honestly? That's... exactly right. 🤍🥹

CHAPTER 15
GRIM DISCOVERY

A few weeks after the grand reopening of Hearth & Quill, the town was gearing up for the Apple Harvest Festival. Banners hung over every street welcoming tourists and townsfolk to 'Fall's 48th Annual Apple Harvest Festival.' They posted the festival schedule of events on every shop door and lamppost.

The festival took place over ten days, but the opening and closing weekends were the busiest. There were events both at the town square and at Sullivan's Orchard. The first weekend included Friday night movie night in the town square. Folks arrived early to set up chairs and blankets and returned to watch 'The Cider House Rules,' eat popcorn and drink warm apple cider. Saturday was the first major festival day, which began with the harvest parade, bobbing for apples, the apple pie baking competition, and then live music and dancing in the square. There was an artisanal market in the town square, a mini farmer's market with autumnal selections, and more.

At the orchard, there were hayrides, a corn maze, apple-pressing demonstrations, and bonfires and s'mores in the evening. Sunday was family day, with apple crafts for the kids, a petting zoo, face painting, and a scarecrow-building activity for families. Throughout the festival, the Fall Trolley ran back and forth daily from 8 a.m. to 10 p.m., providing access to the orchard and easing traffic around the town square.

The apple pie contest was one of the biggest attractions at the festival. Each year, half a dozen bakers would enter their apple pie into the contest, and 4 judges would vote for the best. The top 3 pies won a prize, but the coveted first - place slot was what everyone was after. The winner would have their name engraved on the town's golden rolling pin, which was displayed at Town Hall, plus a beautiful ceramic pie dish customized with their name and "Best Apple Pie–Harvest Festival" and the year engraved on it. It was an incredible honor and something the bakers were excited about every year.

Harper had gotten into the festival spirit and decorated her picture windows with apple-themed displays. She put sandwich-board signs out in front of the bookshop, inviting tourists and locals alike inside. To encourage folks to sit awhile and relax, Harper added several cafe tables and chairs out front. She was excited about the boost in business the Harvest Festival promised.

On Friday, the first day of the festival, Harper was pleasantly busy all afternoon. She barely had time to watch as townspeople spent the day setting up in the square across the street. People brought in tables and decorations, erected a giant inflatable movie screen in the gazebo, and assembled an artisan market on the south side of the lawn. Some balanced on ladders while others shouted directions at them: "...pull the sign up on the right...now down a little...perfect!"

At 6 pm, Harper finished serving her last customer. She popped a few gummy bears into her mouth, turned the sign to 'Closed', left the shop and walked through the square. As she walked, she passed four long tables covered with red and white gingham tablecloths and acrylic signs arranged in a row, announcing each participant in this year's pie contest. A small stack of plates and forks was on each table for the judges to try each entry.

Harper crossed the square, looking for Maggie. Gabe was unloading crates of apples from the bed of his truck. As she got closer, he caught her eye and gave her a slow smile. Her stomach did a little flip-flop at the sight of him. His smile just melted her. And in those jeans, hat backwards with little tendrils of hair curling up around the edges, she was weak in the knees. Harper smiled and waved.

"Hi, Harper," he said, wiping his hands on the front of his jeans.

"Hi, Gabe. How are you?"

"Great," he said with a grin. "What are you up to?"

"Just getting ready for my first Apple Harvest Festival. I'm excited. I was going to ask if I could get a bushel of McIntosh apples from you. My "Local Business" table is running low. Probably because I keep eating them," she said with a laugh.

"Sure! But I don't have any with me right now. Luke and Ryan are back at the orchard harvesting some, though. I'm headed back there now - want to join me?" He took his hat off, wiped his brow and replaced the hat in a move that Harper could tell he'd done a thousand times.

"Um, sure, if you don't mind the company, " she asked.

"I'd love the company. Give me two minutes and we'll be on the way. "

Gabe wasted no time. He unloaded the last two wooden crates of apples from the bed of his truck and placed them in the stack with the others. He chatted with Mary and Greg, the organizers of the Apple Harvest Festival, and they signed a form. Gabe rolled it up and shoved it in his back pocket.

He opened the passenger door for Harper, then circled around to the driver's side and climbed in next to her.

The sun was falling lower in the sky, bathing the apple orchard in a warm, golden glow. Gabe needed to check something in the cider shed, and told Harper to go on ahead and promised to meet her, Luke and Ryan in the McIntosh rows. Harper walked through the rows of trees, their branches heavy with ripe red apples. The soft crunch of leaves beneath her feet was comforting, and the crisp autumn air smelled sweet and musky, like fresh fruit and damp earth. She took a deep breath, feeling the peacefulness settle over her like a warm blanket. It would be a quick stop—she'd just pick up a crate of apples for the bookstore's cider event, and she and Gabe would be on their way. Suddenly, Harper became aware that something felt off. She couldn't quite put her finger on it, but as she wandered deeper into the orchard, she noticed how quiet it was—unnaturally so. Usually, at this time of year, the place was bustling with families, the chatter of children and parents filling the air. Today, though, everyone was in town for the festival. The orchard felt abandoned and deserted, which was unsettling as the sun was sinking lower in the sky. Harper told herself that was all it was. But Gabe said Luke and Ryan were harvesting the McIntosh trees, didn't he? He said she could join them and pick out her own bushel. So where were they?

Harper wandered up and down the rows of trees, passing little red signs in the ground that said Honey Crisp, Ambrosia and Fuji before she found the McIntosh area. The trees were beautiful, medium-sized, with their trunks smooth and straight. But Harper realized it was just as quiet here as it was in the rest of the orchard.

"Hello?" Harper called out tentatively, her voice startling in the quiet. "Luke? Ryan?"

No one answered.

She was about to call out again when she saw it—half-hidden beneath one of the largest trees, the pale cream color of an apple basket overturned, and something reddish purple on the ground beneath the branches. The shape was unusual.

She moved closer, her heart beginning to pound. As she stepped around the side of the tree, her eyes locked on a figure lying on the ground. At first, all Harper saw was color—the deep burgundy of a woolen coat, the silver-gray hair splayed out like a halo on the earth. For a moment, Harper didn't recognize the person. Her heart started racing, and a sickly feeling grew in her belly. Finally, it clicked. The body on the ground was Prudence Sherman.

Prudence lay completely still, her usually rosy cheeks ghostly white, and Harper knew instantly that she was dead. She lay on her back in the dirt, her eyes wide open, staring blankly at the darkening sky. The scowl she normally wore was missing, and in its place was a surprised look, frozen in place. Her burgundy coat was splayed out messily underneath her. She wore a pair of black pants and a cream-colored knit top. Overripe apples were all over the ground around and underneath her, their sharp smell mixing with the earthy aroma of the orchard.

But what drew Harper's gaze most of all was the long, cream feather quill sticking out of Prudence's neck at an angle. The feather had gold veining throughout it, glimmering in the last rays of afternoon sunlight. It was the stolen feather quill from Harper's shop! Prudence had been murdered. How? When? Who did this? And how did the killer get Harper's quill?

Harper felt dizzy, and she knelt down for a moment, careful not to disturb anything.

"Gabe..." Harper whispered, her voice catching in her throat. She cleared her throat desperately. "Gabe!" she shouted, her voice cutting through the thick, warm evening air. Harper's heart hammered in her chest as she fumbled in her pocket for her phone, her hands shaking so much that she almost dropped it. The display read 6:21.

"Gabe!" she shouted desperately, even as she dialed 911. "Luke! Ryan!" The ringing in her ear was too loud in the orchard's silence.

Was this really happening? Who could have done this? Why would anyone hurt Prudence? Who would do this?

"911, what's your emergency?" came the voice on the other end, pulling Harper out of her spiraling thoughts.

She forced herself to articulate, though her voice trembled.

"I'm in the apple orchard, and I... I... I found something. I found some*one*. I found a dea-. I found Prudence Sherman. She's... dead."

The dispatcher's calm voice guided Harper through the next steps, but it all felt surreal, like she was watching someone else live this moment. The dispatcher asked a few questions and asked if Harper had felt for a pulse. She hadn't, and she said she couldn't. Harper knew there was no point. Her eyes were locked on Prudence's lifeless face and unblinking eyes. When Harper finally stood, waiting for the police to arrive, she could see the trees around her sway in the gentle breeze, and she had strange sensation of swaying herself. It occurred to her she was going to faint just before she saw the earth headed toward her.

Within minutes of Harper's call to 911, the small orchard was crowded with people. The red and blue lights of the ambulance and two sheriff squad cars cast an eerie glow on everyone gathered in the orchard as dusk fell.

Harper was sitting on the ground on top of a blanket, wrapped in another blanket. She had no recollection of sitting down. For that matter, she didn't remember anyone spreading out a blanket for her or draping the blanket around her shoulders. Harper was holding a small jug of apple cider and a donut, but she didn't know who had handed them to her. So she just held them, still in shock. She was trying to process everything that had happened in the last few minutes. She felt a chill deep in her bones and, despite the blanket, she continued shaking, her teeth chattering.

"Let's back up, folks," said one of the sheriff's deputies.

He was talking to the small group of people who had gathered about ten or fifteen feet away from Harper. There was Gabe, Luke, Ryan and Becky, who worked the register in the orchard market and had helped Harper at the grand reopening. Their faces were all a mix of shock and sadness, and Becky's red - rimmed eyes looked as though she'd been crying.

The sense of quiet was further shattered as Sheriff Ben Carlisle quickly pulled up in his cruiser. His heavy boots planted in the grass underfoot, his hulking frame and weathered face framed by graying hair. His gravelly voice immediately began barking orders to the two deputies who scrambled to his side as he got out of the car. Sheriff Carlisle had been keeping order in Fall for far longer than anyone could remember. He had a no-nonsense aura about him, and his eyes—dark and sharp—were all business as they took in the scene.

Sheriff Carlisle approached the scene slowly, his eyes scanning everything—every tree, every leaf, every piece of fallen fruit. He moved with an authority that told you he'd done this before. When he reached the tree, he removed his hat, running a hand through his thick silver hair as he took a deep breath.

"Prudence Sherman," he muttered, mostly to himself, but his voice carried through the orchard like a low rumble. He crouched down beside her, the blanket doing little to hide the lifeless form underneath. "That's a shame."

Sheriff Carlisle's expression was one of grim determination, the corners of his mouth set into a deep frown. He knew Prudence about as much as anyone in the town knew her. She'd been a constant presence for years—prickly around the edges, opinionated, but a good woman. As much a part of Fall as the orchard itself. The thought of her ending up like this weighed heavily on his mind.

One of his deputies, a young, nervous man named Greg Hart, hovered nearby, his notepad out and ready. "Uh, hello sir. It looks like the, uh, victim was out here, possibly picking apples," Greg said, glancing at the scattered fruit.

"Yes, deputy," Sheriff Carlisle said, his voice low and steady. "I can see that."

"Uh. Right. Well, there's a feather quill sticking out of her neck. The scene does not appear to be a natural death," Deputy Hart continued, flipping through the pages in his book.

The Sheriff shot a glance at his deputy, then knelt down next to Prudence's body, carefully lifting the blanket to examine her neck. There was a tiny pool of blood at the base of the feather quill, which stood out starkly against her pale skin. Carlisle's face hardened. He hated this part—the way people became evidence, the way a person's entire life could be reduced to marks on a body, to questions of "who" and "why." He took in every detail, from the position of her hands and fingers to the fruit on the ground.

"Did you find anything else on her?" Sheriff Carlisle asked, without looking up.

"Just what you see there," Deputy Hart replied, clearing his throat nervously. "We haven't touched anything—just covered her until you arrived."

"Good," the Sheriff said, standing up and surveying the small group of people watching. They were murmuring amongst themselves, their faces pale and tight with shock. Sheriff Carlisle's eyes found Harper's, sitting on a blanket. He knew who she was—Eleanor's niece, the new bookstore owner. She looked pale and he could see the distress in her eyes.

Carlisle walked over to the group, his face softening slightly as he addressed Harper. "You alright there, Miss Whitmore?"

Harper nodded, gripping the blanket around her tightly. "Yes, I'm fine. I just..." She swallowed hard. "I found her. Prudence. I thought maybe she'd just fallen or something... I didn't know what to—"

"You did exactly what you were supposed to do, calling 911," the sheriff said gently. "Can you tell me what happened? Anything you remember might be helpful, big or small."

She nodded again, biting her lip as she looked back toward the tree. "I... I don't know much. I was just here to pick up some apples, and then I—" Harper's voice faltered, and she felt Gabe's reassuring hand on her shoulder.

"Let's hold off for now," Sheriff Carlisle said, his voice turning businesslike once more. "Stay close. We'll take you into town shortly to take your statement."

"Sheriff, "Gabe said quietly. "Could Harper come into the station in the morning? She's a bit shaken up."

Carlisle looked at Harper, then back to Gabe. "That's fine. Why don't you make sure she gets home safely?"

Sheriff Carlisle turned back to the scene, jaw clenched as he took in the sight. The shadows made the orchard feel darker, like a blanket was being pulled over the scene, urging everyone to hurry and leave before night fell. The sheriff knew he'd need to work quickly— evidence gathered, statements taken, the body examined. Carlisle couldn't believe he had a murderer on his hands, right here in his own town of Fall.

Harper shivered violently despite the warm evening, her teeth chattering. *Why was the quill from my bookstore in Prudence's neck?* The question stood out sharply against the fogginess of her brain. *What if someone thinks I put it there?* Her stomach churned, and she felt a wave of nausea. Harper needed answers -fast. Not just for her own peace of mind, but so she didn't end up in handcuffs.

"Here," Gabe said, striding over to where she was sitting. He took off his flannel jacket and gingerly took the blanket from her shoulders. He wrapped his jacket around her, then replaced the blanket. She was tempted to protest, saying he didn't need to do that, but the warmth of his body radiated off the shirt and she immediately felt comforted. The weight of the blanket added another layer for warmth. She snuggled deeper into both and murmured an almost inaudible 'thank you'.

The deputies motioned Gabe over to ask a few questions about the orchard. They jotted notes in their notebooks, listening intently, and nodding as Gabe talked. Their radios cracked and filled the dusk air with unintelligible updates from dispatch.

By the time Deputy Jake Russell arrived, the stillness of the orchard felt as though it was holding its breath. Sheriff Carlisle stood near the body, his face grim.

"Where is she?" he asked quietly.

Carlisle nodded toward the clearing ahead. "Under that apple tree there."

Jake stepped into the space and froze.

Prudence Sherman lay sprawled on the ground, arms at her sides, her neck tilted at an unnatural angle. The handle of a quill protruded from the side of her neck, its gold tip catching the last of the sun like a cruel decoration.

Jake let out a slow breath. "Is that what I think it is?"

Carlisle nodded. "Looks like one of the display pieces from Hearth & Quill."

Jake crouched beside the body, studying the placement of the quill, the faint drag marks in the dirt, the scattered apples bruised around her.

"Who found her?"

"Harper Whitmore, the new bookstore owner," Deputy Hart answered.

Harper waited for her turn to talk to the deputies. *Who could have done this?* Absentmindedly, she took out her phone and started making a list of people she saw in the town square just before she and Gabe headed to the orchard. There were the Mayor and his two assistants, Paul, Gabe, Patty, Maggie, Caroline, Grace and Lena. There were two older men who were helping hang the banner... Harper didn't know their names, but she could point them out to the sheriff by way of identification. She continued jotting down names, and for those she didn't know, she wrote down physical descriptions.

Before long, she had 35 to 40 people she could vouch for being in the town square just before Prudence was discovered. Of course, she didn't know how long Prudence had been there.

Finished with his conversation with the sheriff, Gabe returned to her and sat down next to her.

"How are you holding up?" he asked.

"I'm okay," Harper said. "I was in shock, but I'm thinking a little more clearly now. Who could have done this...and why?"

"I have no idea," Gabe admitted.

CHAPTER 16
SLEEP

The drive to Harper's house was quick but tense. Gabe kept his eyes on the road, though he couldn't help glancing sideways at Harper—she was pale, her arms wrapped around herself, staring straight ahead. He wanted to ask if she was okay, but the words felt useless in the wake of what had happened tonight.

He pulled up to the bookstore and killed the engine. "Let me help you inside." Gabe's voice was low, confident and reassuring.

Harper hesitated, then nodded, her eyes flickering toward him. She wasn't very good at asking for help, and sometimes would push away people who offered it. She had to resist that urge now. Gabe got out, went around to her side, and helped her down from the truck. Harper took his hand—resisting the urge to say, *'I'm fine by myself'*—and together they headed to the front door of the bookstore together.

At the door, her hands shook as she fumbled with the keys. Harper was annoyed with herself. She felt calm, but the adrenaline was still coursing through her body and betraying her. She allowed Gabe to gently take the keys from her, unlock the door and push it open. The bell chimed softly above their heads. She stood frozen, like she didn't know where to go next.

Gabe reached out and tentatively put his arm around her waist, leading her to the back of the store, through the grandfather clock and up the stairs. He kept her steady as she walked, neither of them saying anything. Gabe lead Harper to her bedroom and pulled back the covers without a word.

"Get some sleep," Gabe said gently. "I'll stay in the bookstore downstairs tonight, in case you need anything."

She looked up, intending to argue that she was fine. But their eyes met for a fleeting moment and something passed between them, vulnerable, and electric. He wasn't just helping her to be kind...he needed to help her somehow.

"Okay," Harper whispered, and crawled into bed, pulling the duvet up to her chin.

Gabe nodded, jaw clenched, and left her bedroom, the door clicking shut behind him. He retreated down the stairs and sank onto the big leather sofa, taking a shaking breath. He wasn't sure what scared him more: seeing Harper so shaken or how much he wanted to be the one to hold her together.

Harper slept hard. When she finally opened her eyes, she felt groggy. She glanced at the bedside clock, which read 8:28am. She grabbed her phone to confirm and was shocked when it said the same time. She couldn't remember the last time she slept this late. What in the...?

And just like that, it all came flooding back to Harper. The orchard. *The dead body.* The quill. Prudence's eyes looking at at the sky in shock.

Harper shuddered and sat up. She went to the living room and threw open the double doors to get some fresh air. Looking down at the square below, she saw the roads were already being closed for the parade that started at 9 a.m. and she saw groups of people setting up for the various Harvest Festival activities of the day. She made her way to the bathroom and when she glanced in the mirror, she was surprised by what she saw. She looked pale and her eyes were all puffy from too much sleep.

Deciding to skip her morning run, she turned on the shower. The room filled with steam as she replayed the events of last night in her head. She was almost halfway through her shower when she remembered Gabe had said he was going to sleep downstairs in the bookstore. *Had he actually stayed?* She hurried to finish her shower, toweling off and coiling her wet hair into a low bun. She threw on a sweatshirt and jeans and headed downstairs.

Gabe wasn't there, but there was a note on the table in front of the hearth. Next to it was a drink carrier from Harvest Roast with two cups in it. The note read:

"I didn't want to wake you, but the sheriff asked me to come down to the station. I left at 8:15, and I put a "closed today" sign on the shop door, so no one will be expecting you to open. I'll check in with you later this morning, but if you need anything in the meantime, call or text. - Gabe P.S. I grabbed you a coffee from Harvest Roast. I hope you enjoy it!"

The shower had cleared the cobwebs from her brain and her thoughts were going at a mile a minute. She didn't know her true crime obsession would come in handy one day, but her brain was scrambling, trying to find connections, thinking about the events of the night before. She suddenly felt determined to find Prudence's killer. Harper was just settling into Fall, and already she knew this community was special. A crime like this could scare people away and destroy the tourist industry. Harper couldn't let that happen. The inns and vacation rentals in town were booked solid through Thanksgiving, then the season slowed. This was the busiest month for the apple orchard, and the shops in town were all set for the Harvest Festival. Hearth & Quill had been enjoying steady business since its grand reopening, and Harper was eager to turn a profit after all her initial expenses. The faster she found the killer, the faster life in Fall would return to normal for everyone.

Harper grabbed the coffee Gabe had left for her, and took a big swig before realizing it was cold... and black ...double yuck. It tasted like sad bean water. She put the coffee in the fridge and headed out the door. She had a crime to solve.

———

The sheriff had asked Harper to meet him at the station that morning to answer some questions. Despite the unease twisting in her stomach, Harper figured she could catch the parade first maybe even clear her head a little before the interrogation. She decided to grab a coffee before finding a spot along the route.

When she walked into Harvest Roast, she couldn't believe how packed it was. Groups of people were huddled around tables, some standing while drinking and eating, others balancing food and cups in their hands. Melanie saw Harper and came around the counter to pull her into a fierce hug.

"I heard you found her," Melanie said quietly, holding Harper out in front of her and searching her face. "I'm so sorry you had to go through that. It must have been awful."

"It was," Harper agreed. "I can't get it out of my head."

"Well of course not - you've been traumatized."

"I have to run over to the sheriff's office now, but wanted to grab a..."

"Of course. Let me get you an extra large coffee...and how about breakfast? Did you eat?" Melanie said, hustling back behind the counter, busying herself.

"Actually, no. I'd love a muffin." Harper admitted.

"You got it. And I'll throw in one of our quiches as well, " she grabbed a pastry out of the display case and popped it and the muffin into a box. "This one is butternut squash and spinach. "

She handed Harper the box and the coffee. When Harper tried to pay, Melanie shook her head.

"Your money is no good here today. You just take good care of yourself."

Harper thanked her and headed out and across the square.

Harper sat on a bench and pulled out her phone and opened the *ATL Girls* group chat. She hesitated for a moment, then started typing.

ATL GIRLS 💅🍸🍷🥪

Harper: There's been a murder in Fall! 😬

There was a pause before her phone buzzed with multiple replies in quick succession.

Amanda: Wait, what do you mean?

Erin: Harper, what? What happened??

Harper took a deep breath before replying, her fingers shaking as she typed.

Harper: I went out to the orchard last night...and I found a body. A local woman named Prudence. Someone killed her.

Amanda: OMG. Harper, that's *insane*. Are you okay?? What did the police say?

Erin: WHAT?! Harper, are you safe? Please tell me you're okay! Call us. Seriously.

Harper looked up at the people walking through the square. She typed back.

Harper: I'm okay. It's just...really overwhelming. The sheriff's involved, and there's an investigation. But I feel like I have to help. I found her.

Amanda: Holy crap, Harp. You're in the middle of a murder investigation?? Be *careful*!

Erin: Harper, we're worried about you. Don't get too caught up in this, like you did with the "case of the missing garbage cans" on my street. Stay safe, please. 💜

Harper: Those garbage cans were never found! It still irks me. But listen…I actually *do* need to get involved here. Remember that quill that was stolen from my shop? It was the murder weapon! I have to help figure out who did this, or it might come back to me.

Amanda: OMG! Okay, if you need us, we'll be there. Drop everything. Just say the word.

Erin: 100%. We love you. Stay safe, ok? Call if you need to talk.

Harper exhaled slowly, comforted by her friends' concern but knowing this situation was far from over.

Harper: Love you guys. Thanks. I'll keep you posted. 💜

Maggie came running up to Harper with a paper cup from Harvest Roast in her hand and gave her a hug that almost knocked Harper off the bench.

"I can't believe I wasn't there. I'm so sorry! How are you?" Maggie squeezed as she talked, her words running together into one big jumble.

"I'm okay," Harper said, laughing at the ferocity of the hug. "I was a little shaken up last night, but I'm okay this morning. I woke up this morning determined to figure out who killed Prudence. Is that crazy?"

"I'm glad you're okay. No, it's not crazy. I want to help, too. I mean, it's truly horrible what happened to Prudence," Maggie said, stalling. "But… is it horrible that I'm also, just like, a *teeny* bit excited because we can be true crime girlies and try figure it out? But, I mean, obviously it's just a horrible tragedy."

"I understand what you mean," said Harper with a little laugh. She took a bite of the quiche. "I feel the same way. I feel absolutely awful for Prudence and her family, but I'm also determined to help find the killer. It could be anyone, which is super weird."

"It could be him," Maggie said, gesturing to the man sitting in front of them on the bench with a young girl around 4 or 5.

"It could be," agreed Harper, wiping her mouth with a napkin. As they watched, he took a used tissue out of his pocket and wiped the girls nose, then replaced it in his pocket. "Yuck. The murder weapon would have snot on it."

"Gross," Maggie whispered, looking around. "It could be her." Maggie gestured to a girl who just walked out of the coffee shop across the street. As they watched, she dropped her bag and a muffin rolled out onto the pavement. The woman let out an exasperated sigh and chased the muffin down, then shoved it into the paper bag, threw it all in the trash and headed back inside, presumably to buy another muffin.

"It could be," Harper said. "She's having a bad morning. What we really need is a way to eliminate people from the list of suspects. I started making a list this morning."

"Ohmygosh, let me see it!" Maggie said, then gasped. "Wait, am I on it?"

"What? Yes, of course you're on the 'all clear' list," Harper pulled a face. "Although, I guess technically everyone in town should be on the guilty list to start. Where were you yesterday afternoon when Prudence was killed?"

"Well, what time was she killed?"

"That's a good point. I don't really know. I found her around 6:15 so sometime before then."

"Okay, well, I was at my house until 2, then I went to the shop and baked four dozen cookies, two pies, three cakes, two tarts and 36 mini tartlets," she ticked off each item on her fingers as she recounted them. "Oh, and then I started a batch of apple croissants for today. Amy was with me. I left just before 8 o'clock."

"Right," Harper said with a nod. "So probably not you, then."

"Not me. How about you? Where were you, Miss Harper Whitmore?" Maggie said theatrically.

"I was at the bookshop helping customers, then I closed up at 6, ran into Gabe and headed out to the orchard. We are there by about 6:15."

"So not you, either. You have an airtight alibi." Maggie sighed.

"Can you tell me who came into your shop yesterday from, say... 12-6?"

Maggie slowly rattled off a list of names and Harper added them to a new note in her phone, labeled 'Maggie - shop visitors.'

"Okay, so we have the two of us, Gabe, everyone I saw in the square just before. And depending on the time she was killed, we can eliminate some of the people who came into your shop."

Maggie nodded and picked at the rim of her coffee cup. "We've got to keep getting alibis."

After a few minutes, a police cruiser drove slowly past them, the mechanical "woo-woo" signaling the beginning of the parade. They turned their attention to the street and tried to enjoy the festivities, both lost in their own thoughts and keenly aware the killer could be anywhere.

CHAPTER 17
MORNING AFTER

Harper stood up and dusted dirt from her jeans. The parade had been a nice break from real life. She said goodbye to Maggie and headed over to the police station.

"Hi Harper, c'mon back," deputy Russell greeted her from the dispatch desk. As he did, he stood and buzzed opened the door just to the side of the desk, which allowed access into the station.

"Thank you," she said, walking through the door.

The Fall Police Department had a tiny force, with four full time officers, two part-time officers and the police chief. Fall's small population soared in the autumn with tourists from all over the Midwest, but the department was largely focused on community policing. The officers had an outstanding relationship with the locals, but the force saw little action. Larger crimes, which were nearly unheard of in Fall, fell under the jurisdiction of the Grand Traverse County Sheriff's department.

The police station was inside of a larger law enforcement building, where one side had the offices for Fall PD and the other held the offices for the Grand Traverse County Sheriff's Department. In the middle of the building were shared spaces - a small holding cell, three interrogation rooms, a lunchroom, bathroom and locker room. Along one wall was a conference room large enough for 10-12 people. On the GTCSD side of the building, the bullpen featured ten desks pushed together in pairs, plus two offices and a larger office for the Sheriff. On the FPD side, there were eight desks pushed together in pairs, plus an office for the Police Chief.

Deputy Russell led Harper to the GTCSD side of the building. He took her to a set of desks, one featuring a plaque that read Deputy Jake Russell, and pointed to a chair for her to have a seat.

After spending 6 years in Iraq and Afghanistan, Jake was perfectly happy to settle down in the small, northwestern Michigan town. He loved his desk, the sleepy locale where not much happened. He also liked the lack of IED's. The quiet town was nearly crime free until someone had murdered Prudence Sherman.

Deputy Russell poked his head into the sheriff's office, and immediately came back out.

"Sheriff Carlisle isn't back just yet - still out at the scene," Deputy Russell explained. "They're trying to get it cleared so that Sullivan's can reopen by this afternoon in time for the apple picking contest and bonfire. We'll see if that happens." He sounded dubious.

He offered Harper a coffee, which he described as 'truly terrible.' She declined.

"Well, let's get down to business. Sheriff Carlisle just wanted to have you come down today to give your statement again. Obviously, you gave your initial statement at the scene, but sometimes after the shock wears off, we remember more detail. We want to collect as much information from you as possible," Deputy Russell pulled out a large legal notepad and clicked his pen. "Now, can you walk me through the events of yesterday afternoon and early evening, please?"

"Sure," Harper shifted in her seat. She recalled the events of the day at a high level, from about the time she approached Gabe asking for the apples right until the sheriff deputies arrived on scene.

After she finished, Deputy Russell kept scribbling for another minute. Then he said, "Now I'm going to ask you a few questions that might sound silly, but might jog any additional memories you may have. Can you think of any sounds or smells right before you made the discovery?"

Harper furrowed her brow, but then a minor detail bubbled to the top of her consciousness.

"Actually, yes. When I was walking in the orchard, I heard a noise deeper back in the orchard. I thought little of it because I thought that Luke and Ryan were in the orchard harvesting."

"Can you describe the sound?" He asked, genuine interest in his expression.

"It sounded like when you shake out a sheet right before you make the bed and there is that flapping, whooshing sound. But there wasn't a harsh snap...just a gentle whooshing."

"Great, and about how long before you discovered the body did you hear that?" The deputy asked.

"Hmmm. I don't know, maybe 1 or 2 minutes before," she said thoughtfully.

"You're doing great. Anything else that you can think of? Smells, sights, other sounds? Even the tiniest details can be meaningful."

"I remember the smell of fruit and the dirt, and then when I was close to her body, the smell of alcohol," Harper said, her eyes closed, lost in her memory.

He wrote everything she said, silently, as if he would break a spell. After a moment, he gently prompted, "...anything else?"

"Yes," Harper said, opening her eyes. "And I'm sorry I didn't mention it sooner...but the feather quill that killed Prudence? That was mine. Well, it was my Aunt's. It went missing from my bookstore about a month ago."

He stared at her for a long time. "I see." He scribbled furiously on his notepad.

"Anything else?

"No, that's everything."

"Alright, Harper," he set his pen down. "When Sheriff Carlisle is back in the office, he is going to have some additional questions for you. So, you know...don't leave town. Alright?"

Harper felt a little ripple of fear go through her. She agreed, thanked him and headed out the door.

Harper sat on a weathered wooden bench in the town square, her gaze fixed on the Apple Bobbing contest happening just a few feet away. Four kids and two adults stood poised in front of metal tubs filled with water, bobbing apples floating on the surface. Prizes were awarded for fastest bob and most apples retrieved in a minute, but the usual lighthearted energy of the contest was missing. Behind the bobbers, clusters of townspeople whispered to one another, their anxious glances and hushed tones betraying their unease. The shadow of Prudence's murder hung over everything, casting a chill over the normally cheerful Harvest Festival.

While Harper was watching the Apple Bobbing contest, her mind wasn't on the apples. Her thoughts were racing, retracing the details of the day before—her conversations with Maggie, Deputy Russell, and the strange things she couldn't make sense of. That odd whooshing sound... it played over and over in her head. Could it be connected to Prudence's death? Every instinct told her it was something she shouldn't ignore.

She sighed and pulled out her phone, opening the notes app. Under a new heading titled, "Questions," she quickly typed "whooshing sound?" The list was growing, and the answers felt as distant as ever.

The bench creaked slightly as someone sat beside her, and Harper looked up, startled to see Gabe settling in next to her. He leaned forward, elbows resting on his knees, his gaze tracking the apple bobbing but his expression serious.

"Morning," he said, his voice low but steady. "How'd you sleep?"

Harper managed a small smile. "Surprisingly well." She hesitated for a moment before touching his arm, grateful for the steadiness his presence brought. "I wanted to thank you for staying downstairs. I don't think I would've slept at all if you hadn't. And the coffee this morning was very thoughtful."

Gabe gave a brief nod, though his eyes remained on the contest in front of them. "I figured you could use it. I knew you'd have a lot on your mind this morning."

Harper watched him for a beat, the quiet between them weighted, but comfortable. They both knew that beneath the surface of friendly conversation, something darker lurked, something they couldn't avoid much longer.

Gabe placed his hand on hers, just for a moment, his touch warm and steady. "I was happy to help," he said, his voice soft but sincere. "How are you holding up today?"

Harper tried to ignore the little flip in her stomach at the warmth of his hand and gave him a quick nod. "I'm okay. I was just going over some notes about things I heard and saw in the orchard, trying to jog my memory. I need to help with the investigation."

"I want to help too," Gabe said, turning to face her fully. "I spent the morning with the sheriff. They've got my entire orchard locked down as a crime scene. I had to cancel all the hayrides, the apple pressing demonstrations... everything." His voice trailed off, frustration clear in his tone.

"I'm really sorry," Harper said, her brow furrowing. "That must be so stressful, on top of everything else."

Gabe ran a hand through his hair, letting out a sigh. "Annie says the market's running low on apples and some items made with the apples, like salsa and jam. It's peak harvest time and I can't harvest, can't access the orchard to get packaged products to restock. But honestly, it's not the business that's bothering me most. I truly feel awful for Prudence. I can't believe this happened in *my* orchard. I feel... responsible somehow. Plus the whole town is on edge. Everyone is scared because there's a murderer in Fall. I feel like I've got to do something to help."

She nodded, her mind already turning over ideas. "Okay, first, you're absolutely not responsible. But I understand how you feel. I started making a list this morning. I'm starting with the people we know didn't do it—the ones who have a solid alibi, like those who were in the square at the time of the murder. I'm going to ask them who they saw, where they were, and see if I can piece together a bigger picture. If I can expand the list of people who are in the clear, maybe it'll help me narrow down the suspects."

Gabe gave her a thoughtful look. "It's a smart approach. The more we narrow it down, the closer we get to figuring out who's behind this."

Harper met his gaze, her determination mirrored in his eyes. She realized he had said *we* instead of *you*. It was comforting to feel like she wasn't alone.

She passed him her phone. He scrolled through and nodded absentmindedly, then said "you forgot Blanche, David and Charlotte. Who is 'the guy with the sunglasses'?

Harper described the man she was thinking of, and without hesitation, Gabe said, "That's Rodney. He works with Hank at the hardware store.

He handed the phone back to her, and she wrote Rodney in parentheses next to her description. After a few minutes, they had a list of people.

"Since you know the people in the town better than me, why don't you make a list of people who might've had issues with Prudence?" Harper suggested, glancing around the square. "She's been in this town for decades—she must have made some enemies."

Gabe gave a wry smile. "Sure, like anyone who's ever had Pru judge their pie."

Harper rolled her eyes. "Ha ha..." she said, then paused. "Wait, you don't really think she was killed over baked goods, do you?"

He shrugged, rubbing his hands together absentmindedly, as if trying to shake off the thought. "No. Well, I don't know. People can get weird when their pride's at stake. But it's probably *not* pie related. I'll start making a list of people who had grievances with her."

Harper nodded. "Maggie told me the *Cider House Rules* screening went on last night, before the news spread about Prudence. But it looks like word is out now." She gestured subtly toward a group of women nearby, their faces tight with whispers. One had a hand pressed to her mouth, on the verge of tears. Another clutched her chest like she'd just heard something too shocking to believe.

Gabe followed her gaze, then turned back to her. "Speaking of Maggie, she's looking for you. They need a new judge for the contest, and she wants to know if you're willing to step in."

Harper's throat tightened. "Me?" she croaked.

Gabe shrugged, his expression neutral but knowing. "I'm heading to the market. Let me know if you need anything."

Harper stood at the long wooden table beneath the towering oak trees in Fall's town square, the faint murmur of the crowd making her feel uneasy. The annual Apple Pie Baking Contest would usually be full of laughter and friendly competition, but this year, it was different. The air was heavy with tension, thick with whispers about Prudence Sherman's murder in the orchard the day before. Continuing with the festival felt like a forced attempt at normalcy, but no one seemed ready for it - not Harper, and definitely not the bakers lined up in front of her, waiting to be judged. They all looked shellshocked.

Harper spotted Maggie and Paul and went over and gave him a big hug.

"How are you, darling? I hear you had quite the scare last night." Paul held her by her shoulders in front of him, inspecting her.

"I'm doing okay. I just feel terrible for Prudence and her family," Harper said.

"Oh, we all do," he said. "Though she had little family, I'm afraid. I'm just glad you're okay. If you're having trouble sleeping, you come back and stay at the inn, okay? I've got a room for you."

"Thank you, Paul. That's really nice. But I think I'm okay," Harper smiled at him.

"Alright, just keep it in mind," he said, with another quick hug. "Now, what are you doing here, dear?"

"I'm a last minute judge, filling in for Prudence. How about you?"

"Well" Paul said. "I'm a judge too...it's my 3rd year!"

"I'm a nervous wreck," Harper admitted.

"Don't be," he laughed. "It's a lot of fun. Just give honest feedback, like you always do with my baked goods."

Harper glanced at the row of pies. Each one was beautiful: some with golden lattice tops, others dusted with cinnamon sugar, or decorated with intricate leaf designs. Normally, Harper would have admired the craftsmanship, but today, her thoughts kept drifting back to Prudence. To the murder investigation. And the disturbing realization that she had no idea who could have done it.

Harper shifted uncomfortably, wishing she hadn't let Maggie talk her into this.

"It'll keep your mind off things," Maggie had said, giving her an encouraging grin. As if tasting apple pies could somehow erase the image from Harper's mind of Prudence laying in the orchard. Or the fact that someone in town had committed murder.

"I can't believe I agreed to this," Harper muttered under her breath, and Maggie gave her a final nudge with her elbow.

Maggie chuckled, not at all concerned. "You're going to be fine. After all, it's just pie."

The head of the Apple Pie Baking Contest, Delaney Connors, stepped up to the microphone, welcoming everyone with a brief introduction.

"We've got a wonderful contest this year," she announced brightly, her tone upbeat, despite the underlying tension no one could ignore. She introduced the judges: Mrs. Shirley Havers, Fall's culinary queen and previous winner of the contest, received a warm round of applause. Paul Winston, owner of The Copper Fox Inn, earned hearty cheers from the crowd.

"And lastly," Delaney said, her smile faltering slightly, "Harper Whitmore, the new owner of Hearth & Quill bookstore." The crowd offered polite, subdued applause. Some curious glances were exchanged as some whispered about the newcomer stepping in for Prudence.

Harper forced a smile as Mrs. Havers took the mic and explained what they'd be looking for - perfect crust, balanced spice, a shining apple filling. Harper barely listened, her thoughts swirling.

As the first pie was presented—Rebecca Rittenhouse's—Harper reached for her fork and froze. A thought struck her like lightning: *What if the killer was one of THIS years bakers?* Harper had asked Gabe to investigate anyone who might have had issues with Prudence, and they'd both thought of people who maybe she judged harshly in past contests. But what if one of these hopeful contestants wanted to avoid being judged by Prudence this year and killed her?

Harper glanced at the bakers standing expectantly before her. *Any of them could have done it.*

She took a bite of Rebecca's pie, the buttery, spiced apple filling offering a momentary distraction from the fear tightening in her chest. Mrs. Havers made polite notes, commenting on the balance of the filling, while Paul Winston nodded approvingly.

But Harper's attention kept darting to the bakers, her mind racing with questions. *Were those smiles genuine? Or were they hiding something? Were the nervous glances just nerves, or something darker?*

"Next," Paul called out, slicing into the second pie. Harper mechanically followed suit, barely tasting the sweet-and-tart blend of apples, her focus far from the contest.

As they worked their way through the lineup, Harper found herself caught between the enjoyable task of tasting pies and the terrifying possibility that the killer was standing just feet away from her. By the fourth pie, she almost started to relax—if only because the caramel drizzle on top surprised her. Maybe Maggie was right. Maybe this would be a distraction after all. But then Prudence's face flashed in her mind, and the suspicion crept back in.

By the time the last pie had been judged, Harper felt dazed. She passed in her notes and the judges scores were compared. The winner was selected - Clara Spencer, a young woman who'd entered for the first time. Her pie was the perfect blend of sweet, spice, and melt-in-your-mouth crust. Mrs. Havers handed her the blue ribbon and golden rolling pin, and the crowd applauded enthusiastically.

But Harper barely noticed.

Maggie sidled up next to her as the crowd dispersed. "See? You did great."

Harper gave her a dry look. "I could hardly focus. What if the killer is one of *this years* bakers?"

Maggie's smile dropped. "What?"

Harper's voice lowered as she scanned the crowd. "Think about it. Maybe someone couldn't stand the thought of being judged by Prudence. Maybe they eliminated her instead."

Maggie's hand rested gently on Harper's shoulder, her face suddenly serious. "Harper, you don't really think..."

"I don't know," Harper replied, the knot of dread tightening in her stomach. "Murder over apple pie sounds pretty wild. Maybe it's more involved than that. I won't know until we can uncover some secrets everyone is keeping around here. "

CHAPTER 18
TIME OF DEATH

Harper hopped into her SUV, her mind buzzing with questions, and headed straight for Gabe's orchard. She couldn't shake the nagging feeling that she needed to talk to him right away. Prudence's murder had cast a long shadow over Fall, and if anyone could offer some insight, it was Gabe. He always seemed to have his finger on the pulse of the town.

As she drove, the tree lined streets were stunning. Nearly all of the leaves had changed from green to a variety of fiery autumn colors. Despite the gorgeous cozy view, Harper couldn't help but feel a creeping unease. The small, picturesque town should feel safe, but since Prudence's murder, it felt anything but.

When she arrived at the orchard, Harper was surprised to see Deputy Russell's cruiser parked near Gabe's barn. Her heart skipped a beat as she spotted the two men standing near the old wooden fence, heads bent together in hushed conversation. Gabe caught her eye and gave a subtle nod in her direction, but Harper hesitated. The gesture wasn't clear—was it a "come over here" nod, or a "wait until I'm done" nod? She hated the uncertainty, feeling awkward as she lingered beside her SUV, unsure whether to approach.

The deputy's deep voice carried on the breeze, though she couldn't make out the words. She watched as Deputy Russell clapped a hand on Gabe's shoulder before turning to leave, his expression serious. Harper's pulse quickened. *What had they been discussing? Why did it feel like there were secrets here, too?*

As Deputy Russell walked away, Harper seized the moment. She hurried over to intercept him, her boots crunching on the gravel path. "Deputy? A quick word, if you don't mind," she called out, trying to keep her tone casual.

Deputy Russell stopped, giving her a measured look as if weighing whether to engage. His brow furrowed slightly, but he didn't brush her off, so Harper pressed on. "I was just wondering if you'd learned anything new about Prudence's murder. Any leads, suspects? Maybe the time of death?"

His eyes narrowed a fraction, clearly not thrilled with her line of questioning. "Hello again, Harper. We're doing everything we can. I suggest you leave the investigation to us." His voice was clipped but not entirely dismissive.

Harper swallowed her frustration, knowing she had to tread carefully. If she wanted any information, she couldn't push too hard. "Of course, Deputy," she said, softening her voice. "I didn't mean to overstep, just... curious. It's a small town, and everyone's on edge."

The deputy seemed to relax slightly, though the stern edge in his eyes remained. "I understand that, but this is a sensitive investigation. The less speculation, the better."

She gave a polite nod, playing along, but she wasn't going to let him off the hook that easily. "I get it. I was just curious about one thing—what time was Prudence killed? I've been hearing rumors, and, well, you know how gossip spreads around here."

Deputy Russell hesitated, then sighed, as though he weighed the information carefully. "We believe the murder took place between 1 and 4 p.m. That's as much as I'm going to say right now."

Harper's mind raced. Between 1 and 4 p.m.? That narrowed things down. She tried to recall what she had been doing that day, but her thoughts shifted immediately to the suspects she'd been considering. Where had each of them been during that time?

The deputy tipped his hat and started walking toward his cruiser, leaving Harper standing in the cool autumn air, a mix of anxiety and curiosity swirling in her chest. She watched him drive off before turning back toward the orchard, where Gabe was waiting near the barn. This time, his nod was clear—it was a "come on over" nod.

Harper walked toward him, her boots kicking up small clouds of dust. "Everything okay?" she asked, trying to sound casual despite the knot of tension in her stomach.

Gabe shrugged, though his eyes flicked to where the sheriff's car had disappeared. "Yeah, just a few more questions he had for me. And he was delivering the good news that said the sheriff cleared the orchard to reopen later this afternoon, so I need to prepare for the apple cider pressing demonstration. What about you? You look like you've got something on your mind."

Harper nodded, glancing around to make sure no one else was nearby. "I'm starting to piece things together, but I'm not sure what to make of it yet. Deputy Russell told me the murder happened between 1 and 4 p.m., so I am wondering who could've been around during that time. It's a small window, but it narrows things down, doesn't it?"

Gabe crossed his arms, leaning back against the fence post. "It does. Just be careful, Harper. Not everyone's going to like that you're digging into this."

"I know," she said, her voice quieter now. "But I can't just sit back and do nothing. Prudence's death wasn't random. I feel like I have to help find the killer so Fall can go back to normal."

Harper sat at a table inside Fall's tea shop, Steeped In Joy, and sipped an incredible chamomile tea. On a small plate alongside it sat two crispy, flaky cookies. Harper was so full of pie, the chamomile was just what she needed to settle her stomach. The cookies remained untouched. Harper had her phone open to the notes section, and she also had a little paper notebook open in front of her. She always had her phone with her, but she remembered things better when she actually wrote them in ink. She had written copious notes about what had happened the day before, what she had seen, her thoughts, questions she had and a possible suspects list, which was currently empty. The teashop was quiet and perfect for getting work done. The only other people in the shop had earbuds in. She glanced up as the bell above the door jingled and saw Mrs. Hastings step in; her face tight with worry.

"Harper, dear," Mrs. Hastings greeted, her voice low and anxious as she took the seat across from Harper. "I can't believe poor Prudence is gone. And from what I hear, in such a... horrible way."

Harper nodded, her grip tightening on the pen in her hand. She felt a mix of emotions, part fear, part determination. She just knew she had to help find the killer.

"It was truly terrible. I just need to be *doing* something, you know? So, I am trying to gather everyone's alibis. I figure it might help narrow down a possible suspect list for the sheriff."

Mrs. Hastings' eyes widened, and she leaned forward, lowering her voice to a conspiratorial whisper. "Of course, of course. I'll do anything I can to help, but I was just at home that evening, color-coding my yarn." She raised her eyebrows and reached for her phone. "Would you like to see a photo, dear?"

Harper shook her head and scribbled a note in her book. "That won't be necessary. Did you see or hear anything unusual?"

Mrs. Hastings shook her head. "No. Well, I walked past the market around 2pm and I saw Prudence through the window—looked like she was arguing with someone. I didn't stop though. Too chilly."

Harper frowned. "Arguing? With who?"

"I couldn't tell from where I was standing," Mrs. Hastings said, adjusting her glasses. "But I thought it sounded like Evelyn Miller. Though I'm not sure."

Harper quickly thanked Mrs. Hastings and made a mental note to talk to Evelyn Miller.

Before Harper could dwell on it, the bell jingled again, and Mr. Thornhill, Fall's resident cheese enthusiast, shuffled in with his usual gruff demeanor, clutching a newspaper under his arm.

"Mr. Thornhill," Harper called out, with a little wave. He gave her a raised eyebrow, but shuffled over to the table, taking a seat without being asked.

"I hear you're playing detective, Miss Whitmore," he said, folding his arms across his chest. "You want to grill me?"

Harper offered a tight smile, tapping her pen against the notebook. "I'm just asking people about their alibis for yesterday. I figure the sooner we find out who did this, the sooner life in Fall can go back to normal."

"Well," he huffed, pulling a chair up and plopping down. " I do want things to go back to normal. The market is closed today. Can you believe that? Closed! I couldn't get my grapefruit. Yesterday, I was in town. I went to the market - I go every day to get the freshest grapefruit, you know. Ran into Mary Cartwright, who wanted to talk my ear off. Then I swung by the hardware store. I visited your shop to pick up the new book on cheese-making - it really is quite good so far. When I left, I saw Prudence in the town square, but we just exchanged hellos in passing. I'd have said more if I'd known it was the last time I'd see her..."

"What time was that?" Harper asked, jotting down notes.

"Just before 2 o'clock," Mr. Thornhill said. Harper thanked him and Mr. Thornill went to the counter to get a cup of tea.

Before she could even process his words, the café door opened yet again, and Maggie burst in, her cheeks flushed from the cold. She made a beeline for Harper's table and sat down without a word.

"How go the alibis?" Maggie said. She grabbed a cookie from the plate and took a big bite.

Harper sighed, meeting Maggie's gaze. "I've got a handful so far. I just got Mrs. Hastings and Mr. Thornhill. Earlier, I talked to a bunch of people who were here. "

Maggie shook her head, her voice softer now. "I hate the feeling that the killer could be anywhere. It's really got me freaked out."

Harper sighed, rubbing her temples. "I know. Plus—there's a lot I don't know right now, and every time I ask someone a question, I end up with two more leads to follow. I need to narrow down the list. Well, I need a list to start with. Then I need to narrow down the list."

Maggie reached across the table and dropped the rest of the cookie on the plate. "I'll be back" she said, and hurried out the door.

The bell over the door rang, and Sheriff Carlisle walked in. He seemed surprised to see her.

"Harper," he greeted, his voice calm but with an edge of formality.

"Hi, Sheriff," Harper replied.

Sheriff Carlisle removed his hat and ordered a cup of tea before turning his attention back to Harper. "I was just grabbing a cup of tea, but I need to chat with you, if you have a minute? "

Harper nodded, her stomach twisting with unease. "About the quill."

"Yes, about the quill," he repeated, his tone sharp but not unkind. "I need to understand why you didn't report it missing the moment you realized it was gone."

Harper bit her lip, gesturing for him to sit at her table. He retrieved his mug of tea and sat. She could tell from his posture that he would not drop this easily, and she couldn't exactly blame him, given it was used in a murder. They sat across from each other, the weight of his question hanging between them.

"Well," Harper began slowly, but steadily. "I didn't realize it was a big deal at first. At first, I wasn't sure what had happened. I wondered if it had been misplaced or borrowed. I thought someone might bring it back."

Sheriff Carlisle leaned forward slightly, his eyes never leaving hers. "When did you realize it was missing? "

Harper answered immediately. "Labor Day weekend, the night of my grand reopening."

"And when was the last time you had seen it prior to that night?" He asked, taking a sip of the hot liquid.

"I had seen it earlier that day. I remember because I was doing some last-minute cleaning, and I wiped the display box," Harper said.

"And when you realized it was stolen, were you alone?" He jotted a few notes into his pad.

"No, Maggie was there. We were having a glass of wine at the end of the night and saw it. We both thought it was odd, but it honestly didn't occur to me to make a police report. I had no idea it would be used in a crime."

Carlisle studied her for a moment before speaking again, his voice gentler now. "Alright. I will check with Maggie to see that her recollection is the same as yours, but, assuming this checks out, I think we can chalk this up to a very unfortunate coincidence."

For a moment, silence filled the tea shop. Harper could feel the weight of the sheriff's gaze on her, but it was no longer accusatory—just concerned.

"I am, however, having forensics run the quill for fingerprints. If your prints are on the quill, we will have a much different discussion," Carlisle said finally. "But for now, what's done is done."

Harper stood as well, relief flooding through her. "That's not possible, Sheriff. I've never touched the quill itself - just outside of the display case. You won't find my prints anywhere on it."

He gave her a small, tight smile. "Okay. Just promise me, Harper, if anything ever goes missing around here—you come make a report. We have little crime in Fall, and that's just how we like it. "

"I promise," Harper said, her voice firm.

Carlisle took another long sip of his tea, then stood and replaced his hat on his head, the usual air of authority returning to him. "Thank you, Miss Whitmore."

As he left and the door closed softly behind him, Harper let out a long breath, her shoulders sagging with relief. She knew he was right —she should have reported the missing quill sooner. However, now he knew she wasn't involved, and Harper could relax because her prints wouldn't be on the murder weapon.

———

The little bell above the door jingled violently as Maggie blew in like a whirlwind, cheeks flushed and hair tousled by the wind.

"Harper! I have something," she announced triumphantly, waving a thick, slightly crumpled stack of paper like she was holding the key to the city.

Harper looked up from the notebook she'd been scribbling in, one brow raised. "What in the world — ?"

"Oh, you're going to absolutely *love me*," Maggie beamed, slapping the papers down on the tea counter. "A list of every single resident in Fall. Full names, addresses, and a few not-so-subtle notes in the margins courtesy of Dolores Franklin's nosy little book club."

Harper blinked. "Oh my gosh...where did you *get* this?"

Maggie leaned in, whispering like she was delivering state secrets. "The library. Dolores has been working on a *town history project* since the Clinton administration. There's a file cabinet in the back with every census, church bulletin, parade committee, and potluck RSVP since 1989. I made a couple of copies."

"You *broke into the town archives* for me?"

"Nooooo," Maggie said slowly, "I *unlocked potential resources* for a citizen-led inquiry. Totally different."

Harper shook her head with a half-laugh. "You are totally unhinged."

"And yet—" Maggie plopped a maple pecan scone onto a napkin and slid it over, "—you love me for it."

"I do love you," Harper laughed, then sighed, staring down at the list. "Okay. We have a list. Now let's narrow it down."

Maggie grinned. "Thought you'd never ask."

CHAPTER 19
THE LIST

They moved to Maggie's shop with the list. The smell of cinnamon rolls wafted through the air as Harper and Maggie huddled over Harper's large spiral notebook and the list of townspeople. Both were spread open across the table. Two cups of coffee sat beside them, half-drunk and definitely cold, but neither seemed to notice.

"Okay," Harper said, tapping the top of the list with her pen. "We start at the top and cross off anyone who's, you know... definitely not the killer."

Maggie raised a brow. "So... dead?"

Harper nodded, deadpan. "Dead, in preschool, or out of town."

Maggie snorted and picked up a black marker. "Alright. Let's see —Eunice Whitaker. Dead. Has been since 2018."

Harper crossed her off with a line that was more aggressive than necessary and wrote *deceased* in the margin. "Bless her heart, but she's definitely not our suspect."

"Next, we've got Timmy Knowles. He's eight."

"Unless he's a very precocious criminal mastermind..." Harper trailed off, then shook her head and drew another line through the name. She jotted the world *child* in the margins.

They worked down the list that way for almost 3 hours, eliminating toddlers, retirees long buried, and the local golden retriever who someone apparently listed as a joke.

Eventually, Maggie sat back, rubbed her eyes and tied her hair up in a ponytail. "Alright, that narrows us down to... ninety-three people. Ish."

Harper groaned. "That's still way too many."

Maggie grinned. "Which is why—ta-da—we need this column." She reached over and scrawled in big block text: **ALIBI.**

Harper leaned in. "Smart. We talk to people. Quietly. Casually."

"Like, 'Hey, where were you during the murder?' over a latte," Maggie said brightly.

Harper smirked. "Exactly like that. Where should we start?"

"How about shop owners?" Maggie offered. "We've already ruled out you and me."

Outside, the wind blew golden leaves against the windows. Inside, two amateur detectives were armed with coffee, curiosity, and a long list of people, one of whom was a murderer.

Harper was sorting bookmarks when Gabe stepped inside Hearth & Quill, brushing a few stray red leaves from his flannel shirt. He carried the crisp scent of autumn air and apple trees with him, along with a bag of fresh cider donuts.

"I come bearing bribes," he said, lifting the bag as he approached the counter where Harper and Maggie were seated.

"That's not a bribe," Maggie said, snatching a donut. "That's breakfast."

Harper grinned and pulled the notebook and list toward her. "You came at the perfect time. We need your brain."

Gabe raised an eyebrow as he took a seat on the stool across from them. "That's not usually what people want from me. Usually it's apples or help to move heavy furniture."

Harper flipped the notebook open to their carefully constructed list. Some names were crossed out. Others had little notes beside them—"out of town," "over 80," "kindergarten."

Maggie leaned in, tapping the top of the page. "We've been narrowing down suspects. Crossed off anyone who's deceased, under the age of ten, things like that."

Harper added, "And now we're working on alibis."

Gabe blinked. "Wait—you actually made a list of the entire town?"

"I didn't make the list," Maggie said. "I just—"

"She borrowed it from the town archives," Harper said. "We made a copy and returned the original. Now we're narrowing the list down."

Gabe glanced at the list, his brows pulling together. "This is... ambitious."

"It is," Harper said. "But it should help us figure out who had motive, means, and opportunity."

He studied her for a beat. "And what happens if we *do* figure it out? You walk up to Sheriff Carlisle and say, 'Here's a notebook full of speculation and donut crumbs'?"

Maggie shoved the rest of her donut in her mouth and mumbled, "Basically."

Gabe sighed and rubbed the back of his neck. "Alright. If we're really doing this, we need to work together. I can ask questions at the orchard, cider stand and market. People talk freely and will just assume I'm making small talk."

"Perfect," Harper said.

Maggie smiled. "And Harper and I are going to start casually interviewing shop owners. Maybe ask the regulars where they were when the murder happened. No pressure, very casual."

"Just a little murder chat over tea," Harper said cheerfully.

Gabe leaned back in his chair, looking between them. "You two are terrifying."

Harper flashed him a smile. "Welcome to the team."

Harper stepped inside the Rustic Pie and was greeted by the savory scent of baking pizzas. She inhaled the smell of dough, melted cheese, and tangy tomato sauce. The hum of conversation and the clatter of dishes filled the cozy pizzeria as people enjoyed their meals. Behind the counter, Ronnie was tossing a pizza crust with practiced ease, his face flushed from the heat of the ovens.

Harper took a deep breath, the familiar smell making her stomach rumble, but she had a job to do. She approached the counter, watching as Ronnie slid a pizza into the oven in one fluid motion.

"Hey, Ronnie," Harper called, giving him a smile.

Ronnie turned, wiping his hands on a towel. "Harper! How's it going? Here for a slice?"

"Not today, but it smells great in here," Harper replied. "Actually, I'm here because I wanted to ask you a few questions about last Friday afternoon."

Ronnie's hands stilled, and his expression shifted slightly. "Figured someone would ask, eventually. It's about Prudence, right?"

Harper nodded, pulling out her notebook. "I am trying to collect information about people's whereabouts when she was killed. I'm starting with shop owners... just want to make sure everyone's accounted for."

"Sure, of course," Ronnie said, leaning on the counter. "I can tell you exactly where I was—right here, from morning till night."

Harper raised an eyebrow. "You didn't leave at all?"

"Nope," Ronnie said, shaking his head. "We had a big delivery order for the festival, and I was in the kitchen prepping pizzas for most of the afternoon. Melanie from Harvest Roast came by a couple of times to pick up food for the crew setting up in the square."

"Any idea what time she came in?" Harper asked, jotting down details.

"She was here around 1:30 and again closer to 3:00." Ronnie said.

"Okay. So that gives Melanie an alibi as well." Harper said quietly, jotting down the details.

"Oh? Well, I could have told you that for free," Ronnie replied, crossing his arms. "She and her assistant were hauling pizzas out of here all afternoon. You can also ask Marco—he's my delivery guy. He took the last of the festival pizzas over around 3:30, I'd say."

"Alright," Harper said, adding Marco to her list of people to check with. "That's all I needed to ask."

Ronnie glanced at the dough in front of him, then back at Harper. "Look, I know Prudence wasn't the easiest person to get along with, but I didn't have any problems with her. Sure, she could be... harsh, but I run a pizza joint. I stay out of all the town politics."

"I get it," Harper said, sighing. "It's weird for a newcomer to be asking all these questions. I know I'm not police or anything...I'm just trying to help. I can't get the image out of my head....and I just feel so bad for Prudence."

Ronnie smiled, though it didn't quite reach his eyes. "Oh, I know you're just trying to help. But trust me, I was elbow-deep in dough and pepperoni that day, not involved in anything else."

Harper tucked her notebook away. "Thanks, Ronnie. I'll follow up with Melanie and Marco just to confirm, but I appreciate you sharing the information."

"No problem," Ronnie said, relaxing a bit. "Before you go, are you sure you don't want a slice? Fresh out of the oven."

Harper chuckled, and her stomach rumbled again. "Actually, I'll take you up on that. Pepperoni, please."

Ronnie grabbed a slice for her, and Harper thanked him. As she headed out the door, her mind was already spinning over the next steps. Every time she scratched someone off the list, she ended up with 2 more people to talk to. Who in Fall had something to hide?

———

The town square buzzed with activity as tourists and townsfolk wandered through the Apple Harvest Artisanal Market. Individual tents and stalls displayed everything from handmade candles to freshly baked apple bread and everything in between. Harper walked through the square, her eyes scanning the familiar faces until she spotted David and Charlotte near their booth, arranging their handcrafted pottery on shelves.

"Hey, David, hey Charlotte," Harper called out as she approached.

David looked up from stacking mugs, flashing a quick smile. "Harper! Good to see you. Can I interest you in a mug?"

Harper stepped closer to their booth. "Maybe a bit later. I'm actually here for something else. I'm following up on a few things about Prudence's death, and I wanted to ask you two about Friday afternoon."

Charlotte paused mid-arrangement, her brow furrowing. "What can we do for you?"

Harper's expression was friendly but serious. "I'm trying to confirm where everyone was during the time of her murder— between 1:00 and 4:00 p.m. I heard you were both setting up for the market in the square?"

David leaned on the booth's counter, nodding. "That's right. We were here all afternoon setting up."

Harper flipped open her notebook. "Did either of you see Melanie's assistant, Hannah, around that time?"

David glanced at Charlotte, then back at Harper. "Yeah, I saw her."

Charlotte nodded, still a bit cautious. "Me too. I remember she was helping Melanie set up the booth for Harvest Roast just across from us. I think that was around 2:30 or so. She was carrying boxes of coffee supplies."

"Did you see her after that?" Harper asked, writing down the time.

"I saw her a little while after that," David said, thoughtfully. "She stayed and was helping move things around. She was here for awhile."

Charlotte chimed in, more certain now. "Yeah, she was chatting with Melanie at one point. I remember because they were talking about how busy Harvest Roast had been with the festival orders."

Harper made a few more notes, nodding. "That's good to know. So you both saw Melanie and Hannah here, working in the square, around the time of the murder?"

David crossed his arms, and frowned slightly. "Well, I don't know what time the murder was, but if you're asking if they were here between 1-4, then yeah. They were here in and out all afternoon and until at least 3:30. Maybe later."

"That's super helpful," Harper said, closing her notebook. "I'm just trying to narrow down everyone's whereabouts, and what you've told me could help clear her."

Charlotte set down a box of mugs and gave a small, uneasy smile. "Glad we could help. It's just hard to believe someone from town could have done this."

"I know," Harper said gently. "I'm new here, but even I can tell Fall isn't the kind of place where this happens."

David and Charlotte exchanged a glance, their expressions softening with a mix of sadness and concern.

"If you need anything else, let us know," David said, shifting the box beside him and beginning to unload.

"Thanks," Harper said, grateful for their openness. She turned to leave but paused, glancing back at the booth. "If you think of anything—no matter how small—don't hesitate to reach out."

"You got it," Charlotte replied, her voice steadier now.

As Harper walked away, she felt a sense of relief. Another piece of the puzzle was falling into place. She had ruled out so many people already....but who wasn't she considering?

CHAPTER 20
CIDER PRESS

The copper kettle on the sideboard let out a gentle hiss as it kept cider warm, filling the parlor of The Copper Fox Inn with the scent of apples and cinnamon. Harper sat in a high-backed armchair near the fireplace, her palms wrapped around a warm mug and Lady in her lap. Across from her, Paul was setting down a plate of shortbread on the low wooden table between them.

"I feel like I should've made something stronger," he said with a tired smile. "Spiced cider doesn't quite cut it after someone's been murdered."

Harper glanced toward the staircase, where footsteps creaked overhead.

"How are your guests doing?" she asked in a low voice, petting the tiny dog.

Paul raised his eyebrows and rubbed the back of his neck. "Room Four's couple tried to check out early, but I talked them into staying. And the woman in Room Two asked if I could recommend a self-defense class." He exhaled. "It's usually maple pancakes and leaf-peeping this time of year. Now I'm giving out crime scene updates over breakfast."

Harper gave him a small, sympathetic smile. "I know the feeling. I was just getting used to people coming into Hearth & Quill to *buy* a cozy mystery. I'm not used to living inside a mystery."

Paul raised an eyebrow. "And yet you're investigating."

She hesitated. "I'm just... trying to make sense of it. Trying to help. For Prudence. For the town."

He studied her for a moment, then nodded. "I get that. But be careful, Harper. This place may look like a postcard, but right now? There's a chill under the leaves. And not just from the weather."

They sat quietly for a moment, the fire crackling between them. The golden light outside had dimmed into a dusky amber, the twilight that made the inn's windows glow like lanterns.

"I hate to even ask, but do you know if any of the guests have an alibi for Friday night?" she asked softly.

Paul's eyes widened, and he shook his head slowly. "I can't believe I'm being asked that. Actually, I can vouch for every single one of my guests. I did an afternoon wine and cheese event before the movie in the park, and every single guest attended. I ran out of brie and French bread."

"Wow," Harper smiled. "And what time was that?"

"We started around 2 and ended just before 5." Paul set down his mug and sighed.

"Thanks for that. I'll cross all of your guests off the list," Harper made a note in her phone. "How are you holding up?"

"You know, I'm worried about our town," Paul admitted. "Fall has weathered more than one storm, sure-but I'm also worried about you. Promise me you won't go poking around any dark corners alone."

She smiled faintly and scratched behind Lady's ears. "No dark corners. Just maybe a dusty file cabinet or two."

Paul chuckled, standing and picking up their mugs. "Come by tomorrow for the cheese and wine hour. Might do the guests good to see a familiar face that isn't mine."

Harper stood too, giving his arm a grateful squeeze. "You're doing a good job, Paul. People feel safe here."

As she stepped outside into the crisp air, the wind rustled the branches overhead, sending a few leaves tumbling to the brick path below.

For now, the town still looked beautiful. But Harper knew beauty could be deceiving.

Sunday morning, the air was crisp for mid-September, biting gently at Harper's cheeks as she adjusted her earbuds and stepped onto the quiet sidewalk in front of Hearth & Quill. The morning fog hung low in the streets, curling around the lampposts and giving an eerie vibe to the normally warm and cozy town. She took a deep breath, smelling the remnants of chimney smoke or burned leaves from the night before. Harper pressed play on her running playlist, and a song from Punch Brothers filled her ears. She took off at a slow pace.

Harper had explored several running routes since she had moved to Fall. This morning, she headed out on one of her new favorite routes, running north towards Traverse City. While the city itself was over twenty miles away, the road was the destination for Harper. It was a peaceful stretch of two-lane highway with tall evergreen trees on either side and zero traffic early in the morning. The trees created a natural corridor that reminded Harper of a trip she took to the Pacific Northwest. She marveled again at the beauty of northern Michigan. The light turned the sky from black to twilight blue, to warmer colors of the sunrise, with oranges, pinks and reds.

As a hawk soared overhead, Harper picked up the pace and settled into a comfortable rhythm, grateful for her muscular legs and strong lungs. Her mind kept flashing back to seeing Prudence lying on the ground. She feared that terrible image was seared into her brain. With each step, her mind circled around the last few days. Her golden quill that had gone missing and then reappeared in Prudence's neck. Alibis that she'd collected so far. All the people she had met in Fall. *Someone wanted Prudence gone, but why?*

Harper turned around after four miles and headed back towards Fall, still lost in thought. *Why would someone use a quill as a murder weapon? Why not a knife or a gun?* As she crested the last hill, the rooftops of town came into view again, cozy and familiar beneath a canopy of gold and crimson. Hearth & Quill stood proudly across from the town square, its third-floor apartment lit with the first rays of sun, as if Aunt Ellie had left a light on just for her.

Harper slowed to a walk, her heart thudding, sweat at her temples, and mind sharper than when she left. She was determined to help find the killer.

The air at Sullivan's Orchard was thick with the familiar scent of apples and an unmistakable tension that had settled over the town. News had spread quickly: Gabe Sullivan was reopening his orchard just in time for the annual apple cider pressing demonstration. It was a beloved tradition that drew both tourists and locals alike. For some, it was exactly what the town needed—a return to normalcy, something to distract and comfort them, a sign that life would go on. But others whispered that it was too soon.

As Harper pulled into the lot, she wasn't sure what to expect. The orchard was quieter than usual, with fewer families wandering between the rows of apple trees. The familiar sight of wooden crates overflowing with apples and the rhythmic creaking of the cider press brought an odd sense of comfort. But the usual festive energy had faded, replaced by small clusters of people speaking in hushed tones, their eyes drifting toward Gabe. A quiet tension hung in the air, a reflection of the uncertainty in the wake of the recent tragedy.

Harper made her way toward the center of the event, where Gabe stood beside the massive cider press, sleeves rolled up, a look of calm determination on his face. The crowd was slowly gathering, eager for the annual tradition—the pressing of fresh apples into golden cider. It was one of the most anticipated moments of the season, and Harper could sense that Gabe was both relieved and anxious to get back to it.

He caught sight of her from across the way and waved, a small smile tugging at the corners of his mouth.

"Hey, Harper," he called out as she approached. "Glad you could make it."

"Wouldn't miss it," Harper replied, returning his smile. "I love apple cider, and this tradition feels even more important considering recent events."

Gabe smiled, clearly proud, then busied himself adjusting the press's wooden frame. Though the orchard had only been closed for less than a day, it felt like much longer, especially with the weight of what had happened. Reopening wasn't just about business. It was a way to reclaim a sense of normalcy.

The crowd grew, with people excited for the traditional cider pressing, the symbolic heart of the season. Gabe was a comforting, steady figure in Fall, and today he seemed to be holding the town together through sheer force of will.

Nearby, Harper spotted Maggie wiping down tables, offering smiles that didn't quite reach her eyes. Harper made her way over, noticing the heaviness in Maggie's expression.

"Gabe's going through with this, huh?" Harper asked quietly as she approached.

Maggie nodded, sighing softly. "Yeah. He says the orchard has to keep going, that people depend on him. But..." She glanced over at Gabe, who was now prepping the apples for the demonstration. "It's different this year. Everyone's still shaken up."

Harper could feel it, too—the unspoken tension that hung over the crowd. Prudence's murder had rattled everyone, leaving the once peaceful town full of quiet fears and suspicions. And now, here they were, trying to pretend life could go on as usual, even though nothing felt normal.

Gabe raised his hands in a gesture for quiet, and a hush fell over the crowd.

"Thank you all for coming out," he began, his voice steady, warm. "I know we're all thinking about Prudence tonight; and keeping her family and friends in our hearts. What happened was a terrible tragedy; and I know a lot of us are feeling shaken. But Fall has always been a town that pulls together. So, tonight, I'm going to press some of the best cider you've ever tasted—fresh from the orchard, and we're going to hug our loved ones a little closer."

The crowd murmured in agreement, offering soft applause. Harper met Gabe's gaze, and for a fleeting moment, the weight of the tragedy lifted. She felt a flutter in her chest and looked down, her cheeks reddening.

Gabe began the demonstration, explaining each step of the cider-making process—from selecting the perfect blend of apples to applying the right amount of pressure for the best flavor. With the sunlight gleaming, the wooden press groaned as Gabe turned the handle, and the first drops of golden cider trickled into the barrel. The sweet, crisp scent of apples filled the air, and Harper watched as levity slowly returned to the gathering.

The cider flowed and, little by little, the crowd relaxed. But Harper's thoughts stayed anchored on Prudence's death, the image of her lying in the orchard still sharp in her mind.

As the gathering was winding down, Harper was standing near Maggie and Gabe, the three of them quietly watching the sunlight filter through the apple trees. The air smelled like cinnamon and leaves and for a moment, Harper felt caught between the comfort of the present and the uneasy of everything still unanswered.

"How's it going, Harper?" Maggie asked.

"It's going well... I've gotten a lot of alibis. I think I need to sit down and go through them all to make sense of it."

"I have a few to share," Maggie said. "How about the three of us sit down later tonight and update the list? Your shop, okay?"

Gabe agreed, and Harper nodded. "Sounds perfect,' she said. "See you both then."

She headed for her SUV, her thoughts swirling.

CHAPTER 21
HELPFUL TROUBLE

ATL GIRLS 🔪🍎🍷📚

Harper: Update from your resident amateur sleuth. The cider event went okay. Everyone was on edge at first, but loosened up when Gabe fired up the press.

Erin: So what you're saying is...cider solves crimes? 😂

Amanda: Or that Gabe presses both cider AND your emotional reset button!

Harper: LOL stop! Although, kind of. Ha I mean, yes he's calm, steady and a little swoon-worthy. But I also can't stop thinking about Prudence.

Erin: Totally fair. That would mess with anyone's vibe.

Harper: Exactly. I'm just starting to feel like part of the community here, and then this horrible thing happened. I want to help, but I'm still new around here, so I'm getting some side-eye for sure.

Amanda: You were born for the investigative bookstore owner life. You've always been interested in mysteries. Tell us what you've got so far.

Harper: I've got a list from Maggie of everyone in the town. I'm writing all my notes there, checking people off when they're cleared. I've collected a bunch of alibis, talked to half the town, and both Maggie and Gabe are helping. We're going over everything tonight, comparing notes and alibis.

Erin: So you're basically living in a cozy mystery novel. 🍁 With cider. And a hot orchard guy.

Amanda: Don't forget to hydrate. And eat. And flirt responsibly.

Harper: LOL. If I crack this case, I'm putting "local hero" on my bookstore sign.

Erin: No! Pumpkin Spice, P.I. ! 😂

Harper: YESSS!

Amanda: Keep us posted. We're invested now in the mystery AND the slow-burn romance.

Harper: Love you both. Back to the clues. 🔍🍎📚

Harper sat on the sofa in front of the hearth, the crackling fire offering a comforting warmth as its flickering light danced across the walls lined with bookshelves. On the table in front of her lay scattered notes, lists, and half-empty cups of coffee and tea. A bag of gummy bears and a bag of red licorice vines lay torn open on the table. She'd been at it for almost 40 minutes when Maggie and then Gabe arrived. Maggie settled beside her, tucking her feet under her, while Gabe took the chair across from them. The air was thick with the smell of cinnamon and coffee.

Harper tapped her pen on her notebook, breaking the silence. "Alright, let's start with the basics. We know Prudence was killed between 1:00 and 4:00 p.m.."

"Yeah," Gabe said, leaning forward. "That was when most of the town was in the square, setting up for *The Cider House Rules* movie night and prepping for Saturday's festivities."

Harper flipped through her notes. "A lot of the shopkeepers were accounted for, and I've now interviewed a ton of people. I have a lot of alibis here in my notepad and on my phone in my notes app. I'm drowning in alibis. Could we maybe shift and start with the people who had a reason to want her dead?" She shot a glance at Gabe, her pen poised over the paper. "Thoughts?"

Gabe sighed and rubbed his jaw. "Alright. First up, I talked to the women Prudence had been especially ruthless with in the past apple contests. That gave us three names: Loretta Sims, Missy Taylor, and Betty Holmes. Loretta's out—she was in Traverse City with her daughter. I confirmed it. Missy has an alibi, too. She was helping Vanessa with inventory at Sweater Weather from noon until about three. Vanessa backed that up. As for Betty... no solid alibi yet, but she's seventy-eight. I doubt she's our killer."

"Can't rule her out," Harper said, making a note on her main list of town residents. "What else?"

Maggie laughed, then glanced at her own notepad, chewing on a piece of licorice. "It always seems easier on the crime podcasts, doesn't it?"

Harper nodded, then paused, her expression shifting as she scanned her notes. "Wait, I forgot about this—Mrs. Hastings mentioned seeing Prudence arguing with someone in the market around 2. She was sure of the time. That narrows the window of the murder to between 2:30 and 4:00.

Maggie's brows lifted. "Do we know who she was arguing with?"

"She couldn't see clearly, Harper said. "But she said it *sounded* like Evelyn."

"Evelyn Miller?" Maggie sat up straighter. "Why would Evelyn and Prudence be fighting?"

"I don't know," Harper replied, scribbling it down. "But if it was Evelyn, we need to find out what it was about."

Maggie glanced at her list again. "I asked around too. Noah and Courtney were picking up the popcorn machine for movie night— they're in the clear. Melanie was working all day at *Harvest Roast*, running pizzas to the town square, and doing payroll after that."

The three of them sat in silence for a moment, the crackling fire their only soundtrack. Harper's brow furrowed as she considered the list of names in front of her.

"Why would anyone want Prudence dead?" Harper said.

"I don't know," Gabe shook his head. He paused thoughtfully, then said, "But something's been bothering me since that night. When we were heading to the orchard, Luke and Ryan were supposed to be harvesting apples."

Harper nodded, leaning forward. "Yeah, I remember you saying that."

"Well, they weren't there when you got there, right? You were the one who found Prudence. The guys weren't there," he said slowly.

Harper's brow furrowed. "You're right. So where were they?"

Gabe looked troubled. "I don't know. When I went into the market to check on things, I didn't see them there. I chatted with Becky, and she didn't mention seeing them, either."

Harper tapped her pen against her paper. "We need answers from them. Adding them to the list."

Gabe nodded.

Maggie pulled out her phone and opened her notes. "Alright, Rebecca Rittenhouse. She's got a solid alibi. She was at the library on Friday, helping organize the fall reading event. Several people saw her there between 1:00 and 4:30 p.m."

Harper jotted it down in her notebook. "That checks out. I didn't have her down as a major suspect, but it's good to confirm."

"Next," Maggie continued, "Clara Cummings. She was at *Rustic Pie* with her husband, Ron. They were having late lunch around 2:30, and she stayed until almost 4:00. I asked Ronnie, and he remembered seeing them."

Harper nodded, adding the details to her notes. "I followed up with Ronnie about his own alibi too-he was in the kitchen most of the afternoon. I checked on Hannah's as well-she was helping Melanie with festival orders are Harvest Roast. Ronnie backed that up."

Maggie jotted a note." Okay, good. That takes two more names off the list."

Maggie leaned back in her chair, crossing her arms. "Now, Mary Flowers. She was working at the elementary school. She had a baking demonstration for the kids that ran from 2 to 4:30 p.m. She couldn't have left, and I talked to the teacher who hosted the event—Leslie Barnes. She vouched for her."

Harper sighed, tapping her pen on her notebook. "So, Mary's clear too. That's ruling out most of this year's bakers."

Maggie nodded, her expression thoughtful. "Exactly. But here's the thing—none of them had any real motive to go after Prudence. Sure, the bakers all know Prudence is a tough judge, but that's not a reason to kill a person. This year's bakers could have just not entered the contest if they were *that* afraid of Prudence's review."

Harper frowned. "Right. That's what I've been struggling with. Prudence had plenty of enemies, but who hated her enough to kill her?"

Maggie leaned in, lowering her voice slightly. "There's something else. I was talking to Dolores, and she mentioned something odd. She said that in the weeks leading up to the contest, Prudence had been on edge. She'd been meeting with someone - Dolores saw her at Harvest Roast a few times, and once she was quietly arguing with someone."

Harper's eyes widened. "Arguing? Did she say who it might've been?"

Maggie shook her head. "She couldn't see who it was, but she said Prudence was acting strange. Like she was worried about something."

Harper leaned back, her mind spinning. "That changes things. Prudence might have been mixed up in something more serious, which makes a lot more sense than this crime being about the pie contest."

"Exactly," Maggie said, her voice dropping. "And whoever she was meeting with might have had more to lose than we thought."

Harper scribbled a few more notes, her heart racing with the possibilities.

Maggie paused mid-chew on her licorice. "There's one more name we need to add—Deputy Jake Russell."

Gabe looked outraged. "Jake? He's a police officer and a war veteran—why would he kill Prudence?"

"I'm not saying he did," Maggie defended, "but if we're looking into seventy-eight-year-old Betty Holmes, why not him? We can't rule anyone out. He wasn't on duty that day, and he was the last deputy to arrive on the scene. What kept him?"

"Alright, alright," Harper said, sensing the rising tension. "Let's not turn on each other. We're just gathering information."

Gabe nodded, though Harper could see the conflict in his eyes. He knew these people well—maybe too well. That one of them could have committed murder was hard to swallow.

"We'll find the truth," Harper said, more to herself than anyone. "We have to."

Maggie nodded, her expression set in determination. "We will. Fall is our town. No one's getting away with this."

The three exchanged a glance, knowing this was just the beginning. Somewhere in that tangled web of alibis and secrets was the key to unlocking the truth. And they wouldn't rest until they found it.

Later that afternoon, Harper spotted Marco near the farmer's market, his delivery car—an aging red hatchback with a giant slice of pizza magnet stuck to the roof—parked crookedly along Main Street. He wasn't in uniform; just jeans, a hoodie, and a knit cap pulled low over his curls. He was holding a caramel apple in one hand and chatting animatedly with the kettle corn vendor.

"Marco!" Harper called as she crossed the street, dodging a pair of toddlers chasing a runaway gourd.

He turned, blinking in surprise. "Hey! Harper Whitmore, mystery woman of the month." He grinned. "Need a pizza? I'm off duty, but I've got connections."

She laughed. "No pizza today. I just had some questions about Friday. I'm sort of confirming everyone's alibis for the day."

His grin dimmed as he realized the topic. "Sure. How can I help?"

"Can you tell me what you were doing on Friday?"

She listened as Marco recounted a very similar story to Ronnie. Both men were working, with Ronnie manning the store and Marco delivering pizzas. Ronnie worked all day. Melanie and her assistant Hannah were in and out several times picking up pizza, and Marco himself delivered the last batch of pizzas to the square around 3:30.

Harper made notes on the list and nodded.

"Is everything okay?" Marco dropped his hand holding the apple stick. "You don't suspect Ronnie, do you, because he could never—"

Harper shook her head. "No, no. I'm just checking timelines. Obviously, I'm not a detective, but I really want to find who did this. I have to help, and I imagine every bit of information I can gather is helpful. And in a small town—everyone notices everything."

"Yeah, they sure do," Marco gave a short laugh. "Well, if you have any more questions, let me know."

"Thanks, Marco. That helps."

He saluted her with the apple stick. "And if you need backup on this investigation, I charge by the hour—plus gas."

Harper walked away smiling, but her thoughts were already churning. Ronnie's alibi was looking solid... but every confirmation just narrowed the suspect list. And the quill in Prudence's neck would not point fingers on its own.

The chilly autumn breeze rustled the leaves as Harper made her way up the narrow cobblestone path to Betty Holmes' small, ivy-covered cottage. The home sat on the edge of Fall, Michigan, a bit secluded from the rest of the town, with a sprawling garden that seemed almost wild, save for the neat rows of late-blooming flowers lining the walk. Betty met Harper at the door, her gray hair pinned up, and a thick wool sweater over a floral dress.

"Harper Whitmore," Betty greeted warmly, though her eyes held a flicker of curiosity. "What brings you all the way out here? You're not here to join my garden club, I assume."

Harper smiled. "Not today, Betty. I actually have a few questions about last Friday afternoon."

Betty raised an eyebrow, stepping aside to let Harper in. "I figured you'd make your way to me, eventually. Word is you've been asking half the town about their whereabouts during Prudence's murder. Her tone was light, but her eyes were sharp with curiosity. "Come on in, then. Let's get some tea going."

Harper stepped into the cozy living room, immediately comforted by the scent of cinnamon and the crackling fire in the hearth. Betty's home was lined with bookshelves, old photos, and the unmistakable warmth of someone who had lived a full life. Betty motioned for Harper to sit as she disappeared into the kitchen for a moment, returning shortly with two steaming cups of tea.

"So, I'm guessing you would like to know where I was on Friday between 1:00 and 4:00?" Betty asked, easing into her armchair with a small sigh.

Harper nodded, setting her notebook on her lap. "I would. I'm trying to confirm where everyone was last Friday. We narrowed down the time to between 2:30 and 4:00 p.m. Do you remember where you were during that time?"

Betty took a sip of tea, her brow furrowed in thought. "Last Friday...," she shook her head sadly. "Terrible thing, what happened to Prudence. I was at home all afternoon. I've been having trouble with my arthritis lately, so I spent most of the day in the garden, trying to prune some shrubs before the frost sets in."

Harper nodded, jotting that down. "Were you alone, or was anyone here with you?"

"I was alone," Betty replied, setting her tea down. "But Mary Cartwright came by. She often brings me groceries when she's out and about. She stayed awhile, chatting."

Harper glanced up from her notes. "Can you think of anyone who may have wanted to hurt Prudence? I understand she could be difficult…"

Betty shook her head firmly. "Oh, Prudence could be a genuine piece of work, no doubt about that. I didn't have any problems with her - we disagreed over the years—mainly over the garden club. She thought my methods were old-fashioned." She waved her hand dismissively. "The only person I know she had a problem with was Evelyn Miller. But she isn't capable of something like this."

Harper drank her tea, and they made small talk for a few minutes. She prodded about Evelyn Miller and the potential issue there, and Betty said it was an old argument about a property line. She encouraged Harper to speak to Dolores Meeks, who apparently knew all about their ongoing feud. When she finished with her tea, Harper took their teacups into the kitchen and washed them. As she went to leave, Betty reached out and touched Harper's arm gently. "Prudence may not have been easy to like, but no one deserves what happened to her."

"I agree," Harper said, feeling the weight of Betty's words settle on her. "That's why I'm trying to help find the killer."

Betty gave Harper a warm hug, and Harper stepped back into the cool air, one more piece of the puzzle falling into place. Betty was in the clear, but as Harper walked back toward her car, she wondered if the property dispute with Evelyn Miller was serious enough to kill over.

The sheriff's office smelled faintly of coffee and lemon-scented cleaning spray. Harper stepped inside and found Deputy Jake Russell at his desk, sleeves rolled up, fingers flying over his keyboard.

"You type surprisingly fast," Harper said, breaking the silence.

"When you're writing up reports about IED's, you've got to hurry," he finished typing, smiling wryly, then glanced up. "Well, well. Look who's trading in books for badges."

"I brought you something," Harper said, holding up a to-go cup from Harvest Roast.

Jake stood, accepting it as if it were a peace offering. "You trying to bribe an officer of the law, Whitmore?"

"Bribe? No, butter up? Definitely."

He chuckled, taking a sip and giving her a nod of approval. "You know my weakness. Excellent coffee instead of the sludge we have. Okay, whatcha got?"

She pulled her well-worn town list from her bag and handed it over. "On the back page you'll see the list of everyone with a motive for wanting Prudence dead. At least, according to myself, Maggie and Gabe. Which, let's be honest, is basically the same as the town census."

Jake scanned it, eyebrows raising. "You actually printed this out?"

"A friend got it for me. But I color-coded it," she said proudly. "Red for motive, green for alibi, yellow for 'Harper's gut says something's fishy.'"

Jake squinted. "Is that... chocolate on the corner?"

"I *may* have had some chocolate," she said sheepishly.

He sat back down, shaking his head but smiling. "You ever set this list down?"

"Nope,"

"You're really serious about this," he said, leaning back in his chair.

"I am. I can't explain why. Maybe it's because I found her. Or because my quill was the murder weapon. I'm new to town, and I already feel protective of this place. It was my aunt's nirvana...and maybe it's mine too. I don't know. That probably sounds weird."

"Actually," Jake said with a small, wistful smile on his face. "It doesn't. I feel the same way. Like I found this perfect little town that not too many people know about, and I want to do everything I can to protect it from the outside world."

"Exactly," Harper agreed, nodding.

She spent several minutes filling him in on everything she knew so far, including who she talked to and her primary suspect...Evelyn.

He chuckled again. "You're trouble."

"I'm helpful."

"Helpful trouble," he said, and took another sip of coffee. "Look, Harper... I don't want to clip your wings or anything, but maybe you should let us handle the murder investigation."

She softened. "I'm not trying to be a hero, Jake. I just feel like I owe it to my Aunt Ellie to protect what she loved. This town. This shop. The people she left behind."

He nodded slowly, then leaned forward, his voice gentle. "And Prudence. I feel like we have to get justice for Prudence."

"Of course," said Harper. "I can't close my eyes without seeing her face. I have to do something to help."

"I get it. I do. But at least promise me you'll be careful? And if things felt dangerous—really dangerous—you'll come to me first."

She offered a small smile. "Deal."

He raised his coffee in a mock toast and sighed heavily. "To helpful trouble."

She clinked her cup against his. "To doing things that make our friends sigh heavily behind their desks."

CHAPTER 22
ELLIES NOTEBOOK

The bell above the door of The Harvest Roast jingled as Harper stepped inside. She was enveloped by the incredible aroma of coffee and scones, with soft jazz in the air. The warmth was a welcome reprieve from the rainy, chilly September day outside. A few locals sat with laptops and steaming mugs, and behind the counter, Melanie was arranging muffins in the display case with the precision of a pastry surgeon.

Harper made her way over after shaking out her umbrella outside the door and propping it against the wall.

"Hey Mel."

Melanie glanced up and smiled. "Hey, stranger. I haven't seen you in a few days. You're due for a maple chai."

"Yum - I'll take one," Harper said, smiling. "And a chat, if you've got a second."

Melanie poured the tea and leaned on the counter, wiping her hands on her apron. "What's on your mind?"

Harper lowered her voice just a touch. "It's about Friday. I'm just... connecting a few dots."

Melanie's expression didn't change, but her posture straightened slightly. "Sure, how can I help."

"Were you working all day?"

"Mostly, yeah. Opened the shop at six like usual. The morning rush was busy—it was market day, so there was lots of foot traffic. I was running pizzas to the crew on the square. Hannah, my assistant manager, was helping me. I took a break around five. Went home, let the dog out, grabbed a shower. Came back by six to get ready for the movie in the square. They always show *The Cider House Rules*, and we serve cider to go with it."

Harper nodded slowly. "Anyone with you when you were home?"

Melanie hesitated for the briefest beat. "Just me. Why?"

"Just checking timelines. You know how it is in Fall - everyone remembers what pie they were eating and who was sitting next to them while they ate it."

That got a chuckle out of Melanie. "True. But honestly, I saw nothing unusual that day. Just your typical Apple Harvest Festival madness. If Ronnie's still under the magnifying glass, you can tell Sheriff Carlisle I was in the pizza shop at least 5 times that day, and Ronnie was there every time."

Harper smiled, but her eyes stayed watchful. "Noted. And how about Marco?"

Melanie leaned in slightly. "Do you really think it was someone we know?"

Harper took her tea, fingers wrapping around the warm cup. "I think whoever did it knew Prudence. And knew exactly where to find her that day."

Melanie's expression darkened. "Then I guess the real question is... who wanted her gone badly enough to plan it? Because it surely wasn't Marco. Who really had a motive to kill Prudence?"

Harper took a slow sip, her eyes drifting toward the fogged-up window. "That's exactly what I'm trying to find out."

Exhausted from her sleuthing and running the bookshop, Harper decided to take an evening off to relax. Surely the murderer could wait one day. She grabbed a sandwich from Golden Crust Sandwich Company and headed back to the bookshop to unwind. She was pleasantly stuffed after devouring an incredible roast turkey sandwich made with stuffing and cranberry sauce and decided to turn her attention to the office. She needed to do something other than think about Prudence and the alibis of every person in town.

She stood in the office doorway, surveying the cluttered space that had been Aunt Ellie's sanctuary. The small room was crammed with decades' worth of paperwork, old furniture, and a faint musty smell. A large oak desk sat against the far wall, its surface hidden beneath a sea of file folders, books, and stacks of faded receipts. Shelves along the walls sagged with old books and knickknacks, while the floor was scattered with boxes that looked as though they hadn't been touched in years.

Harper pulled her curls into a ponytail and turned on some music. She started by tackling the desk, its drawers full of papers and office supplies. Harper sifted through everything, letting most of it go, but keeping items with special significance. She found pieces of her aunt's life tucked away—an old keychain with the bookstore logo, a handwritten list of favorite authors, even a crumpled postcard from a customer thanking Ellie for her book recommendations for her honeymoon in 1974.

Several hours later, the desk was free of clutter both inside and out. Harper wiped down the wood with a damp cloth, organized the drawers with fresh notepads, pens, and a plant she'd recused.

Next, Harper moved to the shelves, dusting and sorting through books and trinkets. Some items, like an old brass clock and a framed photo of Ellie with the shop's first customer, Harper decided to keep. Others, she packed away into boxes for storage, leaving the shelves open and ready for new life. She placed a few potted plants along the top, the green leaves brightening the space instantly.

Harper moved an armchair into the corner, draping a soft blanket over the back for when she needed a cozy place to read. She brought a small side table with a brass lamp from the apartment down to the office, its warm glow making the room feel inviting. On the walls, she hung prints of vintage illustrations of books and typewriters she had found on Etsy the previous week. Lastly, she set her MacBook on the desk, an oversized mug for coffee, a jar for candy and a notebook.

When she finished, the transformation was undeniable. The office had become a light-filled, inspiring space. Harper sank into the armchair for a moment, letting out a satisfied sigh. It wasn't just the physical changes that made the room feel different—it was the fact that, like the rest of the bookstore, this space now felt like hers.

Harper's eyes roamed over the large wooden desk and her gaze landed on a faint groove she'd not noticed before. She sat up, inspecting it closely. It wasn't a simple scratch; it was deliberate, like a seam carefully hidden in plain sight. Harper pressed gently against the side of the desk, letting her fingers slide along the edge until she heard a faint — click. A hidden drawer sprang open with a soft, mechanical sound. Harper's breath caught as she pulled it open slowly and peered inside. She saw a slim, leather-bound notebook and a large manila folder with "Harper" scrawled across it. She recognized her Aunt Ellie's handwriting instantly.

Harper carefully pulled both items from the hiding place and placed them on the desk. Harper turned the manila folder over, ripped open the seal and poured the contents onto the desk.

Dear Harper,

If you're reading this, then you've spoken to my attorney and received the will. Hearth & Quill is now yours.

Though I planned for this day, I wish I could be there to see you walk through those doors. I trust you'll carry on our family's legacy. I know you'll see this place for what it really is: a home for stories, a sanctuary, and maybe even a bit of magic wrapped in brick.

I imagine you're feeling overwhelmed. Maybe you're unsure of why I've left all of this to you, or how you're going to fit into this cozy, small town. As far as 'why you?'...there are two reasons. You always loved books as much as I did, and I've always adored you, my dear. I believe you belong in Fall. This town has a magical way of welcoming people and making them a part of the fabric of the community.

You'll find a delightful cast of characters in our quaint town. Mrs. Hastings believes we should color code the store. Mr. Thornhill comes in at least twice a week for some obscure title, usually on cheese-making. (But he buys a lot, so humor him.) And Maggie, who will show up when you least expect it, probably with a cup of coffee and some wild story to share. She's a lovely soul. They're all characters in their own right, and they've been part of the bookstore's world for a long time. They'll welcome you and help you find your footing.

*When I took over from my father, I worried I couldn't live up to the shop's legacy. my grandpa's But I came to understand something: Hearth & Quill doesn't need perfection. It needs presence. Curiosity. Care. It's a place for people to come lose themselves, find themselves, or just **be** themselves. The bookshop will always be full of people who are curious, dreaming or seeking. And now, it's yours.*

Last, the building has its quirks. There are secrets tucked into corners—sometimes literal ones. My father adored hidden doors and passages. You've probably already discovered one or two. (He used to say, "Time to go home" when he disappeared into one.) There's a trapdoor in the stockroom I never opened, and a few creaky floorboards that still surprise me.

Make it your own. Move things. Add your voice to the story. The bookstore will thrive with you at the helm. Trust it—and trust yourself.

I believe in you, Harper. More than you know.

With love,

Aunt Ellie

P.S. The quill collection was built over decades by my father and me. Please don't part with it. The golden quill once belonged to Ernest Hemingway—he summered at Walloon Lake every year and even visited this bookstore a few times. That quill is priceless, and my favorite. The others hold stories too... ones I hope you'll uncover in time.

Harper reached up and wiped away a tear from her cheek. She missed her aunt terribly, and reading her words felt like such a gift.

After a few moments of reminiscing, Harper turned her attention to the leather book, opening it slowly. The cover was worn and soft, the pages slightly yellowed. She read her aunts's familiar, loopy, flowing cursive handwriting that filled the margins, detailing what seemed like ordinary business records - sales, expenses, inventory notes. But as Harper turned the pages, her eyebrows raised. There, in the middle of the ledger, was a name that kept appearing repeatedly: *Vivian Hawthorn.*

Harper read the entries:

June 5, 1993

Vivian has asked to buy Hemingway's Quill. I told her it wasn't for sale. She seemed disappointed but left without fuss. Strange request.

August 21, 1998

Vivian offered to buy the Quill again, offering more money this time. She didn't seem pleased at my answer.

As Harper continued reading, the offers Vivian made grew larger, and the language Ellie used grew warier.

October 10, 2013

It's been years and now Vivian is back, begging now, offering triple what she first proposed for the Quill. I refused again, but she's not letting this go. I told her it's a historical piece, not for sale.

November 12, 2019

Once again, Vivian sent a note offering an outrageous sum for Hemingway's Quill. She said that its "her family's right." I don't understand, but I feel like I need to be careful.

Harper's hands shook as she flipped to the final entry, dated less than a month before her aunt's death:

April 3, 2024

Vivian was here again—this time more desperate than ever. She said she wouldn't take "no" for an answer. I don't understand why, but something about her feels dangerous. I told her I bought the Quill fairly and wouldn't be parting with it.

Harper's heart pounded in her chest as she closed the book. This wasn't just some quirky piece of local history—Vivian had been chasing Hemingway's Quill for 30 years, growing more frantic with each refusal. Ellie had sensed danger.

Harper's mind raced as she pieced things together. Vivian's obsession, her escalating desperation—what lengths would she go to in order to get it?

She thought back to the night of the grand reopening when Vivian had glided over in a subtle waft of perfume and glittering jewelry. *"Eleanor and I shared a love of old things."* That line echoed in Harper's head now, darker somehow. Had that "love" turned into an obsession? Had it twisted into something more dangerous?

Harper swallowed hard against a terrifying thought. Perhaps Vivian Hawthorn had stolen the quill. But if Harper was right and Vivian *had* stolen it, why had she murdered Prudence?

CHAPTER 23
HEMLOCK RIDGE

Harper had gone for her morning run and stopped by Maple and Crumb for a warm cinnamon scone. She was stepping out with her scone in hand when she saw Dolores Meeks, the town's unofficial historian and avid people-watcher. Dolores was perched on her usual bench outside the bakery, wrapped in a rust-colored shawl and sipping something from a steaming thermos labeled "Pumpkin Spice and Gossip."

"Well, if it isn't Harper Whitmore," Dolores drawled, her eyes crinkling with curiosity. "Come sit a spell. You've been digging into all kinds of things lately—books, alibis, secrets."

Harper smiled warily and took a seat. "I'm just trying to understand this town. Seems like everyone's got a story."

Dolores laughed and nodded. "They certainly do!"

Harper cleared her throat. "You're actually on my list of people to talk to. Betty said you might give me some background on the conflict between Prudence Sherman and Evelyn Miller? I understand they didn't get along."

Dolores chuckled, dry and low. "Didn't get along is putting it politely. Those two hadn't exchanged a civil word in over thirty years.

All started with a piece of land on Hemlock Ridge. Belonged to Evelyn's late husband—a beautiful stretch with a sugar maple grove and a little red barn that looked like it popped out of a painting."

Harper leaned in. "And Prudence wanted it?"

"Well, she thought she was *entitled* to it. Claimed her cousin had sold it unfairly to Evelyn's husband way back when. But it was legal and done. That didn't stop Prudence from holding a grudge so long it practically fossilized."

Harper blinked. "Over a maple grove?"

"Well, and the old springhouse," Dolores added. "Rumor was there was something valuable buried near it—an old box, gold coins, a deed to even more land, depending on who's telling the story. But whatever it was, Prudence never found it. Drove her half mad with spite."

"She really believed there was treasure?" Harper asked.

"Treasure or not, she wanted that land back so badly she'd call Evelyn a thief right to her face. Took her to court twice. Lost both times. Then, she stopped speaking to her entirely. At the Harvest Bonfire last year, Evelyn brought caramel apples to share, and Prudence told everyone not to eat them because they were 'poison from a snake.'"

Harper's eyebrows rose. "Wow."

Dolores gave a slow nod. "That feud was old and as bitter as over-steeped tea. And now they're both gone—one buried, one grieving, and the land still sitting quiet on Hemlock Ridge." She glanced sideways at Harper. "But if you ever go poking around that old springhouse... well. Just watch your back."

Harper smiled tightly and took a bite of her scone, but her mind was already spinning.

Treasure. Land disputes. And a feud that might've led to murder.

Fall, Michigan had layers. And Harper was peeling them back.

The aroma of burnt coffee hung in the air as Harper stepped into the law enforcement building. The front desk was empty. She spotted Deputy Jake Russell in the back, his boots propped up on his desk, flipping through a notepad with a pen stuck behind his ear.

He looked up and gave her a slow grin. "Well, if it isn't our resident bookstore detective. Come to turn yourself in?"

Harper raised an eyebrow. "Only if being nosy is a crime."

Jake stood up, buzzed her in and gestured to the chair across from him. "Alright, Whitmore. What've you got?"

She dropped a folded piece of paper on his desk. "I've been asking around—just casually—and I confirmed a bunch of alibis for the day of Prudence's murder."

Jake leaned forward, his face falling into a more serious expression. "Let's hear it."

Harper talked him through the list, ticking off names on her fingers as she went. She could recite the list from memory at this point, having read it over and over repeatedly. After 10 or 12 names, Harper paused to take a breath.

"What about Ronnie?" Jake asked.

"Ronnie was working at Rustic Pie all afternoon. I spoke with Marco and Melanie. Both said they remembered Ronnie being there the whole shift. Said he was elbow-deep in flour all day."

Jake nodded, scribbling something. "Alright, that lines up with what we got from Marco's time logs. Go on."

"Melanie also said she was prepping for the cider tasting for the *Cider House Rules* showing. I talked to her directly. She was at the shop from morning until five when she went home to shower. By then, Prudence was already dead. Gabe stopped in for a cider to-go and saw Melanie there at a few minutes before 5 o'clock, so she's got multiple witnesses"

"Solid. Anything else?"

Harper hesitated, chewing on her bottom lip. "Well, that just leaves the people who don't have an alibi so far. Or, the people that I'm still concerned about."

Jake studied her carefully. "Go on," he urged.

Harper told him about Ellie's letter and how it seemed to point to Vivian having an interest in the quill that was the murder weapon.

"I haven't pinned down her timeline for that day. She claims she was at home, working on a proposal for the historical society, but no one seems to have seen her until the bonfire that night."

Jake leaned back in his chair, rubbing a hand over his jaw. "Interesting. What else you got?"

"That's it for now. But I'm still digging. I've got loads more people to interview," harper said.

Jake interlaced his hands behind his head and said, "You've done good work, Harper, but why don't you let us take it from here?"

She smiled, but it didn't quite reach her eyes. "With all due respect, Deputy, it's thanks to me that we have this stack of verified alibis. Like it or not, my crime junkie skills are helping you here."

Jake chuckled, shaking his head. "Fair enough. Just...be careful."

"I will," Harper said, rising to her feet. "Thanks."

After a long and busy day collecting alibis, Harper sank into the sofa in front of the hearth. The complete list of residents she got from Maggie was full of notes, alibis and reminders about who had corroborated others' alibis. She had transferred all the notes from her phone to the list and she'd added a few blank pieces of paper as well. It was an intricate web of people, places and intersecting timelines. She made little check marks next to names where an alibi was confirmed, and small X's if something couldn't be verified.

Harper had a massive list of people who had *not* killed Prudence Sherman, and a much shorter list of possible suspects. That was divided into two piles - people for whom she simply hadn't collected an alibi yet, and those who seemed to have some motive to kill Prudence. The top of that suspect list was Evelyn Miller.

Mrs. Hastings had seen Evelyn fighting with Prudence just before her death. It was too much of a coincidence to ignore. Harper had talked to several people in town about Evelyn, casually asking about her history with Prudence. One of them encouraged her to check the library archives. There, Harper dug through old articles and found an interview Prudence had once given about a long-standing property dispute with Evelyn.

They'd fought over land before Hemlock Ridge, but the grudge never truly ended. When Evelyn proposed building an art studio on land bordering the Sherman estate, Prudence saw it as another betrayal. Another battle line.

Prudence had been a vocal opponent of the project, accusing Evelyn of trying to ruin the town's charm with her "modern monstrosities." The tension between them turned bitter and public, evolving into a feud that stretched over a decade.

The article painted Prudence as a guardian of tradition, but to Harper, it was clear this wasn't just about zoning laws. The bitterness had sunk deeper...personal, emotional. Maybe even dangerous.

In a more recent article, *The Fall Gazette* reported that Evelyn was once again bringing the idea up to the planning commission and would be holding a public notice meeting in November, just a few weeks away. The timing of Prudence's death now seemed less like a coincidence and more like the culmination of old wounds that had never healed. Evelyn's art studio had been a sore point for years, and Prudence had done everything she could to block the project. Harper could easily imagine the frustration boiling over. But did it boil over enough for murder?

She scribbled a note on one of the blank sheets of her list, underlining property dispute and Evelyn's studio. This was more than just old gossip. It was a potential motive, and Harper knew she had to dig deeper into Evelyn's past and present.

CHAPTER 24
EVELYN

Harper glanced at the clock above the mantel. It was late, the streets of Fall already silent under a blanket of mist settling in for the night. But her curiosity had taken root. With Evelyn Miller's name circled and underlined in her notebook, it was impossible to ignore the itch to keep going. Evelyn had motive, proximity, and—if Mrs. Hastings was to be believed—a temper hot enough to confront Prudence just before her death.

She reached for her phone and sent a quick text to Maggie. Harper's phone rang less than a minute later.

"Hey, Harper," Maggie answered, a yawn audible in her voice. "You said you needed help? What's up?"

Harper paused. "Did I wake you? I'm so sorry!"

"Nah, I'm in bed, but not asleep yet. What's up?"

Harper hesitated, not wanting to bother her friend but desperate to make progress.

"Well, I need some local history...."

"You're in luck. I know all the town's skeletons. Lay it on me," Maggie said.

"Evelyn Miller," Harper said, her tone more serious. "I know about her feud with Prudence over the art studio. Do you know if they ever resolved it?"

Maggie let out a low whistle. "Oh, no, definitely not. Evelyn and Prudence didn't just fight over that studio—they fought over everything. Halloween decorations, who would host the town's holiday gala... even the way Prudence judged the apple pie contest was a sore spot. And then, of course, there was the property feud. Supposedly, Prudence actually threatened to have the property condemned if Evelyn started building."

"Condemned?" Harper said, surprised. "That's pretty intense."

"Exactly. Prudence had friends in high places. She could make life miserable for Evelyn if she wanted to, and I'm pretty sure she did. It got ugly," Maggie said. "People literally stopped inviting them both to the same functions. They could hardly be in the same room without someone leaving in a huff."

Harper jotted down a quick note about Prudence's influence around town. "Is Evelyn...well..."

Maggie's voice softened. "The kind of person who might snap? I don't know. I was thinking about her the last few days. I don't think so, but we should check her alibi for sure."

"That was my next question," Harper said. "Did you or Gabe talk to her? "

Maggie paused. "I didn't, but I think Gabe did. I think she was seen chatting with the mayor, but I wouldn't swear to it."

Harper perked up, scribbling another note. "That might be the confirmation I need. Thanks, Mags. I owe you one."

"Nah, what are friends for?" Maggie said with a yawn. "I'm off to bed now. Talk tomorrow."

Harper hung up, her mind whirring. If Evelyn was meeting with the mayor, she'd have an alibi. But if not, could she have followed Prudence to the orchard where years of frustration boiled over?

Harper closed her notebook, feeling the weight of what she'd learned. She'd have to find Evelyn, dig a little deeper, and see what she could find. For now, though, the flickering fireplace and the promise of sleep called her. She locked up, turned out the lights, and headed into the grandfather clock, and upstairs to her apartment.

After verifying with Gabe that he hadn't spoken to Evelyn, the next morning Harper made her way over to Evelyn Miller's art studio. It was an imposing building nestled just outside Fall's historic district. The studio was sleek and modern-all glass and steel—a stark contrast to the quaint charm of the town. As Harper stepped inside, she was greeted by the smell of fresh paint and the faint sound of jazz playing softly in the background.

Evelyn looked up from her easel, where she was working on a large canvas swirled with fiery reds and oranges. Her expression shifted to mild irritation as Harper approached, but she quickly masked it, setting her brush down with deliberate calm.

"Ms. Whitmore," Evelyn said, crossing her arms. "What can I do for you?"

Harper returned her gaze, choosing her words carefully. "I'm just following up on some questions regarding Prudence's...well, passing."

Evelyn's lips pressed into a thin line. "I'd think that would be the sheriff's job."

"Yes, but I'm just helping them gather information," Harper replied, unfazed. "This is just a routine question. I understand you were meeting with the mayor and the council members on Friday afternoon?"

Evelyn let out a sigh, feigning boredom. "Yes, I was. We met for nearly thirty minutes about the studio's expansion. Why is that necessary to confirm?"

"Well, someone saw you arguing with Prudence Friday afternoon,"Harper said pointedly. "So your alibi is pretty important.
"

Evelyn's gaze grew colder. "We were *not* arguing. I had some words with her in passing, but that's all. Prudence Sherman has been a thorn in my side, yes. But I have no reason to kill her, Ms. Whitmore. All her meddling only made me more determined to succeed. Unlike some people, I don't get rattled that easily."

Harper noted the tightness in Evelyn's voice, her defensive posture. "So the mayor and the council can vouch for you?"

"Yes," Evelyn said through gritted teeth. "Not that I should need a whole crowd to confirm my whereabouts."

Harper raised an eyebrow. "I suppose not. But Prudence's death wasn't just some accident, Evelyn. People have been...talking. And your history with Prudence is well-known. I'm sure you understand why I had to ask."

Evelyn's expression shifted from irritation to something darker. She leaned forward, her voice low and fierce. "You didn't *have* to ask. You want to *play* detective, be my guest. You have your answer. Unless you plan to start painting with me, I suggest you get back to your little investigation elsewhere. I have work to do."

Harper gave a polite nod. "Thank you for your time, Evelyn. I'll make sure to confirm with the mayor."

As she turned to leave, she couldn't shake the feeling that Evelyn's reaction was more than simple irritation. It was as though Evelyn's alibi was indeed solid—but there was something else lurking beneath the surface, a bitterness Evelyn couldn't quite hide.

Outside, Harper made a note to talk to the mayor and see what time they had chatted. If Evelyn had a verifiable alibi, she was clear. But if anyone contradicted her... well, that might be the crack Harper needed to solve this once and for all.

Harper found Mayor Tom Gillespie outside the town hall, standing under the bronze statue of Fall's founder as he checked his watch, looking every bit the part in his crisp navy suit and polished caramel brown shoes. She quickened her step, hoping he wouldn't slip away before she got a chance to speak to him.

"Mayor Gillespie!" she called, waving as she approached.

The mayor turned, squinting slightly. "Ah, yes? Good morning."

Harper gave him a polite smile, determined to keep things friendly. "Hi, I'm Harper Whitmore, Ellie's great niece — "

The mayor smiled and offered his hand for Harper to shake. "Ah, of course, Miss Whitmore. We're so pleased to have you in our little town. All the way from, Savannah, was it?"

"Atlanta, actually." Harper shook his hand. It was soft and moisturized.

"Yes, of course. Lovely city, Atlanta," he said. "Now, what can I do for you, young lady?"

"Oh, um, I'm just doing a bit of follow-up on...recent events. Specifically, Friday afternoon. I understand you met with Evelyn Miller to discuss her studio expansion?"

The mayor's expression softened with recognition, and he nodded. "Yes, I remember that meeting quite well. I'd have to check with my assistant Henry for the specific time, as he keeps my diary. Evelyn was in fine form that afternoon—had plenty to say about the project, as always."

Harper tilted her head, trying to keep her tone casual. "And how long would you say you chatted with Evelyn?"

"It was just under 30 minutes," he replied, without hesitation. "That part I remember because I tried to limit it to 15 minutes. Evelyn's the type who digs in and doesn't let go. Once she started talking about that studio, there was no way anyone was going to get a word in edgewise. There was no way to keep her to just 15 minutes." He paused, raising an eyebrow. "Is that...relevant?"

"I'm just collecting information, trying to help the investigation," Harper replied. "Thank you, Mayor Gillespie. I'll let you get back to your day."

As he walked off, Harper glanced around, spotting Councilwoman Jenkins chatting with a few townspeople by the post office across the square. Harper approached, waiting for a pause in their conversation before stepping in.

"Councilwoman Jenkins, do you have a moment?"

"Of course, dear!" Councilwoman Jenkins greeted her with a warm smile. "What can I do for you?"

"I just had a quick question about the day Prudence was killed. I understand you and the Mayor met with Evelyn Miller?"

"Oh, yes," Councilwoman Jenkins said, eyes widening slightly. "I remember it well."

"Do you remember the time, or how long you chatted?" Harper asked eagerly.

"Let me check my phone," Councilwoman Jenkins said, looking down at her iPhone. "I can't do anything without Google calendar. "Yes, here it is. We met at 2:30 for 30 minutes. Evelyn had a lot to say about that expansion. She talked our ears off about it!"

Harper nodded, taking mental note of the consistency. "Thank you for confirming. I appreciate your time."

She continued her rounds, tracking down Councilman Perez, who confirmed Evelyn's presence as well. Every council member she spoke to gave the same answer: Evelyn had been there rallying for her studio expansion.

By the time Harper finished her rounds, her initial suspicions had shifted. Evelyn's alibi seemed airtight. With each confirmation, the image of Evelyn as the culprit faded, leaving Harper to reconsider her suspect list. Evelyn might have been at odds with Prudence, but as each witness reaffirmed her presence at the meeting, it became obvious she hadn't killed her longtime rival.

Harper tucked her notebook away, her mind buzzing with possibilities. Evelyn was out. But if not Evelyn...then who killed Prudence?

ATL GIRLS

Harper: Thought I had it. Seriously. I was *this* close to solving it. I had a whole theory mapped out on my list of residents and notes app 😩

Erin: Wait WHAT. Who was it?? Spill immediately.

Amanda: Don't tell me it was the PTA president. I *knew* she had murder vibes under that J.Crew sweater. 😷

Harper: Nope. Evelyn. Thought I had motive, means, *and* a feud that dated back to the Reagan administration. But... her alibi checks out. Of course it does. 🫠

Erin: Ugh. That's so frustrating. You're basically carrying this investigation. Can they at least give you a badge or a cider coupon or something??

Amanda: Hold up... where's Gabe in all this? Still being rugged and emotionally supportive and smelling like fall??

Harper: He is. We've been going through the alibis together. He's been really helpful. And also... very distracting. 😳

Erin: Distracting like "I can't focus on murder because I'm thinking about kissing him" distracting?

Harper: ...I plead the fifth. 😅

Amanda: YOU'RE GUILTY. Guilty of catching feelings. 😏

Erin: Forget the killer. We're invested in the romance subplot now. Keep us updated. On both.

Harper: Promise. Just need to figure out who killed Prudence *and* how not to fall face-first into a cider barrel next time I talk to him.

CHAPTER 25
CINNAMON STICK

The scent of cinnamon rolls and maple syrup wrapped around Harper like a hug the second she stepped into The Cinnamon Stick Café. Golden morning light filtered through lace curtains, glinting off the copper kettles lining the window shelf. Gabe was already there in a corner booth, sipping coffee, his flannel sleeves rolled to the elbows. Maggie sat across from him, stirring her pumpkin chai latte with the intensity of someone trying to decode a message from the foam.

Harper slid into the booth beside Maggie and let out a sigh as she set her tote bag on the seat next to her. "Sorry I'm late. I got caught up with something...unexpected."

Maggie perked up immediately. "What kind of unexpected? Spill."

Harper waved over the waitress—Tina, who wore a cinnamon stick pin on her apron—before turning back to her friends. "Okay. But first, let me order before my stomach eats itself."

Once her coffee and pumpkin spice pancakes were en route, she leaned forward, lowering her voice. "The other night, I was cleaning out Aunt Ellie's desk again, and I noticed this tiny groove on the side. It didn't look like a scratch—more like a seam."

Gabe raised an eyebrow. "A seam in wood?"

Maggie clapped her hands excitedly "Ohmygosh, was it a secret compartment?!"

Harper grinned. "Yes! When I pressed the seam, this hidden drawer popped open. Inside was a book-a leather-bound journal. And it had *my* name on an envelope with a letter from my Aunt."

Maggie's eyes went wide. "A book - like Aunt Ellie's secret musings?"

"More like...a log," Harper said, fishing it out of her tote. She set it on the table between their plates. "She kept a record of every quill she purchased for her collection. More importantly, she wrote down every time Vivian Hawthorn tried to buy the golden quill from her. It goes back decades. Vivian was obsessed with it and I have no idea why."

Gabe leaned in, his brow furrowed. "That's really odd."

"Aunt Ellie knew Vivian wasn't going to give up," Harper added. "One of the last entries said, *She's getting desperate.*"

The pancakes arrived, momentarily halting the intensity as they all dug in. Maple syrup dripped and conversation resumed with full mouths and flying theories.

Maggie pointed her fork at Harper. "Okay, so you think she stole your quill and murdered Prudence?"

Harper hesitated, chewing her food. "Well, I'm not sure. She seems to have a motive to steal the quill, but I can't find any connection between her and Prudence that would make her want to hurt her. By all accounts, Prudence and Vivian actually got along just fine."

"Hmmm," said Maggie thoughtfully. "So we have a thief, but no murderer. So back to the alibi hunt."

"It's been bothering me all night," Harper said, setting down her fork and wiping her mouth with her napkin. "If Vivian stole the quill from me just two weeks ago, and Vivian isn't the murderer....then how did the murderer get the quill? And why did the murderer kill Prudence with something so valuable?"

Maggie paused, bacon halfway to her mouth. "Right," she said slowly, lost in thought. "Why kill with a valuable item?"

"I need to confront Vivian. But first, let's compare notes and alibis.... go!" Harper said, and picked up her coffee to take a sip.

"Okay," Gabe said, rubbing his hands together. "I talked to Noah and Courtney. Solid alibis. "

Gabe rattled off a list of 10-12 other people he had verified alibis for, and as he explained them, Harper made notes in her notebook and phone. There were several places where people's alibis from Gabe matched up with information she'd gotten from others, making her feel even more confident about their work.

"Okay, this is great," Harper said.

She set down her coffee and took out her list, notebook and phone. She began filling the pair in on all the people she'd spoken with, explaining her interest in Evelyn, the feud about the studio, and Evelyn's verified alibi from the Major and the council members. After a few minutes, they were all caught up.

"Five minutes is enough time to do a lot of things," Maggie muttered. "But still. We need more."

Harper flipped to a fresh page in her notebook. "That leaves us with a few shaky spots."

She tapped her pen against the margin. "I'm starting with Vivian."

Gabe's jaw tightened. "Then we need to be careful. Especially you."

Harper smiled at him, heart thumping a little too loudly for this early in the day. "Careful's not really my thing. But I do have good friends watching my back."

Maggie raised her mug. "To friends. And pancakes. And solving murders before lunch."

They clinked mugs, and Harper allowed herself one quiet moment of comfort before diving back into the swirl of secrets and suspicions. The stack of clues was growing—and so was the danger.

The little brass bell jingled overhead as Harper, Gabe, and Maggie stepped out into the crisp morning air. The sun had risen high enough to burn off the last of the mist, and Main Street buzzed with sleepy small-town energy—someone sweeping their porch, a couple walking a golden retriever, the scent of firewood drifting from a nearby chimney.

Harper wrapped her scarf a little tighter as she crossed toward her SUV, parked along the curb just down from the café's window boxes still bursting with late-season mums.

"Alright," she said, keys in hand. "I'll head back to the shop and go through the rest of that ledger. Maybe there's something else I missed."

"I'll come by after I check on the orchard," Gabe offered. "We can go through it together."

"And I'll bring snacks," Maggie added, skipping a step ahead. "Or coffee. Or emergency doughnuts."

But Harper's steps slowed.

Something was off.

A small, sharp glint caught her eye—and then her stomach dropped.

"Uh... guys?"

They both turned just as she crouched near the back passenger-side tire.

Sticking out from the thick tread was a long, curved blade—kitchen knife by the look of it—buried deep enough to flatten the tire. Attached to the handle was a slip of folded paper, speared by the metal like a pinned moth.

Harper tugged the paper free, her fingers suddenly ice cold despite the sun on her back.

Maggie hovered over her shoulder. "What does it say?"

Harper unfolded it slowly. The handwriting was jagged and uneven, like it had been scrawled in a rush.

"Stop digging. You won't like what you find."

A beat of silence.

Then Gabe let out a slow, steady exhale. "Well. That's subtle."

Harper stared at the note, her heart thudding in her ears. The words looked like they were written in black marker, but the edges were smudged—maybe with rain, or... sweat?

Maggie glanced around, suddenly wary. "Someone saw us in there. Followed us. That means they're watching."

Harper folded the note and shoved it into her coat pocket. "Good. Let them."

Gabe placed a hand gently on her arm. "Harper—"

"No," she said, her voice low but steady. "I'm not stopping. Not now. Someone is scared. That means we're getting close."

Behind her, the breeze rattled the café's hanging sign, the metal bracket creaking just slightly. In the distance, church bells chimed the hour—but the warm charm of Fall felt just a little colder now.

Maggie crossed her arms. "Okay then. What's our next move?"

Harper stood up, her eyes narrowing toward the far end of Main Street.

"I'll call Deputy Russell to let him know what happened. Then, we try to find out who's watching. And what they're so desperate to hide."

The tire was flat. The threat was clear.

But Harper Whitmore wasn't going anywhere.

———

The tires hummed against the pavement as Gabe's truck cruised north on the winding two-lane highway. The local mechanic shop didn't have a new tire in Harper's size, so Gabe agreed to drive her to the closest major town, Traverse City, to get one. Orange and gold leaves fluttered across the windshield, catching on the wipers like confetti.

Gabe had a to-go coffee in hand, his flannel sleeves rolled up to his elbows and a Sullivan's Apple Orchard hat on. "You know," he said, "I didn't think tire shopping would make my top ten list of fall activities, but here we are."

Harper raised her eyebrows at him from the passenger seat. "It's a very exclusive bucket list. Right between apple pressing and being threatened by a murderer."

He glanced at her, one brow raised. "You're making jokes. That's either a good sign or a terrifying one."

"I've decided mild sarcasm is my coping mechanism," she said. "That, and baked goods."

"Speaking of baked goods," Gabe said. "Maggie told me you and Paul had some...quality control time yesterday."

Harper shot him a look. "Are you jealous of shortbread?"

"I mean, I can't compete with buttery carbs, Harper. I know my limits."

She laughed, the sound easy and light despite the tension of the past few days.

"For what it's worth, you rank higher than shortbread. Slightly."

"That's the nicest thing anyone's said to me all week."

She laughed and they fell into comfortable silence for a minute. Harper watched the trees blur past, a steady stream of color and sky.

Then Harper said, more quietly, "Do you think I'm doing the wrong thing? Poking around the case like this?"

Gabe was quiet for a beat, then said, "I think you're brave. And stubborn. And probably making the sheriff grind his teeth at night."

She smiled. "He's very good at silent disapproval."

"But I also think," Gabe continued, "you care about this place already. And you care about people you barely know, like Prudence. That tells me a lot about who you are."

As they crossed a rise in the road, Lake Michigan came into view —shimmering blue beneath the soft gray clouds.

"Thanks for coming with me to get my tire," she said.

Gabe turned toward her, a smirk on his face. "You didn't really give me a choice. You called me and said, 'Could you help me replace my tire or should I ask Maggie,' which—honestly—was one of the more aggressive flirtations I've received."

"I wasn't flirting," Harper feigned outrage. "I was being efficient."

"You were being adorable," Gabe said, taking his hat off and dropping it on the console between them. He ran his hand through his dark brown hair, and a few curls fell across his forehead.

Harper's pulse skipped a beat as she watched him. He looked at her and held her gaze a second longer than necessary. Then he gave a little sideways smile and put his hat on his head backwards. Her stomach flip flopped.

Traverse City lay ahead, and soon enough, they'd be headed back to Fall. For now, though, Harper enjoyed feeling like she was in her own little world with the gorgeous Gabe Sullivan.

CHAPTER 26
IN THE FAMILY

The next day, Harper paced the narrow aisle between the bookshelves, clutching the leather-bound book to her chest. Her heart pounded in her ears as she replayed the entries about Vivian Hawthorn over and over in her mind. She didn't enjoy confrontation, but now that the truth—or at least part of it—was in her hands, there was no turning back. The bell above the bookstore's door jingled, and Harper froze. There she was—Vivian Hawthorn, sweeping into Hearth & Quill with her usual air of confidence, her tailored coat impeccable, and her sharp eyes scanning the shop as if she owned the place. She almost seemed surprised to see Harper in her own store.

"Harper," Vivian said smoothly, a polite smile on her face. "You said it was a matter of life or death?"

Harper straightened, feeling the weight of the ledger in her hands. Her fingers tightened around the worn leather, and her jaw clenched. This wasn't going to be a polite conversation, and she knew it.

"Yes. I wanted to talk to you about something. I found..." Harper said, closing the distance and walking toward Vivian. She held up the ledger, "...this. Something in my aunt's desk...about you. About your repeated attempts to buy Hemingways Quill from her."

Vivian's smile faltered for just a moment, but she quickly recovered, her expression tightening into one of mild interest. "Is that so? Ellie was always quite thorough in her records."

"Yeah, she was," Harper said, her voice firm. "This doesn't paint a very pretty picture of you. You seemed determined to get the quill."

"I'm not sure why my past dealings with Eleanor are of any concern to you," she purred, picking an imaginary lint off of her jacket.

"You've been chasing this quill for years, throwing more money at it, practically begging my aunt for it. Why?"

Vivian's eyes darkened, her polished exterior cracking just slightly. "It's none of your concern, Harper. I made offers, your aunt refused. That's how business works."

"This isn't business," Harper cut her off, waving the leather book in the air, her pulse racing. "This is an obsession, Vivian. You were desperate—my aunt even thought you were dangerous."

Vivian's lips thinned and her gaze became stony. "Your aunt didn't know what she was talking about."

"Didn't she?" Harper shot back. She opened the ledger to one of the later entries and read aloud: "'Vivian seems obsessed with the quill. Why? What lengths will she go to to get it?'" Harper snapped the book shut, her eyes locked on Vivian's.

For a moment, the two women stood in tense silence, the air thick with unspoken threats. Vivian's eyes flickered toward the ledger, then back to Harper's face. She took a step forward, her voice low and cold.

"Your aunt was a fool," Vivian hissed, her poised demeanor evaporating. "I offered her a more than reasonable amount for the quill!"

"It doesn't matter. It didn't belong to you!" Harper shot back. "You couldn't *buy* it from my aunt, so you *stole* it from me?!"

Vivian's calm facade cracked just slightly, her voice lowering, hardening. "That quill belongs *to my* family, Harper. We own the house on Walloon Lake where Hemingway spent his summers. It belongs to me!

Harper's brow furrowed as she processed Vivian's words. "So you think that because Hemingway lived in that house, the quill is rightfully yours?"

"You don't even know what happened, do you?" She laughed scornfully. "It's not a matter of 'thinking,' Harper. It *is* ours. Your aunt—" she spat the word with disdain, "—stole it from us!"

Harper shook her head, feeling her anger rise. "What? Aunt Ellie was a good woman, she wouldn't have—"

"I'm not going to continue discussing this," Vivian said, turning to leave.

"You're a thief and I'm going to talk to the sheriff," Harper said quietly.

"You twit!" Vivian spat, spinning back around. "Your aunt stole the quill from under my family *decades* ago. My family bought the house from the Hemingway family. The price negotiated included all contents of the home, but the person managing the estate held a small sale prior to handing over the keys. Your aunt and her father attended the estate sale, and bought the quill and a handful of other items for dirt cheap. They knew what they were doing - they knew anything owned by Hemingway would be an object of "literary tourism" and worth a fortune. She did it anyway. The executor tracked down most of the items that had been accidentally purchased and returned them to my family, but some people refused to return the items. Like your aunt and her father. So we even offered to buy it back at a profit, and they *still* refused. And that's gone on for decades."

Spit was forming at the corners of Vivian's mouth and her eyes looked wild. Harper was starting to feel a bit nervous.

"I...I didn't know," Harper said, quietly, the ledger still clutched in her hands. "None of that was ever - my aunt didn't...," she trailed off, her voice faltering.

For a moment, there was silence. Vivian stared at Harper, her expression unreadable. But then, slowly, her lips curled into a smile—cold and calculating.

"It's not just about sentiment, Harper," she said quietly. "The quill has...a certain influence. I'm a writer. Hemingway would want a writer to have it, not to have it sitting in a box in a dusty old bookstore. The quill should be mine!"

"Vivian, do you really believe that this quill—an old pen—can give you some kind of advantage, like it's magical or something?"

Vivian smiled cooly. "You can scoff if you like, but the world is filled with objects that inspire others and carry meaning. And yes, Hemingway's quill is one of them."

Harper's stomach churned. It was clear now—Vivian wasn't just obsessed with the quill because of its historical connection to her family. She believed it held some sort of power, some kind of mystical influence over the words it wrote. And Harper had the sinking feeling that this obsession had pushed Vivian to dangerous lengths.

"I'm sorry that this happened, Vivian. But that doesn't make what you did right," Harper said calmly. "When all is said and done, I believe the quill should be returned to me."

"You already have it, now give it to me!" Vivian shrieked.

"What?" Harper was confused. "I don't have it. You used it to murder Prudence!"

Vivian's eyes widened with shock. "What? No- I didn't murder anybody."

"I'm running out of patience, Vivian," Harper said, exasperated. "Let's just call the sheriff and let them clear this all up."

Vivian looked completely confused. "You can call the sheriff. I admit that I stole the quill. But I would never hurt anybody, certainly not Prudence. Wait a minute — are you saying you don't have the quill?"

Harper didn't respond.

Vivian shook her head, as if to clear it of thoughts.

"If you don't have the quill, who does?" Vivian asked, confused.

"It was found in Prudence's neck," Harper said quietly, watching Vivian's reaction. She gasped and her hand flew to cover her mouth.

"Harper - I swear...I would never! My nephew saw the quill in your shop in an unlocked case. When he told me, I was tempted, I'll admit. And then at the grand reopening celebration, I just snatched it. I know that what I did was wrong, but I didn't kill anyone. I only had the quill a few days before it went missing. I thought you stole it back. That's why I came into your shop a few times over the last few weeks. I figured I'd see it back in the case and I'd know what had happened. Harper - I would never hurt anyone."

Harper's head was spinning. If Vivian was telling the truth, then she had stolen the quill from Harper- only for someone else to steal it from her and use it to murder Prudence?

CHAPTER 27
FRIENDSHIP

The next day was a busy day at Hearth & Quill, and Harper was shelving a new shipment of books when the front door jingled open, and Paul stepped inside. Lady pranced along behind him, a bright smile on her tiny face.

"Am I interrupting?" he asked, smiling. He was holding a small white bakery box.

Harper looked up and smiled. "Never! Come here, Lady!"

The small dog trotted over to Harper happily, accepting pets and few scratches behind the ears. When she was satisfied, she turned and cheerfully returned to stand at Paul's feet.

Harper said, "Ooh! What did you bring me?"

Paul lifted the box like a prized offering. "New item. Cinnamon-maple shortbread. I need an honest opinion before I add it to the inn's rotation."

She opened the lid and took a whiff. "Paul, this smells like a hug."

He chuckled. "High praise. Try it and tell me if it tastes like a *hug* or a *slightly disappointing handshake.*"

Harper took a pastry and a napkin. She took a large bite and closed her eyes. "Definitely a hug. Maybe even a warm flannel hug."

Paul grinned, then hesitated before sliding into one of the overstuffed chairs near the stone fireplace. "I need to sit a spell."

"I'll join you for a bit," Harper said as she sat across from him. Lady walked over, curling up at Harper's feet.

"Now that's high praise," Paul said, indicating Lady's position at her feet with raised eyebrows. "She really likes you!"

"The feeling is mutual," Harper said, smiling warmly.

Paul leaned forward and looked concerned. "I heard about the... incident with your tire. Word's getting around."

Harper began playing with the napkin in her hand, twisting and untwisting it.

"Yeah," she admitted. "Can you believe that? "

Harper filled Paul in with the recent developments, from Ellie's letter and the notebook, to the various alibis that she, Maggie and Gabe had collected.

"You've been busy," he said, sounding impressed.

"I have. Now Mags and Gabe want me to back off, but I feel like I'm really onto something if the murderer is feeling threatened."

Paul thought for a moment and said, "So... who do you think is the murderer?"

"I thought it was Vivian. I confronted her yesterday," Harper replied.

Paul's brows lifted. "That was... bold."

"She stole something from my shop. A quill that belonged to Ernest Hemingway." Harper's voice was steady, but her hands gave her away— restlessly twisting the napkin. "I thought she killed Prudence over it. But now... I'm not so sure."

Paul's eyebrows raised dramatically. He leaned in. "Did she admit to anything?"

"Yes, Vivian admitted to stealing the quill. But she was shocked to learn that it was used to kill Prudence. I thought it was common knowledge, but I forget not everyone was there that night, and details haven't been shared with the public. Vivian seemed shocked. I don't think she did it."

Paul frowned slightly. "So if she stole the quill...and the quill was used to kill Prudence..."

"Exactly," Harper said exasperatedly. "What the heck happened? Vivian steals the quill and within days, someone steals it from her? What are the odds of that? And *why* was it used to murder Prudence?"

Paul was quiet for a long moment. Then he said gently, "You don't have to carry all this alone, Harper. Just let the police take care of this."

She looked up at him, meeting his steady gaze. "I know. But I also can't stop now. Not when the truth is so close."

Paul reached over and pushed the rest of the shortbread toward her. "Then at least stay fueled. Cinnamon-maple flannel hugs for courage."

She smiled, grateful. "You're a good person, Paul."

"And you," he said, standing to leave, "are a very stubborn one. But I like that."

After a quick wink and a hug, Paul scooped up Lady Von Trapp and left Harper alone with her thoughts, her shortbread, and her books.

CHAPTER 28
VIVIAN

By late morning, Harper walked into Harvest Roast for a much needed coffee break. She absentmindedly flipped through her notes while breathing in the aroma of freshly brewed coffee. The list she'd gotten from Maggie at the tea shop looked like a detective's murder board, notes in the margins, names circled and linked to other names, times and locations scribbled sideways and multiple different colored pens. She was deep in thought, trying to piece together the scattered bits of information about Prudence's murder, when the door swung open, and Gabe stepped inside.

He spotted her at the corner table and made his way over, a serious look on his face. Harper raised her eyebrows in silent question as he slid into the seat across from her.

"I have confirmed alibis for Luke and Matt," Gabe said without preamble, his tone low but deliberate. "They were seen at the time of Prudence's murder. First they were at the market dropping off a load of our new apple cilantro salsa... and then they went to Harvest Roast for a coffee before they headed back to the orchard."

Harper sat up a little straighter, her pen hovering over her notebook and the resident list. "Okay...two less people to worry about."

Gabe leaned forward, resting his forearms on the table.

Harper nodded and said, "I've been going back over everything and I'm more convinced than ever." She had filled him in on the details of her confrontation with Vivian when he stopped by the bookstore the day before.

"I think it's time you involved the sheriff," Gabe said. "Vivian is the link to the quill. And even though she seemed surprised when she found out it was the murder weapon, she might have been lying - and she might have murdered Prudence."

The late afternoon shadows stretched across the winding road as Harper led Sheriff Carlisle to Vivian's estate. The closer they got, the heavier Harper's dread grew. Every clue had pointed back to Vivian: her strange behavior, her obsession with Harper's bookstore, and the fact that she stole the murder weapon. Harper was convinced that whatever secrets Vivian had been keeping were at the heart of everything.

As they pulled up to the iron gates, Harper felt a shiver of anticipation. Sheriff Carlisle parked behind her, stepping out of his patrol car with a cautious look on his face.

"Harper, I want to be clear we are just here to chat with Vivian," he reminded her, giving the dark, silent house a wary glance.

"I know. She admitted she stole the quill, Sheriff," Harper replied, swallowing the lump in her throat. "But I think she's somehow involved with Prudence's murder. She was the last one with the quill."

The sheriff nodded, resting a hand on his holster. "Alright. But stay behind me."

They walked up the stone path together, Harper's heartbeat pounding in her ears. When they reached the front door, they found it slightly ajar. Sheriff Carlisle glanced back at her, unclipping his gun. Harper's unease grew.

"Who would leave their door open?" Harper whispered, her heart pounding.

"Don't touch anything," he whispered, stepping inside first and scanning the dimly lit entryway. He called out. "Vivian? It's Sheriff Carlisle. We need to talk."

There was only silence, thick and oppressive. They moved cautiously through the grand hallway, each step amplifying the ominous stillness that hung in the air. The faint scent of lavender lingered, but it was tinged with something metallic that sent a chill up Harper's spine.

"Vivian?" Harper called out, her voice trembling. They approached her study, the door slightly open, and a dim light spilling out.

Sheriff Carlisle held out a hand, gesturing for Harper to wait behind him as he carefully pushed open the door. But when they both stepped inside, Harper's breath caught in her throat, her blood turning to ice.

Vivian lay slumped over her desk, her hair disheveled and her hand stretched toward a scattered pile of papers, as if she'd been reaching for something just as she collapsed. Her silk blouse was stained with blood, pooling darkly beneath her and spreading across the polished wood.

"Oh my God," Harper whispered, stumbling back, her hand clamping over her mouth.

Sheriff Carlisle moved closer, his face a mask of grim determination. He pressed two fingers to Vivian's wrist, then looked at Harper, his expression confirming what she already knew. "She's dead."

Harper's head was swimming, trying to reconcile the scene before her.

Her gaze fell to the scattered papers on Vivian's desk, her eyes catching on a half-written letter in Vivian's unmistakable cursive.

Harper turned her head to the side to read the hastily written lines.

"Harper, I'm so sorry. Please be caref—..."

The ink smeared, but her message was chillingly clear. Vivian had been trying to leave Harper a note, a desperate attempt to reveal something before she was silenced.

Sheriff Carlisle moved to her side, glancing at the note. "She was writing you a note..."

Harper nodded, the horror of her realization settling over her. "Yes. And it looks like she was trying to warn me."

Sheriff Carlisle's face darkened. "Then we need to follow this trail. Whoever's behind this isn't done yet."

Before they left the study, Sheriff Carlisle slid the letter to the side. Underneath was Vivian's last will and testament. *Why would Vivian be reading her own will while writing Harper a letter,* he thought. They left the study, as the weight of the truth bore down on Harper. Vivian's murder had torn open everything she thought she knew, leaving only one undeniable conclusion: the real killer was still out there, and they were closer than she'd ever realized.

Harper sat on the floor of her apartment, back pressed against the brick wall beneath the window, knees drawn up to her chest. Her hands were still trembling and her mind was going a mile a minute. She kept picturing Vivian's body —cold, pale, lifeless. Not sophisticated or beautiful or polished. Just... gone.

A soft knock at the door was followed by the gentle creak of it opening. Maggie stepped inside without waiting for a response, holding two mugs, each with little tea bags hanging over the edge. She looked around, spotted Harper by the window, and exhaled a breath so full of heartbreak it barely made a sound.

She crossed the room slowly and set the mugs down on the table before sliding to the floor beside her friend.

"Here," Maggie whispered, slipping a cozy knit blanket from the back of the couch around Harper's shoulders. "It's the one you love. Smells like vanilla and firewood."

Harper didn't respond.

Maggie didn't push.

Instead, she reached for one of the mugs, wrapped Harper's hands around the warm ceramic, and nudged gently, like she was coaxing a kitten out of the rain.

"It's chamomile. It'll help..." Maggie said softly.

"She wasn't the killer, Mags," Harper finally said, her voice cracking. "Vivian didn't kill Prudence."

"I know," Maggie said softly.

"I was so sure when I was talking to her. She was so vicious and angry when she was talking about Aunt Ellie, and I got a glimpse...I thought she could have...I mean—she lied, she stole the quill, she threatened me—"

"But she didn't kill anyone," Maggie said, brushing a loose strand of Harper's hair behind her ear.

"No." Harper agreed.

Maggie exhaled. "And whoever did... just killed again."

Harper's eyes brimmed with tears she refused to let fall. "This is my fault."

"No." Maggie's voice was firm. "No, it's not."

"If I hadn't pushed, if I hadn't asked questions, maybe she'd still—"

Maggie grabbed her shoulders gently and made Harper face her. "Harper Whitmore, listen to me. Vivian Hawthorn was already in danger. She got too close to something, just like Prudence did. This isn't about you. This is about a killer who's willing to do anything to stay hidden."

"But I am getting close," Harper whispered. "Someone's scared, and now they've killed twice. What if I'm next?"

Maggie swallowed hard and held Harper tighter. "I think you should stop."

Harper blinked.

"I'm serious," Maggie said, her voice cracking for the first time. "Please, Harp. Let the authorities handle it. Let Sheriff Carlisle figure it out. You've done more than enough."

Harper was quiet for a long time, her gaze drifting to the worn journal from Aunt Ellie on the table, next to the teacups. She thought of the hidden drawer, of Vivian's obsession, of Prudence, of the knife she found in her own tire.

"Ellie would want me to finish it," she said quietly.

"Harper, no. No she wouldn't. She would want you to stay safe," Maggie said, her eyes glassy. "That's what *I* want. That's what all of your friends want."

The sun had dipped below the rooftops, casting the room in amber shadows. From below, faint laughter rose from the street, where life in Fall went on—unaware, or maybe unwilling to acknowledge that something dark was growing in their golden little town.

Maggie said nothing else. She just stayed beside Harper, wrapping an arm around her as they sat in silence, two friends clinging to any semblance of calm as the storm came crashing in.

ATL GIRLS 🖋️🫖🍷📖

Harper: You guys. I just found someone dead. Again.

Erin: WHAT! AGAIN?!?! HARPER!!!

Amanda: Wait, wait, wait. Start from the beginning. Are you okay?? Like *actually* okay?

Harper: Not really. It was Vivian. And she was writing ME a letter when she was killed!

Erin: Holy shit. Vivian as in "This Quill Is Rightfully Mine" Vivian?? She was *so* suspicious, though!!

Amanda: She was! I thought it was her for sure. Harper, are the police there? Did you call the sheriff?

Harper: Yes, the sheriff and the deputy both came. And the whole town has probably heard by now because she was writing me a letter. How weird is that?

Amanda: Oh, sweetie 😔 Do you want us to come up there? I can bring wine. And Erin can bring snacks. And sarcasm.

Erin: And pepper spray. And a portable fingerprint kit I found online because CLEARLY YOU'RE LIVING IN A TRUE CRIME PODCAST. 🕵️

Harper: I want you to come, but not in the middle of all of this mess. And not with a fingerprint kit. LOL Maggie would flip for that, though.

Amanda: How's she holding up?

Harper: She made me tea, wrapped me in a blanket, and begged me to stop investigating. Which I *totally understand* but also...there's now a *double* murderer on the loose.

Erin: And they're getting scared.

Amanda: And that means YOU need to be careful. Like, next-level careful. Maybe even... *cautious,* which I know is not your thing. 😶

Harper: I know. I just don't know how to walk away now. Vivian didn't kill Prudence. Which means someone killed *both* of them. And that someone is still pretending to be one of my quirky neighbors who runs a shop, or bakes apple pie or talks about the weather like they don't have a body count.

Erin: UGH. Small towns sound terrifying.

Amanda: Okay, let's stop spiraling. Harper - take a bath. Eat something. And please, please have someone come over to your place tonight.

Harper: Gabe's coming over. He bringing apple cider donuts.

Erin: The man *gets it.* Marry him immediately. 😂

Amanda: Stay safe, Harp. We love you. And we're here. Always.

Harper: Love you both. Also, if I get murdered, *please* make sure I get a really good podcast episode.

And *no one* better say "she lit up a room."

Erin: Don't even joke about that! But absolutely not. Your episode title will be: "The Bookstore Babe Who Refused to Die Quietly."

Amanda: Tagline: "She had a latte questions and one killer instinct." ☕🔍

Harper: 😄 Okay fine. If I go down, at least let me go down *with a good pun.*

CHAPTER 29
BACK OFF

Harper glanced around the nearly empty orchard, the sky overhead darkening as evening began to settle in. She spotted Luke near the old barn, stacking crates from the day's harvest, his face flushed from the work. Normally, she'd have no problem striking up a conversation with him, but today, a knot of dread twisted in her stomach. She couldn't control the doubt that was creeping into her head about everyone and everything.

Her suspicions had begun small—a passing thought she couldn't shake, a lingering feeling that something didn't add up. Luke was at the orchard on the day Prudence was murdered, and he was near the McIntosh trees where she died. He must know something.

She took a deep breath and walked toward him, steeling herself. "Hey, Luke," she called, trying to keep her tone casual.

He looked up, brushing his hands off on his jeans, his expression friendly as usual. "Hey, Harper. What brings you out here this late?"

"Just getting more McIntosh for the Local Business display at my shop," she said, forcing a smile. "I keep thinking back to the day Prudence was killed, and, well, it's hard to let go of all these unanswered questions, you know?"

Luke nodded, his brow furrowing slightly. "I get that. It's been strange around here since then. And now Vivian."

Harper nodded. She took a tentative step closer, her heart pounding. "That day, you didn't happen to see anything unusual, did you? I mean, anything out of the ordinary?"

Luke paused, his gaze drifting to the barn, as if replaying the day in his mind. "Nothing that I'd call unusual. Just a typical day in the orchard until we shut down the McIntosh section. Why?"

Harper forced a shrug, though her pulse quickened. "Just wondering, I guess. It's strange, isn't it? Why would Gabe shut down the very section that the murder happened in?"

Luke nodded, his expression thoughtful. "Not really. We shut down sections a lot, if we're cleaning, spraying, harvesting, something like that. At the time, I just thought that we must have been doing something there. But now that I think about it, and knowing Prudence died in that area... it's hard _not_ to question it."

She took another step closer, feeling her palms grow clammy. "Luke, did you see anyone here at the orchard between 2-4 on Friday?" The question hung heavy in the air, and Harper braced herself, her nerves prickling with each second that passed.

"No," he said. "Just us and Jake."

"Jake?" Harper asked, surprised. "Why was the deputy here?"

"He's a buddy of ours. He and Connor were up front by the orchard, while we cleaned up the tarps."

Harper swallowed and as she looked at him, her blood ran cold. It came rushing back to her...the flapping sound the night she found Prudence's body. It had been the sound of a tarp snapping in the wind.

Harper paced around Hearth & Quill's back office, her thoughts racing. Her conversation with Luke had rattled her more than she wanted to admit, and the weight of the new suspicion pressing down on her shoulders was almost too much to bear alone. She had to confirm Jake's whereabouts. Harper locked the front door of the shop, the click echoing through the quiet bookstore. She sighed, slipping the key into her coat pocket and turning toward the back staircase.

Something caught her eye on the checkout counter.

A folded piece of parchment.

It wasn't hers.

She approached slowly, heart thudding. The paper was thick, yellowed slightly at the edges—stationery she recognized. It had come from the vintage writing desk in the children's loft. She hadn't touched that drawer in days.

Harper's name was written in neat block letters on the front. Nothing else...just *HARPER*.

She unfolded it with cautious fingers.

Some stories are better left unfinished. Back off.

No signature. Eight words in dark black ink.

Harper's throat tightened and she dropped the paper to the ground. She scanned around the dim shop, shadows stretching long across the floorboards, the corners suddenly too dark, too still.

Someone had been here, inside her shop.

Someone who didn't want her digging deeper.

Her hands trembled as she reached for her phone. She called Deputy Russell, then quickly typed out messages to Maggie and Gabe. She was trembling so much she pressed her hand against the counter to steady herself.

This wasn't just a mystery anymore.

It was a warning.

And it was personal.

CHAPTER 30
DEPUTY RUSSELL

After just a few minutes, a sharp knock echoed through the quiet shop and Harper froze, her heart leaping into her throat. She wasn't expecting anyone this soon. The shop was closed, and it was already dark outside. Her hand instinctively moved to her phone on the counter as she turned towards the door, every nerve on edge.

Harper hesitated for a moment, then crossed the shop floor and unlocked the door. It creaked slightly as she pulled it open.

Deputy Jake Russell stood on the threshold, his silhouette framed by the dim light from the street outside. His expression was unreadable, but his posture was tense. Without a word, he stepped inside as Harper closed the door behind him, the click of the latch echoing in the stillness of the room.

"Harper," Jake said, his voice low, eerily calm. "We need to talk."

Her pulse quickened, a cold knot tightening in her chest. She'd called Jake, but now that he was actually here, something felt...off. He'd arrived so fast. Too fast. She had quiet, gnawing doubts that maybe Jake wasn't as trustworthy as he seemed. The way he'd been on the outskirts of the investigation, the fact that he was the last to arrive on the scene when Prudence was found... And now he shows up almost immediately after she called. Was he just lurking in the shadows, waiting for her to be alone?

"Jake," Harper managed, her voice barely above a whisper. "How did you get here so fast?"

His eyes flicked around the shop before settling on her again, unreadable. "It's about the investigation," he said, stepping forward. "I've been thinking."

Harper took a subtle step back, her mind racing. She suddenly felt vulnerable and afraid of Deputy Russell. She was alone in the shop and there was a double murderer on the loose.

"Thinking about what?" she asked, trying to keep her voice steady, even as her heart hammered in her chest.

Jake's boots scuffed against the wooden floor as he took another step closer, his face cast in shadow. "About you," he said softly. "About the way you've been getting involved in the investigation."

Her hand inched toward the phone, her eyes darting toward the back door, calculating how quickly she could make a run for it. But Jake was standing between her and the exit.

"You shouldn't have been poking around so much, Harper," he continued, his tone taking on a hard edge. "People in this town don't like their secrets being exposed."

Harper's breath hitched. *Oh my gosh. It's him! Jake's the killer!*

"Jake..." she began, her voice shaking now. "What are you trying to say?"

He took another step forward, his face illuminated briefly by the flickering fire. The tension was suffocating, every muscle in Harper's body screaming for her to run, but she was rooted in place. She could feel her pulse pounding in her ears as she reached for her phone, her fingers trembling.

Jake's eyes flicked down to her hand, and for a split second, his expression changed—something softer, almost concerned. "Harper, wait—"

Before he could finish, Harper's phone slipped from her grasp and clattered onto the floor. The noise shattered the tension, and in a panicked motion, Harper turned to bolt for the back door.

"Harper, stop!" Jake called out, his voice urgent now.

Her hand was on the door handle when she felt his grip on her arm, firm but not harsh. She screamed, the adrenaline coursing through her making it come out in a ragged stutter. Her stomach dropped and she realized she was trapped.

But Jake's grip loosened almost immediately, and when she turned to face him, she saw something she hadn't expected—worry. His eyes, once cold and unreadable, were filled with genuine concern.

"I'm not going to hurt you," Jake said quietly, his voice steady but sincere. He held up his hands, showing her his palms. "I'm trying to protect you."

Harper's breath came in short, shallow bursts, her heart still racing as she searched his face for any sign of deception. But there was none. He stepped back, giving her space. The fear that had been coiling inside her began to unravel, replaced by confusion.

"Protect me?" she repeated, her voice barely above a whisper.

Jake nodded, his gaze unwavering. "I came because you called, Harper. And I think you're right to be afraid. Someone in this town killed Prudence, and then Vivian and I'm afraid you might be next."

Harper swallowed hard, her mind reeling. "Why me?"

"Because everyone in town knows you've been trying to solve the case," Jake admitted, running a hand through his hair. "You've been questioning everyone and I'm worried that the killer knows you've been getting closer to the truth and will see you as a threat. Plus the tire and now the note. Can I see it?"

The tension between them eased slightly, though Harper's pulse still thrummed in her ears. She felt a mixture of relief and lingering suspicion, but the more she looked at Jake, the more convinced she became that he wasn't lying.

"I'm sorry," she said quietly, her voice trembling. "I think this is all getting to me a little bit. I thought you were the killer."

Jake's expression softened, and he shook his head. "It's not me.

I'm sorry I scared you, but you can trust me. I raced over because I was concerned about you. Now can you show me the note?"

Harper hesitated for a long moment, the fear still clinging to her. But the sincerity in his voice, the concern in his eyes, and her own instinct told her she could believe Jake Russell.

"Okay," she said finally, her voice steadying. She held out the note to him. "I trust you."

Jake let out a breath of relief and nodded. "Good. Because whoever's behind this isn't going to stop until they're caught. And we're running out of time."

Less than 10 minutes later, the door burst open with a violent jingle of the bell, followed by the unmistakable sounds of boots and hurried footsteps. Maggie swept in first, cheeks flushed and scarf trailing behind her like a cape. Gabe followed close behind, his expression dark with concern.

"Okay," Maggie said, hands on her hips, "where's the note, and who do I have to throat-punch?"

Harper stepped out from behind the counter, retrieved the folded parchment from the floor and held it out to Maggie. "Good to see you too."

Gabe crossed the room in three long strides and pulled her into a hug. She felt his heart hammering through his shirt. "Are you okay?"

"I'm fine," Harper said softly, relaxing for a moment into Gabe's firm embrace. "Just a little... rattled."

Maggie snatched the note from Harper's hand and read it, her eyes narrowing. "'Some stories are better left unfinished. Back off.'" She held it out as if it was toxic. "Rude *and* cliché. Coward."

Gabe gave Harper one more squeeze, then let her go gently. He took the note next, frowning. "Whoever left this wasn't just trying to scare you. They're warning you. That means you're close to something."

Harper nodded. "It was left on the counter. I'd just locked up and was coming down from the loft when I saw it."

"Which means," Maggie said, spinning toward the door, "whoever left it was *in here*. While you were upstairs. That's not just creepy—it's brazen."

They all went quiet for a moment, the only sound the low hum of the space heater and the faint creak of the old wooden floors settling.

Harper crossed her arms, cold now that Gabe wasn't holding her. "What if I really am getting too close? What if I saw something—*or someone*—and didn't even realize it?"

"Then you're in more danger than we thought," Gabe said, his voice low.

Maggie plopped onto the arm of one of the reading chairs. "Okay, let's run this down. Who knew you were here tonight? Who's been acting twitchy? Who has just enough of a flair for melodrama to write something like this?"

Harper managed a small smile. "Hmm... just everyone in Fall?"

"Exactly," Maggie replied. "This is a town where people still label their casserole dishes with embossed initials and leave anonymous notes in church pews."

Gabe's brow furrowed. "Let's think smaller. Who benefits from the case going cold? Who had something to lose if Prudence started talking? And if Vivian didn't kill her... then someone else did. Someone who's still out there."

They all exchanged glances.

The warmth of the bookstore had suddenly taken on a different edge—like the cozy glow had dimmed just slightly, shadows stretching into corners that hadn't seemed suspicious before.

Harper straightened. "I'm not backing down. Whoever left that note clearly thinks I'm on the right trail. And that means I need to keep going."

Maggie groaned. "Of course you do. You're a tiny, autumn-themed freight train."

Gabe gave her a look of half-warning, half-resignation. "Just promise me you won't do anything alone. Not again."

Harper met his eyes. "Deal. We do it together."

Maggie raised her hand. "By 'we,' I assume you mean me too. I've already cleared my schedule."

Harper smiled, her heart buoyed by their presence. "Then let's figure out who wants this story silenced."

CHAPTER 31
FAMILY TIES

As Harper opened the store the next morning, she saw a Sullivan's Orchard truck sitting out front of the bookshop. She walked outside, leaning down to peer inside, seeing Luke and Ryan. "Hey guys," Harper said, confused. "What brings you to my little corner of town?"

"Uh, hey Harper, " Luke said, drumming his fingers on the steering wheel. "Gabe sent us over to do a few things for your shop. Install some cameras and change your locks."

"Oh, he did, huh?" Harper said, surprised.

"He did," Ryan said, getting out of the truck and closing the door.

"And I suppose it would be rude to turn down such a generous offer of help?" Harper said.

"Indeed it would," said Ryan. "But we'll be fast. We've installed similar cameras all over the orchard lately. I think I could do this in my sleep."

"Thank you," she said.

"Don't thank us... we go where the boss tells us," Luke said, jumping out of the truck and grabbing his tool belt.

"Still," Harper said. "Can I at least get you guys a coffee or something?"

"That'd be great, thanks," Ryan said, grabbing his gear.

Harper headed over to Harvest Roast and when she walked in, she found Gabe sitting in the window, looking out and watching her store.

"Ummm...hi?" She said questioningly.

Gabe laughed. "I'm caught, huh?"

"How long have you been here?" Harper asked, sliding into the chair across from him.

"Not long," Gabe said.

At the same time Melanie said "... since we opened."

Harper laughed. "Look, I appreciate your concern, I really do. But this is a little overboard. The cameras, the locks, and you're staking out my business? You have your own business to run."

"It's true. But that's the beauty of being the boss," he chuckled. "I shut down the orchard for today."

"That's incredibly generous of you, but you don't have to do that for me—"Harper said, looking at her lap.

"Harper?" Gabe said with a clear voice. "I don't have to do it, but I want to. I don't think it's overboard. Someone in town knows you're onto them and wants to scare you. I have to help keep you safe."

Their eyes met, just for a moment, but it was enough. Gabe reached out his hand. Without hesitation, Harper slid her hand into his. Their fingers laced together in an unspoken understanding that neither of them dared to name. It was a simple touch, but it carried a quiet promise that settled into Harper's chest like the first ember of something that might soon catch fire.

Melanie interrupted the moment by arriving at the table. Seeing

Gabe and Harper's intertwined fingers, she raised her eyebrows and smiled. "Okay, then," she said and handed over three coffees to-go. She offered to refill Gabe's cup.

"Oh no. If I drink any more coffee today, I'll never sleep again," he laughed, covering the cup with his free hand.

He squeezed Harper's hand before letting go, then took two of the cups of coffee to help carry them back to the bookstore. Together they strolled to the bookshop, grins on both of their faces.

Harper and Gabe sat in the cozy chairs in the bookshop's window, watching Luke and Ryan work. Before long, they started talking about the murder and Luke and Ryan joined them in the nook, sitting and chatting. Harper tapped her pencil against the page of notes, then looked at Gabe.

"One thing has been bothering me. You told Luke and Ryan not to harvest the McIntosh apples the afternoon that Prudence was killed, but you told me they *were* harvesting them when we drove over there to get a bushel."

Luke nodded, leaning back in his chair as if it were the most ordinary thing in the world. "Yup," he said, glancing at Ryan, who nodded in agreement.

Gabe's brow furrowed, his confusion turning into something sharper, more intense. "*I* told you not to harvest?" he repeated slowly, staring at Luke. "That doesn't sound right. I was working with the Honey Crisps that morning before I headed to the square. I never said a thing about leaving the McIntosh trees alone. Why would I?"

Ryan blinked, exchanging a glance with Luke. "I thought it was strange," he said, scratching his head. "But when Connor said you didn't want us near the McIntoshes, we weren't going to argue with you. There's always something to harvest! We just moved onto — well, now I don't remember."

Luke laughed and took a sip of his now cold coffee. "Yeah, the harvest days all start to blend together, don't they?"

Harper felt her stomach twist, a chill crawling up her spine. "Wait," she said, her voice barely above a whisper. "Gabe didn't tell you not to harvest? Not Gabe, but Connor? You're sure?"

Luke nodded, his face showing the first hint of unease. "Yeah, Connor. But Connor was just passing on Gabe's order. It's all the same, we didn't question it."

Harper glanced at Gabe, whose face had gone pale, his gaze fixed on the table as if he were piecing together something truly horrifying.

"I didn't ask Connor to tell you that," Gabe said slowly, his voice a mix of shock and anger. "Connor cleared the orchard. He didn't want anyone near the McIntosh trees..."

"...because he knew Prudence would be there, " Harper finished quietly.

The full weight of her words settled over the room, filling the silence with a dreadful tension. Harper's mind raced, pieces of the puzzle snapping into place with a terrifying clarity.

"Wait - what's Connor's last name?" Harper asked, flipping through her sheet of names.

"Hawthorn," Gabe said. And then his eyes went wide.

The realization hit her like a cold slap. Vivian had said she had a nephew who had seen the quill at Harper's shop. Connor was Vivian's nephew! Her heart started pounding. Connor had been at the bookshop when she first arrived in town, helping Harper clean up to get ready to reopen. He must seen the quill and told his aunt about it. Connor worked at the orchard, and that gave him the ability to ensure the orchard was empty when he met up with Prudence. She still didn't understand what happened between those two events, but Harper suddenly felt certain that Connor was behind Prudence's death.

"Connor Hawthorn...," Harper said, talking in choppy half sentences. "Vivian's nephew. He cleared the orchard. He killed Prudence. "

Ryan and Luke's eyes widened, dawning horror flickering in their faces. "Connor? You think Connor is the killer...?" Ryan stammered, his voice trailing off as the truth set in.

But Harper's mind was already racing ahead. "Where is he?" she asked, her voice urgent.

"I think..." Luke's face drained of color as he remembered. "He's supposed to be meeting with Maggie at the orchard. She mentioned something about discussing plans for the autumn showcase."

Harper's heart dropped, and she whipped her gaze to Gabe. The fear in his eyes mirrored her own. "Maggie," she said, her voice barely concealing the panic building in her chest.

Gabe didn't hesitate. "We need to get to the orchard. Now."

They bolted for the door. Gabe shouted, "Truck keys!" Luke fished them from his pocket and tossed them over. Ryan stood frozen, eyebrows furrowed, still processing what they'd uncovered.

Harper couldn't wait. "Stay here in case Maggie comes here...and call the sheriff!" she called over her shoulder before dashing out the door and jumping into the truck.

Gabe slid behind the wheel and started it with practiced ease. The two of them locked eyes for one second, long enough to register the panic on both of their faces. Gabe took off towards the orchard. Every scenario flashed through Harper's mind—the orchard silent and secluded, Maggie meeting Connor there, unaware of the danger. Her pulse thundered, and she felt a sickening fear clawing at her throat.

"Maybe we're wrong..." Gabe's voice was rough and thick with worry.

"We aren't," Harper replied, breathless. She pulled her phone out of her pocket and dialed Maggie, but no answer. She fired off several texts in quick succession: "call me," "where are you," "Please respond, Mags." Harper couldn't shake the mental image of Maggie, alone with Connor, unaware that she was with the killer.

As they neared the edge of town, the rows of apple trees began to come into view, their branches casting dark, twisted shadows over the ground. Harper spotted the faint glow of the barn's exterior light, and a new wave of fear surged through her. She had to get to Maggie —before it was too late.

CHAPTER 32
INTO THE CIDER SHED

Harper's heart raced as she and Gabe parked the truck and sprinted out towards the cider making barn. Harper had called Maggie at least 10 times on the drive over, but she hadn't answered the calls or texts. A sinking feeling had settled in Harper's stomach.

Gabe called out "Maggie?" his voice low but urgent. They both stood still, listening. No response.

Harper exchanged a worried glance with Gabe before running towards the cider press barn. When they got there, Gabe threw open the door and Harper noticed something that made her stomach twist: broken glass jars near the cider press, a shattered wooden case, and a few dark stains on the floor.

"Oh no..." Harper's voice was barely a whisper.

A faint sound—a soft, strangled sob—came from the back of the barn. Harper's heart lurched. She and Gabe rushed toward the sound, slipping past the oversized barrels of ripening fruit and into the corner of the large space. There, huddled on the floor, was Maggie. Her hair was disheveled, and her hands trembled as she hugged herself tightly. Her face was pale, eyes wide with fear. The sight was enough to send a chill through Harper's entire body.

"Maggie," Harper whispered, crouching beside her friend, careful not to startle her. "It's me. It's Harper. You're safe now."

Maggie looked up slowly, her eyes darting between Harper and Gabe, as if not quite believing they were real. A shudder went through her, and she let out a broken breath, her voice trembling. "It's... Connor. He killed Prudence. He was here. I was so scar—"

"I know," Harper broke in. "We figured it out."

Gabe knelt beside her, his jaw clenched with anger, but he softened his tone as he spoke. "What did he do, Maggie? Did he hurt you?"

She shook her head, but fresh tears brimmed in her eyes.

"No, but... he made it clear he could if he wanted to. He said he needed to talk, but then... then he started saying these awful things, how I shouldn't interfere, how I didn't know what I was getting myself into. I got scared and said I wanted to leave, but he wouldn't let me leave. He cornered me here in the back. I've never been so scared, Harper. I thought..."

Harper took Maggie's hands in hers, feeling the faint tremors that ran through her friend's fingers. "I'm so sorry, Maggie. We're here now. We're not going to let him get away with this."

Maggie looked between them, her eyes clouded with fear but also a glimmer of strength. "He said if I didn't stop helping you—if I didn't stop asking questions—that he'd... he'd make me pay for it. He took my phone and smashed it. He said he'd do worse if I didn't stay quiet."

A low, simmering rage flickered in Gabe's eyes. "The Sheriff is on his way, but I'm not going to let him get away."

Maggie squeezed Harper's hand, her voice a soft, timid whisper. "I thought... I thought I was brave, that I could stand up to anyone. But the look in his eyes... Harper, he was like a different person."

Harper's heart broke at the fear in her friend's eyes, and she wrapped her arms around Maggie, pulling her close. "You *are* brave, Mags. I'm so proud of you. You survived."

Gabe reached out, placing a reassuring hand on Maggie's shoulder. "It's going to be okay. We're here."

Maggie nodded, her breath slowly evening out as she leaned into Harper's embrace. The warmth of her friends was enough to chase away a fraction of the terror Connor had left behind, but Harper could see in her eyes that it would be a long time before that shadow fully lifted.

Together, they helped Maggie to her feet, steadying her as she wiped her tears away. Harper looked over at Gabe, her eyes hardening with resolve. Connor had pushed them all to the edge, but he'd made one mistake—they weren't about to back down.

CHAPTER 33
CONFRONTATION

"I want to get Maggie safely back to my truck." Gabe said. "Let's go - stay behind me."

"Why don't you go ahead and I'll wait here for you?" Harper said. " I can clean some of this up and find her phone."

"And my keys, Harper. My keys are somewhere in here." Maggie said.

"I'm on it," Harper said with a nod.

Gabe hesitated.

"Alright. But Harper - don't go out there alone. It's not safe." His eyes searched hers and she nodded.

"I'll be right here," she promised with a soft smile. "Hurry back."

They exchanged one more look before Harper smiled and said "go!"

After they were gone, Harper furiously searched through the mess. She found the keys first, then moved broken crates and pieces of wood to find Maggie's phone. She tucked it into her pocket and paced the floor anxiously. A minute went by. Then two. Then five. Harper was growing impatient. *Where was Gabe? Had something happened to him?*

Just then, Harper saw movement by the old barn across the field. *Had Gabe gone without her? Was she supposed to meet him over there?* As she watched, the door to the barn slid open five or six feet, then slid closed. *What should I do*, she thought. She gave it another minute, then decided to check it out.

Harper's pulse raced as she made her way through the darkening orchard, the fading autumn light casting long shadows between the rows of trees. The cool evening air bit at her skin, but she ignored it, her focus set on the small barn ahead. She had pieced everything together, and now it was time for her and Gabe to confront Connor —once and for all.

She'd figured out part of the puzzle: Connor had kept Luke and Ryan away from the orchard on the day Prudence was murdered. And Vivian had stolen Hemingway's Quill, trying to cover up whatever secrets it held. But what Harper hadn't expected was that Connor had a deeper role in all of this—one that still eluded her.

The barn door creaked as she pushed it open, the musty scent of hay and apples wafting toward her. Inside, Connor was crouched by a workbench, his back to her, sorting through some tools. Gabe was nowhere in sight. Connor didn't hear her at first, so Harper took a deep breath, steadying herself.

"Connor."

The single word was enough to make him stiffen, his movements halting. Slowly, he stood and turned, his face half-obscured by the dim light filtering through the open door.

"Harper," he greeted, his voice flat. "What are you doing here?"

"I could ask you the same thing," she said, stepping inside, her boots crunching against the straw-strewn floor.

Harper shook her head, her hand tightening around the notebook she carried. "I talked to Luke and Ryan. You told them not to harvest the McIntosh apples on the day Prudence was killed. You deliberately kept them away from the orchard."

Connor's gaze darkened, and for a moment, Harper thought he

might bolt. But, he squared his shoulders and took a step toward her. "I didn't want them to overhear me talking to Prudence. "

She stepped closer, her heart pounding in her chest. "I know you told your Aunt Vivian about Hemingway's Quill, and I know she stole it."

"That quill belonged to our family." A grimace tugged at the corner of Connor's mouth. "I saw it in your shop the night we cleaned, in an *unlocked* case. It was clear you were clueless about the value of what you had on your hands."

"Okay, so you and your aunt decided to steal Hemingway's quill. What did it have to do with Prudence? Why did you kill her?"

Connor's eyes flashed, but he remained silent.

"It wasn't planned," Connor said, his voice quiet. He looked almost remorseful. "I didn't mean to hurt her. One day, a few weeks after my aunt stole the quill, Prudence came by to ask for my aunt to help her fight against some building of Evelyn's. Prudence saw the quill on my aunt's fireplace. She threatened to expose Aunt Viv as a thief. It would have destroyed her reputation. I couldn't let that happen."

Harper felt her pulse hammering in her ears. "Why? Why did her reputation matter so much to you?"

"My parents are dead. My aunt's writing proceeds are my inheritance. She couldn't be exposed as a common thief... it was humiliating, but it would also ruin her career."

"Her *career* is what you worried about?"

"I didn't want my aunt's name dragged through the mud. When Prudence took the quill from my aunt's house, she said she was going to return it to you and tell you everything. I knew I had to act fast. I asked her to meet me, and I thought I could convince her to give it back. I thought since I worked at the bookstore, I could return it to the case and you'd never be the wiser. The quill would be returned, and my aunt wouldn't get into any trouble, and her writing career would continue. So I setup the meeting in the orchard that night. I thought it would be empty because everyone would be at the Harvest

Festival. But Prudence wouldn't give up the quill. She was determined to come see you and tell you what really happened. "

"So you killed her?"

"I didn't plan to. But she just wouldn't let it go, wouldn't give me the quill. She was always so sanctimonious and perfect. She wanted to ruin my aunt, tell you and the police about how my aunt stole the quill and I couldn't let that happen. We fought and then... I ended up stabbing her with the quill."

"But you made sure no one would be around ," Harper said slowly.

Connor's expression darkened, and the air in the barn seemed to thicken with tension. "I didn't plan to kill her, Harper. All I wanted was privacy so no one would know what my aunt did. My plan was to confront her, get the quill, and move on. But Prudence was too nosy for her own good. She was going to ruin everything."

"You had a choice," Harper shot back, her voice shaking with anger and fear. "Whatever happened that night, you could have stopped. You didn't have to kill her."

Connor's face twisted into a sneer. "She left me no choice. But I screwed up leaving the quill behind. I should have taken it with me."

Harper narrowed her eyes. "But why kill your aunt? Why kill her, Connor? Your own family."

"She was going to confess everything," Connor screamed suddenly. "She was going to destroy her career! I couldn't let her do that."

"So...all of this was... for money?" Harper whispered.

"Yeah, well not everyone was just handed a massive bookstore and an apartment, *Harper*," he sneered. " Do you know that I have four jobs around town? I work in your little shop, the pizza parlor, the orchard, *and* the hardware store. I'm always picking up extra work, helping everyone with odd jobs. I'm so tired of working hard and still having so little. I kept going because I knew that one day I would inherit her house and her estate."

Harper's heart pounded in her chest, panic rising as Connor

stepped closer. "You can have the quill," she said frantically. Her mind raced, trying to figure out how to escape. She had to get out of here, had to get to Sheriff Carlisle—but Connor was blocking her only way out.

"It's too late for that, Harper," he hissed, moving towards her ominously.

"Connor, don't do this," Harper said, trying to keep her voice calm. "You can turn yourself in. You don't have to make this worse."

But Connor's face was set in grim determination. "I'm not turning myself in. I'm getting that quill back...it's my inheritance."

Before Harper could react, Connor lunged at her, but Harper darted to the side, her adrenaline surging. She grabbed the closest thing she could find—a rusty pitchfork leaning against the wall—and brandished it between them.

"Stay back!" Harper warned, her voice shaky but fierce.

Connor hesitated for a split second, his eyes flickering to the pitchfork. It was just enough time for Harper to make her move. She dashed toward the door, heart pounding as she flung it open and bolted into the orchard, the cool night air hitting her like a shock.

Behind her, she could hear Connor's footsteps, but she didn't look back. She ran as fast as her legs would carry her, weaving between the apple trees, her breath ragged and her mind focused on one thing—getting out of there alive.

CHAPTER 34

RUN

Harper's legs burned as she tore through the orchard, the cool autumn air stinging her lungs. Her breath came in sharp, shallow bursts, and her heart thundered in her chest. The darkened rows of apple trees stretched out before her like a labyrinth, their branches clawing at her as she ran. Behind her, she could hear Connor crashing through the underbrush, his footsteps heavy and relentless.

"Harper!" Connor's voice rang out through the orchard, sharp and dangerous. "You can't outrun me! You should've stayed out of it!"

But Harper didn't stop. She couldn't. Fear surged through her, adrenaline pumping, as she sprinted between the trees, her mind racing with the single, terrifying thought: *I need to get out of here.*

The orchard was a blur around her. She stumbled over a twisted root, barely catching herself before she fell face-first into the dirt. Gritting her teeth, Harper pushed herself harder, knowing Connor was closing in. The barn had been too isolated. No one would hear her scream if he caught her out here. *Where was Gabe?*

The moon hung low in the sky, casting eerie shadows that made the trees look like looming figures. She darted between rows, disoriented, trying to remember which way would lead her back to the road. But the orchard seemed endless, a maze of darkened paths and indistinguishable rows of apple trees.

Her foot snagged on a low branch, and she fell hard, her hands slamming into the cold earth. She cried out, pain shooting up her wrists, but she forced herself to scramble back to her feet, every muscle screaming in protest. Behind her, Connor's footsteps grew louder, closer.

Panic clawed at her chest. She wasn't going to make it.

"Harper!" Connor's voice was closer now, filled with an icy rage. "You're not getting away from me!"

She could hear the menace in his voice, the unhinged edge that made her blood run cold. Harper's mind spun, desperate for an escape. She could barely see in the dark, but she needed to keep moving—find a hiding spot, anything to put some distance between them.

And then, just ahead, she saw a faint glow through the trees—a light.

Hope flickered in her chest. The road. It had to be the road. Or maybe—*Gabe.*

Without another thought, Harper sprinted toward the light, her legs trembling from exhaustion but refusing to give up. She heard Connor's pace quicken behind her, his breathing harsh and furious.

But then, a new sound broke through the night—the distant roar of an engine. A truck.

Harper's heart soared. Gabe.

She burst through the last row of trees, stumbling into the open, her vision swimming. The headlights of a truck were cutting through the dark, barreling down the dirt road toward her. She waved her arms frantically, the desperation rising in her throat like a scream. "Gabe!"

The truck screeched to a halt just feet away from her, and the door flew open. Gabe jumped out, his eyes wide with panic as he ran toward her. "Harper!"

"Connor is right behind me!" Harper gasped, grabbing his arm.

Gabe didn't need any more explanation. His expression hardened, and he immediately pulled Harper behind him, turning to face the orchard. He reached into the truck and grabbed the flashlight from the seat, the beam cutting through the darkness just as Connor emerged from the trees, his face twisted with rage.

"Stay out of this, Gabe!" Connor shouted, advancing toward them, his eyes wild. "You don't know what's going on!"

"I know enough," Gabe growled, stepping in front of Harper, his broad frame blocking her from Connor's view. "And you're not getting any closer."

Connor stopped, his eyes narrowing, chest heaving with exertion. For a moment, Harper thought he might back down, but then his hand twitched toward his pocket.

Gabe caught the movement and acted in a flash. He lunged forward, grabbing Connor's arm and twisting it behind his back before Connor could reach for anything. Connor let out a howl of pain, but Gabe didn't let up, forcing him to the ground and pinning him there with his knee.

Harper watched, breathless, as Gabe held Connor down with a strength she hadn't fully appreciated before. "You're done, Connor," Gabe said, his voice low and menacing. "It's over."

Connor writhed beneath him, his face contorted with fury. "You don't understand! She—she was going to destroy everything! I had no choice!"

Harper staggered forward, clutching her side as she struggled to catch her breath. "You killed her, Connor. You murdered Prudence because she was going to expose you and Vivian."

Connor's eyes blazed with a mix of hatred and fear, but he stopped fighting, realizing he was trapped.

Harper felt her knees weaken, the adrenaline finally ebbing away as the reality of what had just happened sank in. Gabe looked back at her, his eyes filled with concern. "Are you alright?"

Harper nodded shakily, though she wasn't sure she believed it herself. "I—I'm okay."

The sound of sirens pierced the night air, distant but growing louder. Gabe kept Connor pinned to the ground as they waited, his grip never loosening.

Harper leaned against the truck, her heart still racing. The nightmare was finally over, but the weight of what had happened lingered in the air. As the flashing lights of the sheriff's car approached, she closed her eyes, grateful that this ordeal was over.

CHAPTER 35
HARVEST ROAST DEBRIEF

Harper sat at the table in Harvest Roast, her hands wrapped around a warm mug of chai, trying to steady her nerves. The coffee shop was quiet now, the rush of the day long gone, leaving just a small group of them—Maggie, Gabe, Harper, Paul and Melanie—gathered in a corner booth. Lady was curled up on the floor beside Paul in a small dog bed he had brought with him. The soft glow of the dimmed lights made the place feel cozy, but the weight of everything Harper had just been through lingered in the air like a storm cloud.

Maggie sat across from her, wide-eyed and pale, her usual spark replaced by exhaustion and uncertainty. Gabe sat next to Harper, his arm resting protectively along the back of the booth behind her. He watched her intently, as if unsure if she was out of danger.

"I'm so glad you're both okay," Paul finally said, looking at Maggie and Harper.

"Me too," Melanie echoed. "But I'm not sure I understand all of it. How the quill ended up with Prudence? What did Prudence have to do with any of it?"

Harper took a deep breath, organizing her thoughts. "It took me a while to figure that out too. But I think I finally see the complete picture."

She glanced at Maggie and Gabe, both leaning in.

"It's really two stories," Harper began. "The first is how my family got the quill and why it's valuable. That goes back to Ernest Hemingway and his connection to Michigan. When he was a kid, early 1900s maybe into the '20s, he vacationed every summer at Walloon Lake, not far from here. My great-great-grandfather opened Hearth & Quill back in 1884 and he remembered the Hemingway family coming into the store many times over the years.

"As we all know, Hemingway went on to become, well, Hemingway. He inherited his family's summer house and when he sold it 1961, he sold it with its contents. The family that bought it didn't realize the value of what they had purchased." She paused to take a sip of her chai.

"They ended up having an estate sale," she went on. "By that time, my great-great-grandfather, Theodore Whitmore, had already passed the store down to my great-grandfather, John. John ran the store from 1932 to 1975, when he handed it down to his daughter, my great-aunt Eleanor. So back to 1961. They held that estate sale and my great-grandfather John bought a bunch of items for cheap. And one of those things was Ernest Hemingway's quill."

They were all listening intently. Harper continued, looking at each person.

"The family that bought Hemingway House...the ones who had the estate sale? That was Vivian's family."

Maggie's brow furrowed. "Wait – so her family sold off a bunch of Ernest Hemingway memorabilia without even realizing it?"

"That's right," Harper explained. "Vivian and her father later realized what they'd done...selling off millions of dollars worth of literary memorabilia. Most of the items were long gone, the items my grandfather bought were right here in Fall. Vivian and her father believed the quill rightfully belonged to them, that it should have stayed with the Hemingway summer cottage. Both of them tried for years to get it back, but my grandfather refused."

Harper took a sip of her chai and continued. "So the entire Hawthorn family knew about this feud. When Connor helped clean the bookshop, he saw Hemingway's quill in an unlocked case. He mentioned it to Vivian and she decided to steal it at the grand reopening."

Melanie nodded. "Okay, I get it. Your family bought the quill, the Hawthorns wanted it back and Vivian ended up stealing it. But what does it have to do with Prudence?"

Harper nodded. "That's the next part of the story. Prudence's involvement was a total accident. There was an upcoming meeting about the property dispute between Prudence and Evelyn. Prudence was going door-to-door trying to drum up support for her side. Prudence stopped by Vivian's house and she happened to see the quill. Prudence knew Hemingways quill was part of Ellie's collection and should now belong to me."

Gabe leaned forward. "Let me guess – Prudence threatened to go public?"

"She did," Harper said. "She took the quill from Vivian and said that Vivian and Connor needed to come clean to me – or she'd go to the police."

"Okay, so now Prudence has the quill and Vivian and Connor are scared," Paul said.

"Right. Which brings us to the murder. Connor told Prudence that Vivian agreed to return the quill to me and confess. He just asked that Prudence let them do it discreetly. Said his aunt was ashamed. And maybe Prudence wanted to believe him – so she agreed to meet Vivian in the orchard before the pie judging to give her the quill. She believed Vivian would return it to me and the matter would be closed."

Harper paused, her voice tightening. "But Vivian was never coming. Connor set it all up."

Silence hung between them, broken only by the faint crackle of the café's fireplace.

"Connor didn't want to return the quill," Gabe said quietly.

"Right. Connor wanted the money the quill could bring his family. Connor and Prudence argued. And when Prudence refused to back down... Connor killed her with the quill."

Melanie covered her mouth.

"Connor claims it was an accident, but he made sure that the orchard was empty. He told Luke and Ryan not to harvest the McIntosh apples."

Gabe's jaw clenched. "And Vivian?"

"She didn't know what Connor had done," Harper said softly. "After I talked to her, I think she had a hunch. She was going to confess – about stealing the quill, about everything. She couldn't live with it anymore."

Harper looked down at her hands.

"And that's why Connor killed her too. He couldn't let her ruin everything. Vivian's reputation. Connor's future, and most important to him, his inheritance. He wanted to sell the quill. So, he silenced his aunt by killing her."

"He wasn't protecting her," Gabe said quietly. "He was protecting himself."

Harper nodded. "Right. Now two people are dead."

They all sat in silence for a moment, the crackle of the fire in the hearth the only sound in the quiet cafe.

"Which brings us to the last few days," Paul said.

"Connor was frustrated that I kept digging about the murder and about the quill," Harper said. "He met with Maggie to get her to persuade me to stop looking.

"I can't believe I was alone with a killer," Maggie said, her voice barely a whisper. "And then he chased you. You could have—"

"But I didn't," Harper cut in, her voice firm but gentle. "Thanks to Gabe."

Gabe gave a small, humble smile, his eyes meeting Harper's. "You were the one who figured it out. I just happened to be in the right place at the right time."

Maggie shook her head, still in disbelief. "Well, I'm just glad you're okay. And that Connor is in custody."

Harper nodded, feeling the exhaustion finally settle into her bones. "I'm glad *you're* okay. It's over now."

But as she sat there with Gabe and Maggie and her friends, safe and warm, she couldn't shake the feeling that the secrets in Fall, Michigan, weren't entirely behind them. The town had always seemed so picturesque, so perfect. But now Harper knew—there were always shadows, even in the brightest places.

CHAPTER 36
STAY OR LEAVE

Harper sat in her cozy nook at Hearth & Quill, sipping a steaming mug of chai tea as she gazed out at the leaves swirling in the breeze outside. The shop was quiet, but her mind was still buzzing from the whirlwind of recent events. She pulled out her phone, feeling the need to reconnect with her girlfriends from Atlanta. It had been too long since she'd caught up with them, and she missed the easy banter and laughter. Plus, she had a lot to catch them up on - and not just about the murders.

ATL GIRLS 💅🍸🍷📚

Harper: Hey ladies! Miss you all. How's everything back in the big city?

It didn't take long before her phone buzzed with replies.

Amanda: OMG Harper! Finally, you remembered we exist! 😂 What's going on in that tiny fall-obsessed town of yours? Did you solve the mystery, Nancy Drew?

Erin: Seriously! I've been waiting for the next chapter of 'Harper Moves to Murderville.' Don't leave us hanging.

Harper hesitated, unsure how much she should reveal. They

might never believe half of what she'd been through with the double murder investigation.

Harper: Let's just say this mystery turned into multiple crime scenes, and I might've gotten a little too involved in figuring out what happened. 😬

Amanda: Classic Harper, solving mysteries! I love it. You really are the new Nancy Drew!

Erin: Wait, wait. Did you crack the case? Did you get the quill back??

Harper: I did. 🕵️ But it was way more intense than I bargained for. I'm still recovering. 😅

Amanda: Sounds like you need a spa day ASAP. Can I convince you to come back to Atlanta for a weekend? We miss you!!

Harper's heart warmed at the thought of seeing her friends, but she looked around the cozy bookstore, the fire crackling in the hearth, and smiled. She missed Atlanta, but Fall felt like a new home for her.

Harper: I miss you guys, too. I'll plan a trip soon, promise. But for now, Fall has me hooked. 🍁 Plus, there's *so* much more to figure out here. 😌

Erin: A mystery woman through and through. 😄 We'll hold you to that trip. Until then, keep us updated on all the small-town drama.

Amanda: And don't forge to update us on you and Gabe next time you decide to text!

Harper: LOL... Oh, there's lots to tell you about that topic, too...

With that, Harper tucked her phone away, feeling a little more connected to her old life but content to stay exactly where she was. Fall had its mysteries, but it also had its charm—and she wasn't ready to leave it behind just yet.

CHAPTER 37
SECRET DOOR

The soft chime of the bell over the door echoed through Hearth & Quill as Harper stepped inside, her boots clicking lightly on the hardwood floor. The late afternoon sun streamed through the large front windows, casting a warm, golden glow over the bookstore. It was quiet, peaceful—just the way she liked it.

In her hands, Harper held the delicate glass case containing Hemingway's quill, cleaned and restored. Its intricate design caught the light as she carried it through the shop. *It really is beautiful*, Harper thought. The weight of the last few weeks still lingered in her mind, but today, for the first time in what felt like forever, there was a sense of closure. The mystery had been solved, Connor was behind bars, and the danger that had hung over Fall, Michigan, had finally lifted. It was almost Halloween, the celebrations that surrounded the holiday, and the bonfire that all Fall residents talked about.

Harper stood in front of the display case that hung above the mantle of the enormous hearth at the center of the room. This was the spot reserved for the largest and most beautiful quills. Gently, she unlocked the cabinet and placed the quill inside, taking a moment to admire it before closing the door with a soft click.

"There you go," she whispered, almost as if the quill could hear her. "Right where you belong."

As she stood and turned to leave, something caught her eye. The quill had shifted slightly in its case, tilting to one side as if something beneath it had moved. Frowning, Harper crouched back down and peered closer at the base of the display.

She ran her fingers along the wooden panel beneath the case, her touch brushing against a faint seam in the wood she hadn't noticed before. Her curiosity piqued, she pressed gently on the edge of the seam. At first, nothing happened, but then—*click*—a soft sound echoed through the quiet room, and the panel beneath the case shifted slightly, revealing a small button.

Harper's heart raced. She glanced around the shop as if expecting someone to appear, though she was alone. Slowly, carefully, she pressed the button and heard another —*click*—. One side of the stone hearth opened a crack, revealing an inset panel door on which the stone was secured.

"Wow..." she breathed, leaning closer to inspect it.

When closed, it was the seamless and invisible side of the stone hearth. But now, a two inch gap was visible. It was a secret door—an old one, judging by the worn hinges and the dust that had settled in the crevices. Harper reached for her phone, turning on the flashlight to illuminate the passage. The extremely narrow spiral staircase twisted down behind the massive hearth, beckoning Harper into the unknown.

Her mind buzzed with questions. *How long had this been here? What was it used for? Did her Aunt Ellie know about this?* And, more importantly, *why was it hidden beneath the very spot where Hemingway's quill had been displayed all these years?*

Harper's pulse quickened, her instincts telling her this discovery was important—another mystery waiting to be solved.

"Well," she murmured to herself with a wry smile, "looks like the bookstore has more secrets than I thought."

For a moment, she considered closing the door and leaving the passage unexplored. She had faced enough danger and intrigue the last few weeks to last her a lifetime. But something about the hidden door and the narrow staircase called to her—a whisper of something left unfinished, a puzzle waiting to be solved.

With one last glance at the bookstore around her, Harper stepped through the secret door and started down the stairs, her flashlight beam cutting through the darkness as she ventured deeper into the unknown. The hidden passage felt cool and damp, the walls lined with old stone, untouched for who knew how long. Harper's footsteps echoed softly as she proceeded downward, the beam of light revealing two or three steps at a time, cobwebs hanging from the walls. She didn't know where the staircase led, but the further she went, the more certain she became that whatever lay at the end of this was tied to her Aunt Ellie—and possibly even to Hemingway himself.

As she pressed onward, the faintest glimmer of excitement sparked in her chest. The mystery of the quill had been solved, but clearly, Fall had more stories to tell.

And Harper was just getting started.

ALSO BY

Book 2 - Bonfires & Betrayal (coming December 2025)

Book 3 - Cinnamon & Conspiracies (coming spring 2026)

ACKNOWLEDGMENTS

Thank you to my husband, Rich, and my terrific kids, Wesley and Lila. Thanks for all of the encouragement and support, and for almost never interrupting me while I was writing. (Well, okay, you interrupted me a lot, but mostly just for snacks). You heard, "Mom is writing" a lot, and you were very understanding. You two are the reason I work so hard. Rich, you've let me live my dream these last 9 months (12 years) and there aren't enough words to thank you for that. Thanks for believing in me, brainstorming with me, and for taking care of the kids/dog/chickens when I was lost in the writing. The kids and dog appreciate it, but the chickens (that you never wanted) really appreciate it, because you give them extra worms.

Thanks to my mom and dad, who are the original supporters in everything I do. Thank you to my mom for telling me I was a brilliant writer... starting at about age 7, when my writing was (probably) terrible. Your words became the voice in my head, telling me I was a talented writer who could do anything. Thanks for encouraging me to write, to read, and to tell stories, but to get a business degree, just in case. That worked out pretty well. I love you both more than you know.

To my sister, Yvette, who encouraged me to make up stories when I was a kid and stayed up way past our bedtime to listen to them. You were my first audience. You have always shown up with I need you, no matter how far apart we may be. I love you.

Thank you to all of my Chicago besties. You are the most unhinged, supportive, crown-straightening, pump-me-up girls I've ever known. You've shown up so many times for me and I am in awe of each of you. Thank you for the 10 different group chats, the laughs, the inspiration and the support. I love that we can talk about everything - from plants, books, dragon riders, trip planning, shopping, parenting, cooking, Rugby videos, and back to books again in three minutes. I appreciate all the advice, guidance, support, reassurance, and hand-holding. Over the months I was writing this book, you've encouraged me, supported me and answered 138 random questions about tiny little details. You have celebrated every tiny achievement as if I'd won a Pulitzer, and there are no words for that kind of friendship.

To the real Atlanta girls. There are a lot of you; I just used two of you to represent the ATL. I'm terrible at keeping in touch, but please know y'all have such a special place in my heart. My 13 years in Atlanta were some of the best years of my life. I think of you all often, and fondly.

A huge thank you to Courtney Aussem for editing my book...five different times. You are an incredible human who does so many things all at the same time and makes it all look effortless. You are a fantastic writer, a phenomenal editor, and a world-class friend. And you're also, like, really pretty, which is just rude.

Thank you to my Reading Between the Wines book club girlies for encouraging me to read, introducing me to new books every month and most of all, for believing that I am worthy of being the October book selection. I hope you loved it!

To my beta readers: Stephanie, Kelsey, Kim, Courtney A, Courtney H., Angel, Therese, and Kimberly S.. Thank you for being my first round of readers, for catching plot holes, typos, and so much more. I couldn't have done this without you.

Thank you to my incredible ARC team who read my book on an incredibly short timeline. It matters more than you know.

And finally, to my readers. I truly cannot believe you are here. I've dreamed of publishing my first book since I was 7 years old, so you are helping to fulfill my lifelong dream. From the bottom of my heart, thank you.

A self-published author like me has about 1% chance of ending up on any bestseller list, going viral, or getting on Reese or Oprah or BookTok's radar...but, hey, a girl can dream, right? Would you **please** tell others about my book? Grab your phone and snap a picture of you reading this book and post it on TikTok, IG or FB? Write a review on Amazon or Goodreads? Those 30 seconds won't matter much to you, but it just might change my entire life.

Thank you for buying, thank you for reading, thank you for making my dreams come true. Onward to book 2 of this series ... (and a **very** spicy book series that's also in progress).

XOXO, Jules

ABOUT THE AUTHOR

Jules Motschall writes cozy mysteries with a twist of charm, heart, romance, and just the right amount of intrigue. When she's not plotting crimes in the fictional town of Fall, Michigan, she's likely curled up with a good book, a strong cup of coffee, and a fall candle.

Autumn & Alibis is her debut novel and the first in the Hearth & Quill Mystery series. Jules lives in Chicago with her husband, children, their six chickens, and a mini Goldendoodle.

Printed in Dunstable, United Kingdom

69199806R00153